Don't Die Under the Apple Tree

Don't Die Under the Apple Tree

AMY PATRICIA
MEADE

KENSINGTON PUBLISHING CORP.

http://www.kensingtonbooks.com

KENSINGTON BOOKS are published by

Kensington Publishing Corp.
119 West 40th Street
New York, NY 10018

All Kensington Titles, Imprints, and Distributed Lines are
available at special quantity discounts for bulk purchases
for sales promotions, premiums, fund-raising, and educa-
tional or institutional use.

Special book excerpts or customized printings can also
be created to fit specific needs. For details, write or
phone the office of the Kensington special sales man-
ager: Kensington Publishing Corp., 119 West 40th Street,
New York, NY 10018, attn: Special Sales Department,
Phone: 1-800-221-2647.

ISBN-13: 978-0-7582-6758-0
ISBN-10: 0-7582-6758-4

First Mass Market Printing: May 2012

10 9 8 7 6 5 4 3 2 1

Printed in the United States of America

Don't Die Under the Apple Tree

Chapter One

"Rose Doyle Keefe." The petite thirty-two-year-old lifted the lapel of her tan wool coat to display the badge that identified her as an employee of the Pushey Shipyard Corporation, Brooklyn.

The uniformed military guard nodded absently as his eyes traced the outline of her coat lapel and came to rest on the open neck of the dark blue canvas coveralls she wore beneath it.

"*Mrs.* Rose Keefe," she amended.

The guard hastily returned his gaze to the badge, scribbled something on a large clipboard, and, without making eye contact, nodded Rosie's admittance.

Stepping from the cobblestones of Beard Street through the doorway of the nineteenth-century red brick building, Rosie followed the sound of male voices to the massive, windowless holding area. There, by the dim glow of the factory lights, foremen issued the day's directives and workers waited for the horn blast that signaled the end of one shift and the start of the next.

Rosie stood in the back of the room with the other female employees. Although the still predominantly male staff of Pushey Shipyard understood that the draft was making young male workers increasingly scarce, they refused to take the new, and decidedly temporary, female hires seriously. Shipbuilding was hard, dirty work and no one of the weaker sex could ever excel at it; to infer otherwise was an insult to the profession.

Fearful that cheap women's labor would replace them or lower their wages, and resentful of the special labor laws that afforded women longer rest periods and newer washroom facilities, even the most decent of men harbored some mistrust or animosity toward the new recruits.

And so, instead of chatting with each other like coworkers, the two genders remained separate. The women huddled together at the back of the room, watching silently as the men told jokes, discussed their families, and regaled each other with tales of their latest sexual conquests.

Even amid the din of boisterous male conversations, one voice rose far above the others, that of self-appointed political pundit Tony Del Vecchio. "Did you hear Roosevelt on the radio last night? Now he's breaking the army into three different groups—one for air, one for land, and one for supplies. It's like tirty tree all over again with one bunch of people doing this, another bunch of people doing that, and no one getting anything done. Next thing you know, he'll be giving them letters of the alphabet, like WPA, NRA, NLRA . . . Jeez, if the guy worried half as much about killing Nips and Krauts as he does about naming things, the war could be over before the year is out."

Michael Delaney, a familiar face from Rosie's childhood, nodded his head in agreement. "You said it, Tony. The *Normandie* burned in the harbor just two month ago and they still haven't figured out who did it. For all we know, it could have been a Nazi. The whole city could be crawling with them, but all FDR cares about is housekeeping. If you ask me, we New Yorkers have to take matters into our own hands."

"Yep," Del Vecchio concurred. "Though my old lady could learn something from Roosevelt. If she did half as good a job at putting things in order, I'd be a happy man." Delaney chuckled in commiseration.

Rosie, meanwhile, shook her head in silence. The only "old lady" in Delaney's life was his elderly, ailing mother. Barring a minor miracle—namely, the demise of every other man on the planet—that situation was not likely to change anytime soon.

Rail thin and ratlike in countenance, Michael Delaney did not possess the genetic traits that most women considered "swoon worthy." On the contrary, his wiry black hair, deep-set eyes, and rather prominent nose had, since childhood, garnered negative attention from both sexes, often earning him such unflattering nicknames as "Ichabod" or "Crow."

Such ridicule might have caused a less determined or less clever child innumerable problems. But Michael Declan Delaney was a master of self-preservation. Adopting the policy of "If you can't lick 'em, join 'em," Delaney learned at an early age that he could ward off potential tormenters by befriending the loudest, biggest, and dumbest kid in St. Cecilia's schoolyard. Due to relocation, rising uniform expenses, and growth spurts, the identity of that "kid" changed from year to year, but Delaney's skill at playing the faithful lackey never wavered. Given his current friendship with Tony Del Vecchio, it still hadn't.

"Now Frankie-Boy—oh, excuse me: 'Mr. President' —is saying the *Normandie* might have been an accident," Del Vecchio continued as the men, now silent, gathered around him and Delaney, their insulated work jackets engulfing the two men in a sea of blue. The women, meanwhile, remained clustered in the back of the room; however, they listened and watched with rapt attention. "Accident? You and I were both there, right, Delaney?"

Delaney nodded his head in earnest. "Sure were."

Again Rosie silently shook her head. Tony Del Vecchio could claim to have kissed both Rita Hayworth and Betty Grable in the same night and Delaney would swear it was true.

"We both saw it, didn't we? First the black smoke, thicker than anything I've ever seen."

"Everyone saw the smoke, Del Vecchio," finally Rosie piped up, causing all eyes to turn toward her. "It covered most of Manhattan."

"Yeah, but not everyone saw the boat go over, did they?" Del Vecchio challenged. "It was the middle of the night, but we saw it, Delaney and me. The fire was out by then, but all of a sudden the thing lurched to the port side and kept on going. I've worked on the docks all my life and I ain't never seen a ship do that."

"Me neither," Delaney said.

"The minute we saw it, we both said that it was no accident. Nope. No way that was an accident," Del Vecchio repeated, much to the delight of his audience. "Mark my words: someone sabotaged that ship. That's why the fire hoses didn't work. Someone cut the hoses so that the fire would be out of control by the time anyone could get there."

"Nazis," Delaney said. "Had to be."

"Of course it was Nazis. You can see their U-boats from Rockaway or Jones Beach."

"The Jersey shore, too," a man remarked from the crowd. "My sister has a place down there."

Delaney again nodded, this time with arrogance.

"What the hell is the navy doing letting the Krauts get that close? How many ships have to burn before ol' FDR takes notice and does something other than housekeeping?"

"Housekeeping," Del Vecchio muttered. "Only thing reorganizing the military does is makes it impossible to find anyone. I got a cousin who signed up for the army and he thinks they might move him to the air force. Do you know where your kid brother's gonna wind up, Delaney?"

"Nah. I don't think they've told anyone for sure yet. But then again, with my brother you never know." Delaney looked in Rosie's direction. "How about you? You know where your husband's gonna be?"

Billy Keefe had been the bane of Michael Delaney's existence ever since their school years. Handsome, charming, and a consummate liar, Billy excelled at everything Delaney didn't, including winning Rosie's heart.

Reluctant to discuss her absent husband and possibly reignite a childhood rivalry, Rosie feigned deafness.

Delaney, however, was his indefatigable self. "Say, Rosie," he persisted. "Rosie. Doyle . . . I mean, Keefe. Rosie Keefe!"

His voice, combined with the stares of her coworkers, proved impossible to ignore.

She leveled a stare at Delaney that was far blacker than the smoke of the *Normandie*.

"Hi . . . Rosie," Delaney grinned nervously. "Say, do you know where your husband's gonna be when they split up the army?"

Like spectators at a tennis match, the seventy-odd employees of Pushey Shipyard turned their attention to Delaney and then back to Rosie, who stood, arms folded across her chest, at the back of the room.

"No," she answered flatly. "I haven't heard from him."

"What?" Delaney put a hand to his ear.

"I don't know," Rosie repeated in a voice just softer than a shout. "I haven't heard from him."

The crowd again turned to Delaney.

He nodded. "Yeah, the mail is slow in coming. Driving my ma nuts. How long's it been since your last letter?"

Volley. Back to Keefe.

Rosie drew a deep breath. "I . . . umm . . . I haven't had a letter. Or a phone call," she added.

"Huh? You saying you haven't heard from your husband since he was called for service?"

Rosie gazed at the faces staring back at her. She wanted to run, hide, bury her head in the ground, but she knew that doing so would cause her to lose her job. "Michael Delaney, your mother is friends with my mother. You know darn well Billy wasn't drafted. He enlisted."

This time all eyes remained focused on Rosie.

"How long ago was that?"

Rosie scratched her head through the dark blue kerchief that covered her auburn hair and avoided all eye contact lest she break into tears. "Let's see . . . when did we declare war on Japan?"

"Before Christmas?" Delaney replied incredulously. "Jeez, I had no idea. . . . That was over four months ago."

Four months, six days, and eleven hours, Rosie thought. Outwardly, however, her response was one of carefree nonchalance. "Over four months? Really? I'd lost track."

"Hey, did you say your husband's name was Billy?" Del Vecchio spoke up. "As in Billy Keefe?"

"Yes," Rosie answered. "Why?"

Del Vecchio convulsed with laughter, his rounded abdomen quivering violently beneath his gray cotton overalls. "The Billy Keefe I know couldn't hold a steady job, let alone make it in the army. Every time I see the guy, he's tying one on with a good-looking dame. Last time it was a tall, cool blonde. The time before that, it was a cute brunette. That's why you haven't heard from him. He's probably shacked up somewhere with some broad."

As the crowd gawked and whispered, Rosie felt the color drain from her face. She had always suspected that Billy stepped out with other women; so long as those suspicions remained unfounded, it was easy to push them aside and focus on the daily business of living. But now, here she was, surrounded by coworkers she had known for less than a week, listening to this odious troll of a man laugh as he confirmed her worst fears.

"Come on, Tony," Delaney chided in an uncharacteristic display of backbone. "You don't have to—"

"It's okay, Delaney," Rosie interrupted. "I'm sure Del Vecchio has my husband confused with someone else."

"I don't think so. This guy's five foot nine, light brown hair, and has a big mouth."

"That describes a lot of men," Rosie argued.

"Yeah, but not all of them hang out at The Cannery Bar on Court Street," Del Vecchio countered. "That's where your Billy liked to go before he 'enlisted,' right?"

"I . . . I don't know where he used to go in the evenings," Rosie stammered.

"This guy probably never worked any job longer than two weeks either. Ring any bells?"

Rosie had no time to confirm or deny the statement. Bob Finch, the shift foreman, stepped to the front of the room to announce the day's work assignments. "Miller . . . Jones . . . Murphy . . . machine shop.

Drummond . . . Gaikowski . . . Phillips . . . Snyder . . .
Wallace . . . graving plate. Nelson . . . Scarlatti . . .
you'll be in the belly of the beast. Owen . . . you'll
assist them."

"Mr. Finch," a Negro woman called from the rear of
the room. "I thought I was assisting at the bottom of the
ship."

"You know the rules, Jackson," Finch admonished.
"You have to weigh less than 120 pounds to be let
down there."

"But I—" Jackson began to argue.

"You heard what I said, sweetheart. Cut back on the
meatloaf sandwiches, fried chicken, or whatever you
people eat, and then we'll talk."

Rosie felt her blood boil. Although she had grown
up in a predominantly Irish Catholic neighborhood in
Greenpoint, childhood visits to a grandmother in the
Bronx had introduced Rosie to people of different
races and religions, many of whom helped to look after
her grandmother when her health began to fail. It was
a life lesson to take people one at a time, instead of as
a group.

As Jackson, eyes wide and blinking back tears,
shrank back into the crowd in stunned silence, Finch
continued the morning's announcements with the cool
reserve of a military sharpshooter. "Hansen, Heater . . .
Keefe, Passer . . . Delaney, Bucker . . . Del Vecchio,
Riveter. Gang one, Pier number two."

A "riveting gang," as it was called, consisted of four
members: heater, passer, bucker, and riveter, each of
whom played a vital role.

At the beginning of the workday, each gang would
be dispatched to their section of the ship. There, a safe
distance from the ship's exterior, the heater would lay
wooden planks across a couple of steel beams placed

on the ground, thus making a platform for the portable, gas-burning forge in which he would heat the rivets. While the heater brought the forge to temperature, the three other gang members scaled the scaffold and laid planking along the area where they were going to work. Once they were firmly ensconced on the planking, the bucker and passer would drop a rope scaffold bearing the riveter into the ship and lower it until it was level with the exterior platform. Comprised of three two-by-ten planks, this rope scaffold provided just enough space for the riveter and his tools.

Once setup was complete, the passer and bucker, tools in hand, took their position on the exterior scaffold, while the riveter, on the rope scaffold, waited on the other side of the steel hull. The heater, standing on his platform, would heat a rivet until red hot. Using tongs, he would pick it from the coals of his forge and toss it to the passer, who caught it in a metal can.

Meanwhile, the bucker had unscrewed and pulled out one of the temporary bolts joining the two pieces of steel, leaving the hole empty. The passer would pick the rivet—which, at this stage, was shaped like a mushroom with a button head and a stem—out of his can with a pair of tongs, stick it in the now-vacant hole, and push it in until the head was flush with the steel and the stem protruded from the riveter's side.

While the passer stepped aside and prepared to catch the next rivet, the bucker fitted a tool over the rivet head and held it in place while the riveter pressed the cupped head of his pneumatic hammer against the rivet stem, which was still red hot and malleable, and formed a button head on that side as well.

The process was repeated until every hole that could be reached from the scaffolds was filled with permanent rivets. The scaffolds would then be moved to a new section. The heater's platform, however, remained in place until all the work within a seventy-foot radius had been completed.

Upon hearing her assignment, Rosie sighed noisily. She had spent the previous week acting as passer to the riveting gang of Hansen, Del Vecchio, and Delaney. It was only Tuesday, but this week looked to be shaping up the same way.

Although working on high scaffolding presented its own risk to workers' safety, that risk was far outweighed by the dangers posed by the red-hot rivets as they sailed approximately forty to seventy feet through the air. In the few days since starting at Pushey, Rosie had heard several employees speak of flying rivets that had burned through their clothes, hair, and flesh. And Delaney, a lifelong bucker, had warned Rosie against allowing the hot metal to fall into the vats of oil, varnish, paint, or any of the vast number of flammable chemicals present at the shipyard on a daily basis.

Indeed, for a riveting gang to avoid injury, it was necessary for all four workers to learn to anticipate each other's movements, but nowhere was this truer than in the relationship between heater and passer. The best heater/passer teams in the yard not only minimized the risk of injury, but they enabled the bucker and riveter to work at maximum efficiency and speed while demonstrating a rhythm and flow typically seen only in Major League catchers and pitchers.

Rudy Hansen was one of the best heaters at Pushey Shipyard. In complete control of the forge at all times, he could heat a rivet to the perfect temperature and do so quickly, so that none of it melted away. Meticulous and highly observant, he could determine whether or not a passer would be good at his job within the first few hours of working with him. Unfortunately, the only thing Hansen could determine about this new passer was that she was female.

Rosie followed the rest of her gang into the shipyard and climbed, along with Delaney, to the scaffold. Working at a height of fifty feet granted her a bird's-eye view of the yard below and the cobblestone streets beyond, but the massive steel hull completely obscured her view of Gowanus Bay. *Just as well*, she thought. Catching Hansen's rivets while balancing herself on the narrow platform was difficult enough; she did not need the added distraction of a waterfront view.

Clutching her rivet cone tightly in her hand, she waited for the first toss of the day, fully aware of Hansen's contempt, and confident that he'd persist in the previous day's behavior of consistently overshooting the bucket. While most of yesterday's tosses could still be caught by taking a step backward toward Delaney, the few that had been thrown overhanded, rather than in the traditional underhanded fashion, proved impossible to either catch or dodge and had left large red welts on Rosie's wrists.

It was, therefore, a genuine surprise to find that today, the first, second, and then a third round of rivets landed softly in the bucket.

Still on guard, yet hoping for the best, she caught every rivet Hansen cast her way that morning. Feeling herself falling into the rhythm the other, more experienced passers had described, she finally understood their love for the trade. There was, amongst the creaks and crackles of the narrow walkways, despite the swinging of the ragged old ropes, a beautiful choreography to the process.

Rosie grabbed a hot rivet from her bucket, placed it in a predrilled hole, and smiled to herself. *Perhaps this job will work out*, she thought. *Perhaps I've been too hasty—*

Her thoughts were interrupted by a sudden and sharp burning sensation in the back of her trousers. Rosie turned her head to see a round hole, just about the size of a rivet, singed into the seat of her coveralls. Fifty feet below her, Hansen and another man laughed.

Furious, Rosie shouted from the scaffold, "The next rivet that hits me, Hansen, is getting thrown right back in your face."

Rosie's warning elicited whistles and catcalls from the male workers in the vicinity.

Hansen's smart-aleck response—"If you can't stand the heat, go back to the kitchen"—brought down the house, prompting Bob Finch to emerge from the ship-yard office.

"That's enough, fellas. Get back to work," he commanded. "And Keefe? You open that piehole of yours again, you're outta here."

Finch marched back into his office, leaving a quiet crew to return to their various tasks.

Rosie drew a deep breath and picked up her rivet bucket, hopeful that Hansen would play fair. But, in her heart of hearts, she knew that things wouldn't be that simple—a feeling borne out when Hansen tossed the next bunch of rivets overhanded instead of underhanded, sending the white-hot pieces of metal hurtling past Rosie's bucket and directly toward her head and torso.

Rosie shielded her face with her forearms and yelped as the rivets, reminiscent of glowing grapeshot, burned tiny holes into her kerchief and coat sleeves and sent her scuttling backward along the narrow wooden planks. Fearful she might lose her balance, Delaney rushed from the other end of the scaffold, reached around her coat, and grabbed hold of the elastic waistband of her coveralls.

"You okay, Rosie?" Delaney asked.

She gave no reply. Her anger at the morning's events—Del Vecchio's taunting, Billy's lies, and Finch's reprimands—rushed forth in a torrent. Hastily, she picked three of the hot rivets up from the floorboards with her tongs and made her way down the scaffold.

"Hey, Hansen," Rosie called when she was a few feet away from the forge.

Hansen, his back turned to the scaffold as he laughed and joked with two other men, had been oblivious to Rosie's descent. At the sound of her voice, he turned to confront his redheaded nemesis, his face registering both surprise and confusion.

With a quick motion of her arm, Rosie released the rivets from her tongs and launched them at Hansen's chest. Two of them bounced off of his asbestos apron and landed on the sleeves of his heavy flannel shirt. The third, however, slipped down the top of Hansen's apron, causing the man to scream obscenities and dance around until the metal object, finally extricated, plopped onto the ground.

A highly agitated Bob Finch exploded from his office door. "What the hell is wrong with you, Keefe? Hansen, you hurt bad?"

Hansen shook his head.

"Thank God for that," Finch uttered in relief. "Everyone back to work. Keefe: my office."

Rosie obediently followed Finch into the shipyard office and stood before his desk. The foreman didn't even bother to close the door before launching into his tirade.

"What the hell were you thinking? Hansen is our best heater. You could have burned him—badly."

"Hansen could have burned me badly, too," Rosie argued as she displayed the holes in her coat sleeves and the blistered red flesh on the arms beneath them. "Besides, you shouldn't yell at me. He's the one who started it."

"Yeah, but there's a whole bunch of crazy broads lining up to take your place. There ain't any men left who can fill in for Hansen. You're fired, Keefe."

Rosie's anger and indignation dissipated, immediately replaced by regret and remorse. "But Mr. Finch—"

"No 'buts,' Keefe. Get outta here and let someone with a family to feed have your job."

"But I have a family to feed, too, Mr. Finch. Most of us women do. That's . . . that's why we're here." Her voice cracked as she fought the urge to cry. "Please. Please, Mr. Finch. My sister and her baby moved in with me just a few weeks ago, right after my brother-in-law was killed. I need to take care of them."

"You don't say?"

"Yes." She drew a deep breath. "Please, Mr. Finch, don't fire me. I'm sorry about Hansen. I lost my temper. It won't happen again."

"Damn right, it won't happen again. You think I'd let you anywhere near Hansen after what you did to him?"

"No," she conceded. "But I'll work anywhere else. I'll paint. I'll sweep up. I'll work in the cafeteria. Anything."

"Anything, huh?" A gleam flickered in Finch's eye.

"Yes. Anything. I just need a job."

Finch grinned and shut the office door. "Maybe there is a spot for you. You're a tiny thing. . . . I never noticed it until now. What do you weigh, 105? Or 110?"

"Around there, I guess. Why?" Rosie stepped backward as she felt a wave of anxiety wash over her.

"We could send you to weld the bottom of the

hull." Finch moved closer, his eyes appraising her with every step.

Rosie took another step away from Finch only to back into his desk. "That sounds good," she responded nervously.

"It should. It pays more than you've been making." Finch continued his approach.

"That's very kind of you. Who should I see about being trained?" she asked in an attempt to extricate herself.

Finch grabbed her by the wrist. "Not so fast."

Rosie's heart began racing and she wondered if she should scream. "What are you doing?"

"You and I need to discuss the terms of our agreement."

"Agreement?" she asked as she tried to yank her wrist free of Finch's grasp.

Finch grabbed her other wrist and pulled her closer. "You owe me, Rosie. That's what Delaney calls you, isn't it? 'Rosie.'"

"Let go of me!"

Finch only tightened his grip, all the while smiling menacingly. "Come on now, that's no way to treat the man who just saved your job, is it?"

"I don't want the job. I don't want this. Let me go!" Rosie struggled to break free, but Finch was incredibly strong.

"Let you go? But we're just getting started. You said you'd do anything to keep your job, didn't you?"

"I meant cleaning up or—or . . . but not this," Rosie explained, all the while trying to free her hands.

Finch pushed her backward against the desk. "So you're gonna let that sister and nephew of yours starve just because you changed your mind about playing? That's silly, don't ya think? Especially when we both know you want to." As Finch moved his mouth closer to hers, Rosie leaned forward and gave his lip a hard bite.

Finch reared back and instinctively brought his right hand to his mouth, leaving Rosie's left hand free to grab the heavy green stapler from the desk behind her. Without a second thought, she lifted it above her head and brought it crashing down just above Finch's right temple.

Finch cried out in agony as Rosie swung open the office door and ran into the yard at breakneck speed, bumping into Michael Delaney on the way.

"Rosie, what happened? Your face—it's white. What happened? What did Finch do to you?"

Rosie stared blankly at Delaney, uncertain of what he was saying or asking, certain only of her desire to run.

Several yards away, Bob Finch leaned out of his office door, a trickle of blood wending its way down the side of his face. "Keefe! You slut! I'll make sure you never get a decent job in this town again!"

The area surrounding the office fell silent as all eyes fell, in turn, from Bob Finch to Rose Doyle Keefe.

"Delaney!" Finch shouted. "I'll do the same to you if you don't get back to work!"

Delaney took Rosie's hands and placed in them a handkerchief, a hipflask, and a one-dollar bill. "The money is for a cab so you get home safe," he instructed before sprinting back to his rivet gun. "The rest is for you—in case you need it. I'll check up on you later."

Rosie pocketed Delaney's gifts, shot a vague smile in his direction, and took off through the Pushey Ship-yard gates.

Chapter Two

It was well past dark by the time Rosie returned to her one-bedroom Manhattan apartment. After sitting near the Brooklyn docks for hours, she'd hopped the Brighton Beach subway line and rode it to Coney Island and back before transferring to the Interborough Rapid Transit train that would take her back across the East River into Manhattan. From the Eighth Avenue/Twenty-third-Street stop, it was a two-block walk to the brownstone she and Billy Keefe called home.

Thirteen years had passed since Billy first carried her over the threshold on their wedding night. During that time, Rosie watched her friends and neighbors marry, have children, and move to more spacious apartments and houses, while she and Billy barely scraped by. Realizing that her husband's nonexistent work ethic and her part-time job at the local bakery would never afford them the opportunity to move, Rosie decided to make their apartment the best it could be. Although the space measured just three hundred square feet, Rosie worked hard to ensure that every precious inch wasn't simply clean, but cozy. Using hardware store paint, she breathed new life into her secondhand bedroom set and coffee table, and, with discounted fabric from Montgomery Ward, she hand-stitched curtains, slip-covers, and throw pillows to conceal the threadbare sofa, dime-store bedspread, and dreary view.

Rosie scaled the bare wooden staircase, consoled by the prospect of collapsing onto the slipcovered couch and sinking into the oblivion that only sleep could offer. However, upon arriving to find her sister, Katie, waiting by the apartment door, she knew that sleep would have to wait.

"Oh, Rosie, thank goodness you're home," Katie cried as she threw her arms around her sister. "I've been so worried about you!"

Rosie fell into Katie's arms and buried her face in her younger sister's long, blond hair. Comforted by her sister's familiar scent of baby powder and Chantilly perfume, Rosie felt the tension in her shoulders ease and a trickle of silent tears stream down her face. It was the first time she had cried all day.

"Shh," Katie soothed. "Let it out. You're home now. Mr. Finch is far, far away."

Rosie lifted her head from Katie's shoulder. "How did you—?"

"Michael Delaney came by to check on you. He told me you'd been fired. He also said that . . . well, he said your boss was bleeding when you left. What happened, Rosie? Are you okay? Did he hurt you?"

Rosie entered the apartment and flopped onto the large, upholstered sofa, which, since Katie's arrival, had been serving as her bed. "No, he didn't hurt me. He . . ." Her voice trailed off.

Katie shut the apartment door and sat beside her sister. "You don't have to talk now if you don't want to," she offered as she helped Rosie off with her coat and shoes. "I know it's been a rough day. That's why I laid your pajamas out on the bed. Go get cleaned up and when you come back, if you feel up to it, we can talk over some tea and some soup. It's your favorite: navy bean, just like Pop used to make."

Rosie's eyes again welled with tears. "Oh, Katie-girl," she exclaimed as she embraced her sister. "I know it's not under the best of circumstances, but I'm so glad you and Charlie are here right now."

"I am, too, Rosie."

Rosie's eyes narrowed. "Say, where is that nephew of mine anyway?"

"Oh, I put him down for the night."

"Of course. Stupid of me. I guess I didn't realize how late it was."

"No matter. I'm sure he'd still like a kiss from his Aunt Rosie," Katie replied as she sent her sister off to the apartment's only bedroom.

Rosie tiptoed through the narrow passage between Charlie's crib and the double bed. Peering over the wooden rails, she watched as the towheaded six-month-old, thumb in mouth, slumbered peacefully. With a proud grin, she smoothed his hair and pulled the blanket over his pajama-clad body before retreating to the bathroom for a much-needed shower and change of clothes.

She emerged from the bathroom a few minutes later, still on edge, but better equipped to face the world. After changing into a set of short-sleeved cotton pajamas and a chenille bathrobe, and after conducting another brief check on Charlie, Rosie returned to the living room to find the whitewashed coffee table set with two cups of tea, sugar, milk, and spoons. From the corner of the room, Glenn Miller's "Serenade in Blue" echoed softly from the 1940 Philco console radio.

"What's all this? You don't have to wait on me."

"Oh yes, I do. You've watched over me my entire

life. It's high time I take care of you for a change,"
Katie explained from the kitchen. "How's Charlie?"

"Sound asleep and beautiful." Rosie sighed.

"You'll have one of your own someday."

"I'm not so sure about that."

"Why not?" Katie challenged as she brought two
steaming bowls of soup from the kitchen.

Rosie settled onto the sofa with her bowl and spoon.
"Thanks. This smells wonderful," she said, purposely
avoiding the question.

"I hope it tastes as good as it smells," Katie replied
as she settled beside her sister. "So what do you mean
you're 'not so sure'? Do you mean because of Billy?"

"Mmmm . . ." Rosie slurped her soup noisily. "Gee,
Katie. I think this might be better than Pop's."

"Thanks," Katie answered absently. "Ummm . . . I
heard about Billy and what that man said about seeing
him. I can't believe it! You don't really think he's still
in town, do you?"

Rosie let her spoon drop into her soup bowl. "I don't
know what to think anymore. Part of me refuses to believe that Billy would stoop so low. His disappearing
for a day or two is nothing new, but four months? Where
could he have gone for so long? But then again, if he
did enlist, I would have heard something by now,
wouldn't I? At least I would have gotten his paychecks."

"Not if he didn't arrange to send them to you."

"True. It's not like I got his paychecks when he was
at home. Why should this be any different? But I . . .
well, I'd like to think he'd write me to tell me where
he was."

"When Jimmy got shipped out, he wrote to me from
the train that same day," Katie recalled with a wistful

smile. "I didn't receive it until two weeks later, but still . . ."

Rosie placed a comforting arm on her sister's shoulder. "I'm sorry, Katie-girl. Here I am going on about Billy when . . ." Her voice grew faint.

"That's all right," Katie assured as she patted Rosie on the knee. "They're good memories. Besides, I was the one who brought up Billy in the first place."

"Yeah, but—" Rosie narrowed her eyes and let her arm slip from Katie's shoulder. "Say, how did you know about Billy anyway?"

"Delaney, of course."

"Of course." Rosie shook her head. "Wow, you two had a regular gabfest, didn't you? I always knew Delaney was sweet on you."

"Sweet on me? Dream on, Macbeth! Delaney's been following you around since grade school." Katie laughed. "Makes you wonder, though, doesn't it? What would your life be like if you had married someone like him instead of Billy Keefe?"

"Given the Delaneys' ability to reproduce, I'd probably have six kids by now."

"All of them with your red hair and Michael's glorious nose!"

"Now, wouldn't that be pretty? But then again, I probably wouldn't be sitting here, feeling like such a fool."

"You're not a fool. You trusted the man you married, the man you love."

"But I shouldn't have trusted him. I've always suspected there were other women. I just didn't want to think about it, that's all." Rosie picked up her spoon and poked at the beans in her soup. "The other thing is . . . well, I'm not sure I do love Billy. Not anymore. I think I fell out of love with him quite some time ago."

"So what are you going to do?"

"I don't know. Right now, I have other things to worry about. Like, for instance, the fact that I no longer have a job."

"You're one of the hardest-working people I know. Why were you fired? And why was your boss bleeding when you left?"

Rosie told Katie about the incident with Hansen and then the scene in Finch's office.

Katie gasped. "Oh, Rosie, honey, I'm so sorry! You wouldn't have taken that job if it weren't for me and Charlie moving in with you."

Rosie shook her head. "It's not your fault. Whether you were here or not, I'd still have to find something to take the place of Billy's paycheck."

"Yeah, but without our mouths to feed you could have taken a shop-clerk job or something that paid less. I never liked the idea of you working at the docks with all those men. It's dangerous."

"No, Katie! I love having you and Charlie here. With Billy gone, I don't know what I'd do if you weren't. As for a shop-clerk job, I would have taken one if there were any. Right now, every job out there has something to do with the war. No, the only person to blame here is me. If I had only kept my cool and not lost my temper, none of this would have happened. I wouldn't have been fired and Finch wouldn't have tried what he did."

"Listen, even if you had managed to keep your cool, I don't think it would have made a single bit of difference. Should you have thrown rivets back at Hansen? Maybe not. But if you hadn't stuck up for yourself, the next batch of rivets he threw at you could have gotten you right in the face or, worse, caused you to fall off that scaffold. No, lamb, the problem isn't with you, it's with them."

"As much as I agree with your sentiments," Rosie said, "part of me thinks I should have tried to tough it out a little longer, especially knowing what that shipyard paycheck would mean to our bank account."

"Well, that shouldn't be entirely on your shoulders," Katie declared. "In fact, from this point on, I'm going to do my share."

"Katie," Rosie admonished, "we already discussed this and we both agreed that your most important job right now is taking care of Charlie."

"And I will take care of him. I'll just have some help doing it."

"We can't afford to pay someone to watch him," Rosie pointed out. "Besides, he's just a baby. I don't like the idea of some stranger helping to raise him."

"It wouldn't be a stranger. Ma would watch him."

"Ma isn't going to take the train from Greenpoint and back everyday."

"No, you're right, she wouldn't want to do that . . . but . . . um . . . well . . . what if she didn't have to?" Katie suggested.

Rosie's eyes grew wide. "Oh no, Katie, you only just got here and I like having you around. Please say you're not moving back with Ma!"

"Okay, I'm not moving back with Ma," Katie reassured.

"Good. That's better."

"All three of us are."

"What?" Rosie put her bowl of soup on the coffee table and threw her head against the back of the sofa.

"Come on, Rosie," Katie coaxed. "Just think about it. Ma has that great big house sitting empty. We could each have our own room—that means no more sleeping on the sofa for you."

Rosie closed her eyes and sighed.

"And," Katie continued, "Ma's house is paid for. If she continues to take in mending, I get a part-time job, and you get a job at another shipyard—"

"I don't know if I can," Rosie interrupted. "Finch has probably bad-mouthed me to every other yard in Brooklyn."

"Then you check the yards here in Manhattan. Or the airplane factories in Queens," Katie said resolutely. "The point is, if the three of us pool our money, we'd have more than enough to make ends meet."

"You're overlooking two very important things: First, Ma drives me crazy."

"Ma drives me crazy, too." Katie shrugged. "She drives everyone crazy. But she loves us and means well. Besides, there's strength in numbers; so long as you and I stick together Ma doesn't stand a chance."

"Second," Rosie went on, "I'm a married woman. I can't just call my landlord and move out."

"Why can't you? Billy packed up his stuff and went off to war without giving you a second thought." Katie added under her breath, "If, in fact, he's even at war."

Rosie sighed noisily. Everything Katie said about Billy made perfect sense, but it still didn't make it any easier for her to let go. "It seems strange, taking off and not telling him."

"Leave a forwarding address. If and when Billy ever sees fit to write you, you can tell him then. If he makes a big stink about it, tell him you would have said something sooner but you had no way of getting in touch with him."

"You're right," Rosie relented. "It's silly to stay here in this tiny apartment struggling until Billy comes home or sends along a paycheck. Moving to Greenpoint would give us more room and more money, and it'd be healthier for Charlie in the long run, what with that big backyard. Still, it's a big decision, Katie, and today has been . . . Just do me a favor and let me sleep on it before you say anything to Ma."

Katie's face flushed bright scarlet.

"Oh no." Rosie bolted upright. "Katie? What did you do?"

"Hmm?" The blond sister feigned innocence.

"You already called Ma, didn't you?"

"Nooo," she sang. "Ma called me. Delaney flapped his gums to his mother about you being fired and Mrs. Delaney called Ma, who, in turn, called me."

"So this was all Ma's idea?"

"Nooo," Katie sang again. "Well, maybe some of it. The rest was mine, though. But no matter who thought of it, I still think it's a good idea."

"And maybe it is," Rosie admitted. "But you know how Ma gets when she's excited. And nothing could be more exciting to her than the thought of both of us and her only grandchild moving back home."

There was a loud knock on the apartment door. "Good grief! That's probably her now."

"It's too late for Ma." Katie dismissed the thought with a wave of her hand.

"Are you kidding? She'd come here in the middle of the night, strap the furniture to her back, and walk it to Brooklyn, if she thought it would get us there faster." Rosie got up and opened the door just wide enough to poke her head through and just narrow enough to obscure Katie's view. She gave a wink to the tall man on the other side of the door and put a finger to her lips in order to ensure he didn't give the game away. "Oh, hi, Ma. We were just talking about you."

"Stop it! I know it's not Ma," Katie shouted from the sofa.

Meanwhile the tall man in the gray tweed overcoat and gray fedora narrowed his blue eyes. "I beg your pardon?"

"I'm sorry," Rosie quickly apologized. "I was playing a joke on my sister."

It was a bit late in the evening for vacuum salesmen, but then again, this man, with medium brown hair that was slightly gray at the temples, finely chiseled features, and a five-o'clock shadow that was four hours past due, didn't look like the type who sold household appliances. "May I help you?" she asked.

"Rose Keefe?"

"Yes."

The man extracted a badge from the top pocket of his overcoat. "Lieutenant Jack Riordan, NYPD. You're wanted for questioning in the murder of Robert Finch."

Chapter Three

Lieutenant Jack Riordan sat in the austere, gray interrogation room and stared across the white enamel tabletop at his suspect. The practice of silently studying individuals prior to questioning them was a process Riordan had learned as a young cadet, and it had served him well in his twenty-five years with the police department.

The purpose behind the exercise was twofold. First, the period of extended silence tended to catch wary suspects off guard, thus setting them off balance and making them far likelier to trip up during questioning. Second, by quietly watching a subject, Riordan often observed body language that might suggest that a person was guilty: lack of eye contact, a lowered head, or fidgeting. If these signals occurred more frequently during the questioning process, it was a clear indication that Riordan was on the right track.

Rose Doyle Keefe, however, demonstrated none of Riordan's "tells." Having changed from her chenille bathrobe and pajamas into a long-sleeved printed gray rayon dress that hugged her narrow waist perfectly, she sat, legs uncrossed, feet together, hands resting openly on the table in front of her. Her peaches-and-cream complexion remained constant and her wide hazel eyes boldly met his unflinching gaze.

Riordan endeavored to continue the exercise a few moments longer, but it was he, not Rosie, who was struck by the overwhelming urge to look away. As a clean-shaven young man came into the room, Riordan cleared his throat awkwardly. "Mrs. Keefe, this is Detective Lynch. He'll be taking notes on our conversation."

Rosie murmured a quiet "hello" to the detective, then returned her eyes to Riordan's.

"Please be advised, Mrs. Keefe," the lieutenant continued, "that if, at any time, you wish to stop the questioning and contact an attorney, you have the right to do so."

Rosie nodded.

"Do you know why you're here, Mrs. Keefe?" Riordan asked.

"Yes. Mr. Finch is dead."

"Not just dead—murdered. At approximately five o'clock this evening, his body was discovered beneath an abandoned pier a short distance from the Pushey Shipyard. His skull was bashed in."

The color drained from Rose's face—an indication of surprise, not guilt. "I didn't do it," she averred.

"No one is suggesting you did, Mrs. Keefe, but excuse me if it doesn't seem to be outside the realm of possibility. We know what happened at the shipyard this morning. After he caught you assaulting a coworker with hot rivets, Finch called you into his office and fired you. Witnesses say he was bleeding after you left."

"That was just so I could get out of there! I never—!"

"No one's saying you do this sort of thing all the time, Mrs. Keefe. Finch assaulted you and you snapped.

It's a very natural reaction. So, here's how I imagined it happened: you became angry and lashed out. You hit him on the side of the head with the heaviest object you could find . . . a telephone, for instance. But then you quickly realized that you couldn't kill him then and there—too many people around. So you came back at the end of the shift, lured Finch beneath the pier, and finished the job."

Rosie felt her face grow hot. "Why do you need me here, then? It's obvious you have the whole thing figured out."

"Because we need to hear it from you."

"You want me to tell you what happened? Fine. I'll tell you what happened. First, I didn't assault anyone—Hansen threw the hot rivets at me first. I simply retaliated. If you don't believe me, take a look at the holes burned into my coat sleeves." She lifted her coat from the back of her chair and held the sleeves aloft. As promised, the cuffs were singed with holes.

"Second"—she resumed as she replaced the coat—"I didn't lose my temper when Finch fired me. On the contrary, I begged for a second chance. Finch used my desperation as an opportunity to force his attentions on me. I hit him on the head—with a stapler, not a telephone—as a means to escape."

"Why didn't you scream?" Riordan countered.

"I don't know," Rosie stated blankly. "I honestly don't know. Perhaps I didn't think I'd be heard or, given the welcome I had received, I didn't think anyone would care."

"Where did you go after that?"

"I ran from Finch's office and bumped into a friend of mine, Michael Delaney, on my way out of the shipyard."

"Did you tell this friend what had happened?"

"No, but he knew something was wrong."

"And after leaving the shipyard, what did you do?"

"I sat by the water. Wandered around town. Rode the train for hours."

"What time did you get home?"

"Thirty, maybe forty minutes before you showed up."

"Did you speak to anyone or run into anyone you knew during this time?"

Rosie shook her head. "No one other than my sister. She was waiting for me when I got back home."

Riordan sat back in his chair and clasped his hands behind his head.

"It looks awfully black against me," she acknowledged.

"You have to admit you had the means, and Finch's advances give you an even stronger motive than we previously thought."

Rosie's eyes grew steely. "A stronger motive? Lieutenant Riordan, if I lured every man who's yelled at me, made a pass at me, or otherwise treated me badly, down to the docks and murdered them, you'd be able to walk across Gowanus Bay on the bodies."

Riordan leaned forward and propped his elbows on the table. "Has life been as bad as that?"

"It's had its moments—most of them today," she replied with a sardonic grin. "I suppose you're going to keep me here, being the main suspect and all."

"I don't think that will be necessary. The detective here will give you a ride home. Just promise me you'll stay put. No wandering to Jersey, huh?"

With an earnest nod of the head, Rosie stood up and donned her coat.

"Oh, and another thing." Riordan's face softened. "Next time you need to hit someone with a piece of office equipment, use a telephone. It will knock him out instead of just making him angry."

Rosie cast Riordan a puzzled glance before leaving with Detective Lynch.

Riordan sank back in his chair and, once again, placed his hands behind his head. To the casual passerby, it was a stance of confidence, perhaps even arrogance, but for Jack Riordan, it was a means of dealing with frustration.

The door of the interrogation room swung open.

"Good evening, Captain," Riordan greeted without looking up.

Short, stocky, and with a ruddy complexion, Captain Richard Kinney always appeared to be one step away from an apoplectic fit. Tonight, however, he seemed to be in its very throes. "Was that the Keefe woman I just saw leaving?"

"It was," Riordan confirmed.

Kinney ran a hand through his thinning hair and inhaled deeply. "Why? Why did you let her go?"

"Because she didn't do it."

"Oh?" Kinney broke into laughter. "So she swivels her hips and lets a tear run down that pretty white face of hers and suddenly she's a saint."

"She's not a saint." Riordan smiled, all the while staring at the chair Rosie had occupied. "But she's far from being a murderer."

"Says who? Need I remind you that this precinct is still facing public ridicule for your public crusade against Frank Costello?"

"You needn't remind me. The people you need to remind are the citizens and politicians of this city. Just because Costello has more manners than his predecessor, Lucky Luciano, it doesn't mean he's any less dangerous. If anything, his nice-guy image makes him even more powerful. But of course, that's exactly why my crusade is so unpopular, isn't it? Because it ruffles the feathers of those he has in his pocket."

"Quit it, Jack. This has nothing to do with the Mafia, and you know it. The Pushey family—as in the owners of Pushey Shipyard—contacted me as soon as they heard about Finch's murder. They want this thing wrapped up, quickly and quietly, before their name gets dragged through the papers."

Riordan withdrew a cigarette from the inside pocket of his jacket, lit it, and took a long drag. "Five days. Considering the press has, or should have, lots of other news to report, it's not unreasonable."

Kinney was nonplussed. "Five days? For what?"

Riordan snuffed his cigarette and rose from his seat. "Five days to follow Keefe and to investigate the case," he stated as he stared down at his captain. "At the end of five days, if I don't have an arrest that will survive a jury, you can have my badge."

"I don't want your badge, Riordan. You're the best I have."

"Then don't hold the Costello case over my head. Had you given me the time I requested, we could have gotten Costello *and* his henchmen, but you and your friends couldn't wait and the charges bounced." Riordan shook his head. "I won't be rushed on this one. I won't send an innocent woman to the gallows just because you and your friends are 'antsy.'"

"No, five days sounds . . . fair, Riordan" Kinney said. "Unless . . ."

Riordan raised an eyebrow in warning. "No stipulations." With that, he strode out of the interrogation room.

Chapter Four

Rosie shut the door of the squad car and watched as it drove away before ascending the wooden brownstone stairs to the second floor. As she had done earlier that night, Katie stood on the other side of the apartment door, awaiting her sister's arrival. Only this time, Rosie didn't feel like chatting.

"There you are!" Katie exclaimed. "What happened? Why did they need to speak to you?"

"Finch was murdered," she replied as she hung her coat on the row of hooks attached to the back of the apartment door.

"I know. I heard Lieutenant what's-his-name. But how? When?"

"Sometime this afternoon. They found him under the docks." Rosie, not wanting to worry her sister, lied about the means of death. "He was stabbed."

"Oh! And you argued with him today—oh! They don't think you did it, do they?"

"No," she lied. "They know I wouldn't have used a knife. They had to question me because I had a motive, but it's okay. Lieutenant Riordan assured me that it would be fine." Rosie pulled the lieutenant's business card from the pocket of her dress and glanced at it. Even in the most serene of moments, she was terrible at remembering names, but for some reason the lieutenant's rolled off her tongue with ease.

"Are you sure? I mean, having a cop come to your door—"

"I'm positive." She embraced Katie tightly. Rosie's need to protect her younger sister had only gotten stronger since Jimmy's death. "It's almost midnight. You should get some sleep. Charlie will be awake before you know it."

Katie relinquished her hold on Rosie's waist and emitted a loud yawn. "It has been a heck of a day, hasn't it?"

"It has," Rosie agreed with a vague smile. "And tomorrow's going to be just as difficult once you tell Ma that we're moving back home."

Katie's lovely face stretched into a wide grin. "You've decided, then?"

Rosie nodded slowly. If she was going to go to jail, she wanted to make sure that Katie and Charlie were settled in and cared for. "Yes. I'll give the landlord notice and try to sell off some of this stuff before I leave, but you and Charlie should go as soon as you can."

"Oh no. We should move together. I can stay and help you pack and—"

"Don't be silly, Katie. We can barely move in this place as it is. It will be a lot easier for me to pack with your stuff over at Ma's. Besides, the weather's getting nicer. Charlie should be out in the fresh air instead of breathing in the city dust and dirt."

"I guess . . . but what about you? Will you be okay here on your own? I feel like I should be helping."

"You will be helping. Once Ma knows for sure we're all moving in, she'll be breathing down our necks nonstop until every stick of furniture is back in Greenpoint.

But if you and Charlie move first, you can keep her occupied while I tie up loose ends here."

"How long will that be?"

"Not long at all. I have a monthly lease. So two more weeks maybe?"

Katie nodded. "I'm glad you decided to move, Rosie. Things'll work out fine. You'll see."

"And if not, at least I'll be with you and Charlie." She smiled wanly. "Now hurry off to bed. You have a busy next few days in store and we can talk more in the morning."

"Okay. Do you need anything before I go?"

"No, my pajamas and robe are there on the couch where I left them."

"Okay. Good night, Rosie."

"Good night, sweetie."

Rosie waited until Katie had shut the bedroom door before changing out of her gray dress and last pair of good stockings and back into her cotton pajamas. Forgoing her robe, she crept to the narrow coat closet and extracted a men's navy blue sports coat from a wire hanger. Burying her face in the soft wool fabric, she was overcome by the familiar scent of Courtlay Cologne.

Oh, Billy, if only you were here, none of this would be happening.

Silent tears streamed down her pink cheeks and plopped softly onto the collar of her floral printed pajamas.

If only you'd come home, she wished. But it didn't take long before she realized the futility of such yearning. The truth was that in their thirteen years of marriage, Billy Keefe had never been there when she needed him. When they couldn't make rent, it was Rosie who spoke to the landlord and then worked to make up the difference. On the few occasions when Billy drank the grocery money, it was Rosie's good name that obtained them a small line of credit. And when Rosie's father died suddenly, of a massive heart attack, Billy was unavailable—until a uniformed policeman found him passed out in an alley and brought him home.

Still, Rosie might overlook all those moments if Billy was here now. She knew that he would be of little help in getting her out of the present situation, but at least he might hold her and try to assuage her sense of fear and loneliness.

Rosie folded the jacket tenderly and, wiping away her tears, placed it on the top shelf of the closet beside her meager collection of hats and gloves. There was no point in waiting for Billy to return, no time to waste waiting for someone to rescue her. She had to rely upon herself to find a way out of this mess and, after having considered her options during the ride from the police station, she decided there was only one way in which she could both pay the bills and clear her name.

She had to get back her job at Pushey Shipyard.

Lieutenant Jack Riordan made the lonely, late-night drive back to the Brooklyn row house owned by Mrs. Anne Marie Accurso. Accurso, a sixty-two-year-old widow and mother of two sons, put the third floor of her house up for rent shortly after her husband, Genarro, passed away three years earlier. Featuring a small hot plate, an icebox, and a full, private bathroom, the space also included use of the house's driveway, all for the price of fifteen dollars a month—a steal for such a safe, quiet, well-established neighborhood.

Riordan, ever mindful that scores of other tenants would be willing to pay twenty dollars and more to live in the Carroll Gardens area, made a point to occasionally slip his landlady a few extra dollars or, when he was in the Little Italy neighborhood, purchase a box of her favorite pignoli cookies. Since the marriage of Mrs. Accurso's elder son, Vincent, and the deployment of her younger son, Bruno, into the army, Riordan had even taken to helping with the traditionally male chores of mowing the lawn, changing lightbulbs, taking out the trash, and, as he had done the past weekend, tilling the soil of Mrs. Accurso's prized rose garden.

Such deeds did not go unnoticed by the widow. And therefore, when Mrs. Accurso saw that her tenant was working late, she would sneak upstairs and leave a foil-covered plate of meatballs, lasagna, braciole, or some other Italian delicacy in his icebox and then, mindful of his privacy, hasten back downstairs again.

And so the pair coexisted peacefully, each performing a certain function in the other's life, but never quite fulfilling the void created by absent family and loved ones. With her scant knowledge of English, Mrs. Accurso didn't provide much in the way of company or conversation, but, after spending his days chasing down mobsters, murderers, and thugs, Riordan found that he seldom felt like talking anyway. Mrs. Accurso, for her part, knew only that her tenant was a policeman who had been in the newspapers, a fact that served to make her feel safe but failed to impress her old world sensibilities. Her focus was on home, hearth, and family; she had no desire to hear, read, or involve herself in the ugliness of the masculine universe.

Likewise, Anne Marie Accurso found Riordan's bachelor status quite confusing. Although no match for her Genarro, God rest his soul, the lieutenant was certainly handsome enough and possessed a strong build that many young women would find appealing. Yet she had never seen him with a lady friend. If the man had no interest in women, then why did he not pursue a career in the priesthood?

Tiptoeing up the red-carpeted stairs to the third floor, Riordan arrived in the space that served as living room, bedroom, and kitchenette. After switching on the light, he flung his hat onto the trundle bed and, with his coat still on, reached into the icebox for a beer. Finding Mrs. Accurso's food parcel instead, he lifted out the plate and peeked under the aluminum foil to find a pair of stuffed green peppers smothered in tomato sauce.

With a sigh, Riordan turned on the hot plate and put the peppers on the burner. As much as he enjoyed Mrs. Accurso's cooking and appreciated her meal deliveries, every now and then he hoped to look beneath the wrapper and find a T-bone steak and a baked potato.

With dinner heating, Riordan removed his overcoat, threw it onto the bed with his hat, and returned to the icebox to retrieve his beer. Using the edge of the counter, he popped the cap from the brown bottle and took a long swig before moving to the set of double windows that looked out onto the front garden and, a few feet beyond it, the street.

The clouds that had cast a pall over the day had finally released their burden, covering the earth below in a fine mist. Riordan, however, had other things on his mind besides the weather. Ever since their interview, he could not stop thinking of Rose Doyle Keefe. There was her beauty, of course—dark red hair set against alabaster skin and a set of pink lips that hypnotized as they moved—but there was something else to that face, a sense of defiance, determination, and quiet strength that he had never before witnessed in a woman.

Riordan took another swig from the bottle and undid his tie. Colleagues had always accused him of being a sucker for damsels in distress and, for the most part, they were right. Abandoned by her husband shortly after their son was born, Riordan's mother had taken any odd job she could find in order to support herself and her child. As soon as Jack was old enough, he contributed to household expenses by selling newspapers and working as a clerk at the corner market. His efforts, however, came too late. Weakened by years of hard labor and poor nutrition, Riordan's mother became ill with pulmonary tuberculosis and was sent to a sanatorium. She died there, two years later, at the age of forty-eight. Her son, Jack, was just seventeen.

Be it due to guilt over his mother's life of struggle and sacrifice or frustration over his inability to save her, Riordan grew to become a man who revered women. Their ability to endure the physical pain of childbirth and to consistently put their children's needs ahead of their own made them, in Riordan's opinion, not just the fairer but the psychologically stronger of the sexes.

And yet, despite their strength, they were socially vulnerable. From birth to marriage to childrearing, it seemed that woman's fate lay perpetually in the hands of men. The good fortune of having a kind father and a loving husband made the difference between a happy life and one of constant toil and heartache.

Riordan's job with the police department had put him in contact with many women who had entrusted their physical and financial well-being to rogues, rapists, and abusers. As always, he followed the letter of the law to ensure that justice was done, but if he appeared to devote a bit more time to their cases, go a bit softer on their interviews and interrogations, or even act as an advocate to ensure their voices were heard, it was because he felt that these women were truly deserving of the extra time and care.

Occasionally, a nefarious female would take advantage of Riordan's kindness, leaving him to doubt the wisdom of his ways. At other times, his desire to protect compromised the other relationships in his life, such as ten years ago when his then-fiancée, citing that Riordan was putting too much time into finding a woman's lost child, cancelled their trip to the altar. Sometimes, as was the case now, defending a female suspect had even put him on the wrong side of the captain's good graces.

Defending Rose Keefe, however, felt different to Riordan. It felt, for lack of a better word, "right." Her reaction in the interrogation room was not the usual display of tears and hysterics. She made no ploy for sympathy nor did she beg for clemency. Other policemen might have taken this as an indication that she was coldly detached from the situation or perhaps even the world around her. Riordan, however, understood it to mean that, whatever hardships she had endured, Rose Keefe was the type of woman who was determined to stand on her own feet.

Riordan polished off the remainder of his beer and wandered back to the hot plate. Lifting off the aluminum-foil cover, he shifted the contents of the plate with the help of a kitchen fork and then re-covered them to continue the reheating process. Depositing the dirty fork on top of the icebox with a frown, he ambled to the trundle bed and perched beside his coat and hat.

Rose Keefe might not have asked, nor even have wanted, Riordan's assistance, but that was probably because she wasn't aware of just how much she needed it. Although, so far, all the evidence in the Finch case was circumstantial, Rose's outburst paired with the assault with the stapler painted a very dark picture for the redhead.

Riordan's men would be at the shipyard and nearby docks until the wee hours, collecting evidence. The problem was, with the shipyard closed until morning, evidence was all they would find. In order to clear Keefe's name, one had to identify other possible suspects.

And that required questioning the employees of Pushey Shipyard.

Chapter Five

Subconsciously aware of the sound of whispers emanating from a space somewhere above her head, Rosie awoke with a start. As she blinked the sleep out of her eyes, the concerned faces of her mother and Katie crystallized through the fog.

"Ma? What are you doing here?" Rosie sat up and ran her hands over her face.

Standing just over five feet tall and weighing in at one hundred and thirty pounds, sixty-two-year-old Evelyn Mary Doyle was, despite her petite size, formidable. Like a small dog who assumes a larger-than-life attitude in order to intimidate larger foes, Evelyn had learned early on that speaking loudly, gazing directly, and standing straight, with hands on hips and nose in the air, went a long way toward making both enemies and strong-minded daughters cry "uncle."

Standing at Rosie's feet, Evelyn combined the hands-on-hips pose with a defiant forward thrust of the chest. "I'm here to take care of my eldest daughter. Where else would I be?"

With a loud yawn, Rosie swung her feet over the side of the couch and onto the tufted floral area rug. She was in no mood to field what would, inevitably, turn into a never-ending stream of questions. "There's nothing to take care of, Ma. I'm fine. Really."

"Fine? Is that why Margaret Delaney called me yesterday? To tell me that everything was fine? Still, at least Michael talks to his mother."

"Ma, please . . ."

"And I suppose that's why you were asleep all morning, eh? Because you're 'fine'?"

Rosie leaped from the sofa in horror. "I've been asleep all morning? What time is it?"

"A little before noon. Katie and I tried to wake you, but you were delirious. Talking in your sleep about things that made no sense. At one point you even shouted at us not to touch you."

"I'm sorry," Rosie muttered as she frantically folded her blankets. She had hoped to get to Pushey before the morning shift started. But if she hurried, she might at least be able to get to Red Hook in time to put in a half-day's work. That is, if Finch's replacement agreed to take her back.

"That's all you have to say for yourself, is it? 'I'm sorry' and 'I'm fine.'"

"For now, yes. Say, why don't you stay here with Katie and Charlie this afternoon? And then, tonight at supper, I'll answer all your questions. I promise."

"But—"

"I don't have time to talk right now, Ma. I should have been at the shipyard hours ago!" Rosie realized her mistake too late, but on the off chance that her mother hadn't caught the name of her intended destination, she turned on one heel and hastened toward the bedroom.

Rosie should have known better. Her father had frequently joked that Evelyn's hearing was so acute that she would complain at night about the neighbor's dog barking, even though it had been six years since both neighbor and dog had moved to Westchester County.

"Rosaleen Elizabeth!" Evelyn exploded, sending wisps of graying auburn hair tumbling from the bun atop her head.

Evelyn had always called her daughters by their Christian names, but combining them with their middle, or Saint's, names meant business. Rosie froze in her tracks.

"Did I just hear you say that you're going back to that . . . that place?"

Rosie turned around slowly and mirrored her mother's hands-on-hips pose. "Yes, you did."

Katie, flaxen haired and even-tempered like her father, had witnessed several of these power plays as a child and, therefore, knew that it was only a matter of time before she was drawn into the middle of the argument. Hoping to escape the apartment unseen, she grabbed an amused Charlie from his blanket on the floor and inched toward the door.

"Katherine Brigid! And just where do you think you're going?" Evelyn boomed.

"I . . . I was just taking Charlie for a walk."

"You're not taking my grandson anywhere. Not until you talk some sense into your sister." Evelyn met her younger daughter at the door and took the baby from her arms.

"Oh, but Ma," Katie whined.

"Don't 'but Ma' me. You've been every bit as worried as I have."

"Ma, leave her out of this," Rosie ordered.

"No," Katie spoke up. "Ma's right. I was sick after Delaney's call yesterday. And then, this morning, with you thrashing around so, I didn't know what to think. That's why I asked Ma to come by."

Rosie recalled Katie's promise from the night before. "Nice job sticking together, sis."

"I'll stick by you when you start making sense. You know Ma and I would be devastated if something were to happen to you. And yet, you want to go back to the shipyard, with all those men. After . . . after what happened."

"I don't like the idea any more than you do, but I have to get my job back."

"There's no need, Rosaleen," Evelyn argued. "You and your sister are moving back home with me. It's already been settled."

"I know, Ma, but I still need the job."

"Why? With the three of us sharing expenses, you can take it easier. I hear the bakery shop over on Bedford is looking for a counter clerk. The hours are good and it's right around the corner. That'll save you money on the train."

"I can't, Ma. Not right now."

"But you can go back to a job you were fired from? Where someone was murdered?"

Rosie shook her head. "You don't understand. I have to."

"Here we go again. That's exactly what you said when your father and I objected to you marrying William." Again Evelyn Doyle ignored the existence of nicknames. "'You don't understand, Ma, I'll just die if I don't marry him!' Your father and I thought you were in trouble, but no. You were just so in love you couldn't see straight. You went off and eloped, and look where it got you. No children, no money, and a husband who's God only knows where."

Rosie glared at her sister.

"Katherine didn't tell me," Evelyn announced. "Mrs. Delaney did. But it didn't take a phone call from her to tell me that you're unhappy. Too late now, though. You made your decision to marry and it can't be undone. Still, you'd think you might have learned something, but now here you are again, not listening to reason, running off to get back a job that might kill you."

Rosie blinked back her tears. "This is a different situation, Ma," she said quietly. "Someday I hope to explain it to you, but right now, there's somewhere I need to be. Will I see you at supper?"

Evelyn folded her arms across her chest and turned her nose up. "I don't know. I haven't decided."

"Well, then, have a good afternoon." With that, Rosie marched off to the bedroom and slammed the door.

Rosie changed into a pale green shirtdress and a cardigan sweater and, with a pair of cotton workcloth coveralls stuffed into her oversized handbag, caught the 12:25 train to Brooklyn. After checking in at Pushey's front gate, she stepped from the unseasonably warm April air and through the heavy metal doors of the main building. The dreary, windowless holding area, typically resonating with laughter and chatter as employees awaited the start of their shift, was now vacant and eerily quiet.

Less than twenty-four hours had elapsed since she'd last stood in this room, and yet it felt like it had been months. In that brief period of time, her marriage, her job, and her freedom had all been compromised. At the moment, Rosie could do nothing to save nor improve her marriage, but she could work on preserving the other two.

She sighed heavily and exited through the heavy steel door to the shipyard, which was abuzz with coverall-clad employees working furiously to make up for the previous day's cancelled night shift. It was not long, however, before attention switched away from production and to the redheaded visitor standing outside the holding area doors.

The shipyard gradually fell silent as all eyes fell on Rosie.

Amid the sea of disapproving stares, Rosie felt her pulse begin to race. *What am I doing here?* she wondered to herself. *Everyone thinks I killed Finch! They're never going to give me my job back. I might as well—*

She was about to retreat back into the employee holding area when she noticed a petite woman in her mid-twenties walking toward her. Her blue coveralls were stained with splotches of black grease in every conceivable size and shape and her cheeks bore traces of dirt and grime, yet her brunette hair, tied in a pink kerchief, and her ruby tinted lips demonstrated that this young woman had no intention of trading in her femininity for a steady paycheck.

"Keefe?" she asked as she offered a gloved right hand.

Rosie, in wonderment, took the hand and nodded.

"Nelson," the younger woman introduced herself. "I just wanted to thank you for sticking up for us."

"I beg your pardon?"

"Hansen and a few of the other guys have been giving us girls a tough time ever since we got here. Lots of us thought about doing what you did, but we were too scared to go through with it. Thanks for being brave. Thanks for showing them that we don't have to take their guff."

"That really wasn't something I planned," Rosie explained. "I just got mad, that's all."

"Doesn't matter why. You still stuck up for yourself. And, for the record, I don't think you did it."

Rosie's face was a question.

"Killed Finch, I mean," Nelson clarified. "But even

if you did, we'll stand behind you. Finch had it coming to him."

"What the hell's goin' on out here?" a man's voice suddenly bellowed. "I didn't call for a break."

Rosie spun around and watched as the figure of Tony Del Vecchio emerged from the shadows of the red brick building behind her.

"What's everyone staring at? Did FDR decide to pay us a—?" At the sight of Rosie, Del Vecchio fell silent.

"So you're the new foreman," Rosie deduced. "I should have guessed."

Del Vecchio cleared his throat before launching back into command mode. "All right, people, back to work. There's nothing to see here. You, too, Nelson. I've had enough of your yappin' for one day."

As Nelson trudged back to the dock and the loud whir of hydraulic guns resumed, Del Vecchio waved Rosie back into the main building and shut the door. "If you're here for your last check, Keefe, I ain't got it. All the hours for the week are still in Finch's office. The cops have had it locked up since they got here last night."

"I'm not here for that. I'm here for a job."

"A job?" Del Vecchio laughed dismissively. "You got one helluva nerve!"

"Finch shouldn't have fired me in the first place, Del Vecchio. You know that. I was on your gang. I kept up with both you and Delaney and never once complained. It was Hansen who started the trouble."

"Hey, I'm not gonna argue with you. Should Hansen have done what he did? No. Were you a hard worker? Sure. But that don't matter now. What does matter is that every guy out there thinks you murdered Finch."

"I sort of gathered that when I walked in."

"Yeah. You wanna face that every day?"

The prospect gave Rosie pause, but she knew she

couldn't waver. "It might be tough at first, but in time, they'll get used to me being here. And by then, the police will have proven I didn't do it."

"Oh yeah? Well, why don't you come back when they have? It'll be easier on both of us."

"Because I need the money now."

Del Vecchio ran a hand over his round, pockmarked face in exasperation. "Look, you're just not gettin' it. I can't have some killer working here."

"But I'm not a killer."

"I don't know that for sure." Del Vecchio pointed to the doors that led to the yard. "The fellas out there don't know that."

"Call me crazy, but doesn't this country believe that a man or, in this case, woman is 'innocent until proven guilty'? Why are we even fighting this war if people like you are so quick to throw away those beliefs?" Rosie felt embarrassed to have used patriotism and propaganda to further her own cause, but she quickly recovered. She had her own war to fight.

"Oh no. Don't you go pinnin' that on me! Not after the trouble you caused me this morning."

"Trouble? What trouble are you in? If anything, it looks to me like you got a promotion. And probably a raise to go along with it."

"Oh yeah, I got a promotion, all right. A promotion, a raise, and a lot of headaches. That thing you did to Hansen got the women all fired up. 'New foreman, new rules,' they said. I spent half the time before lunch trying to get them to work. And Jackson? She didn't even show up today. No note. No phone call. No nothin'."

"Really?" Rosie grinned. "Well, it's only going to get worse, you know. Once the girls around here learn that you wouldn't hire me back—"

"How would they find out?"

"Well, everyone saw me here today. It's not too hard to guess what I wanted. Besides, some of the girls live in my neighborhood. I'm bound to run into one of them while on the train or at the market or . . ."

"And you'd tell them? You'd tell them that I wouldn't give you your job back?"

Rosie shrugged. "I have no reason to lie. If someone asks, I'm going to tell them the truth."

"Go ahead." Del Vecchio folded his arms across his chest. "Go ahead and tell 'em. I'm not gonna let a few women scare me."

"A few?" Rosie laughed. "You read the news, don't you? FDR expects to be drafting 200,000 men a month by summer. What are you going to do when the guys out there get called up? Who's going to replace them? Unless the Pusheys try to revoke child labor laws, there's going to be an awful lot of women in this shipyard."

"So?"

"So pretty soon, you're going to have to convince those women to rivet and weld and climb scaffolds and do a whole lot of things they've never done before. That won't go smoothly if they think you're a creep."

"And hirin' you back will make 'em think otherwise?"

"It couldn't hurt, could it? 'New foreman, new rules.' Now's your chance to prove it."

"What makes you think they care what happens to you? For all you know, they think you murdered Finch, too."

"I don't *think* they're on my side. I *know* it. Nelson surprised me a little while ago by thanking me for standing up to Hansen. She said it was like I was sticking up for the other women here at the yard. She also said that she didn't care if I murdered Finch. All that mattered was that I stuck up for myself and for them."

"They don't care if you're a murderer? Aw, come on, that's just crazy."

"I agree. I'm just telling you what Nelson told me. But imagine how pleased those women would be if you stick up for the person who stuck up for them? Why, after that, I'm sure they'd give you no trouble at all."

Del Vecchio rolled his eyes and drew a deep breath. "Okay, Keefe. You drive a hard bargain, you know that?"

Again Rosie shrugged. "I said I wasn't a murderer. I never said anything about blackmail."

"Yeah, yeah. You can start first thing in the morning." Del Vecchio moved to the back doors of the building and paused. "Oh, and Keefe, I don't mind you sticking up for yourself, but if you pull that hot rivet routine again—"

"I know. I'm fired. Again."

With a solemn nod, Del Vecchio opened the steel doors and exited to the shipyard, leaving Rosie alone in the windowless holding area.

When the doors had shut, Rosie exhaled loudly and threw her head back in triumph. She'd done it. Where and how she'd had found the nerve to boldly coerce Del Vecchio into rehiring her, she wasn't quite sure, but she had managed to get her job back. Now, to get down to the business of investigating Finch's murder, but where should she begin?

Without knowing it, Tony Del Vecchio had provided Rosie with two solid leads. First, there was the matter of the missing Jackson. Where was she and why hadn't she shown up for work? Between the Normandie fire and Finch's murder, many women were certain to be scared off of working by the docks. However, it was doubtful that word of Finch's death had spread so rapidly that Jackson would have known about it prior to the start of her shift.

Although it was very possible that Jackson was at home in bed with a cold or even the grippe, the timing of her absence was curious. Had she witnessed Finch's murder? Did she know something that she did not wish to disclose? Or perhaps she, herself, was the murderer. She had sufficient motive. Not only had Finch stripped her of her welding duties—a job that, even for a Negro woman, must have paid reasonably well—but he had humiliated her in front of her coworkers.

Jackson could have easily met Finch by the docks after their shift, perhaps even under the pretense of discussing her demotion. Whether she snuck a tool from the yard into her handbag with the intention of murdering Finch or the discussion simply got out of control and she grabbed a piece of driftwood from the shore, Finch would never have anticipated the death blow she delivered.

Then there was Finch's successor as foreman. At age thirty-eight, Tony Del Vecchio did not possess the seniority to fill the position. And to be certain, there were men at the yard who were better liked. So why was he next in line for the job? Had Del Vecchio, himself, known that he would replace Finch? Pushey Shipyard was selling tugs and tankers galore to the navy and coast guard. Any foreman who managed a tight, productive shift was sure to be handsomely rewarded for his efforts. Those financial benefits, combined with the prestige of the position, would have been very tempting to a man like Del Vecchio.

Unfortunately, looking into Jackson's and Del Vecchio's motives and alibis would have to wait until Rosie was back on the job, when she had the opportunity to glean information from other shipyard employees.

Until then, however, there had to be something she could do to launch her investigation.

Rosie eyed the empty holding room and the doors that led to the men's and newly installed women's facilities. The police had probably swept this entire area before letting the day shift begin, but that didn't mean that she shouldn't have a look around. Having some shipbuilding experience under her belt, she might notice some small detail that the police overlooked. But even if she didn't, the act of searching would, at the very least, make her feel as if she was being productive.

She walked to the men's room and placed a tentative hand on the door. Should she? Rosie glanced from side to side and then chided herself for such foolishness. The room would, invariably, be empty since employees used the facilities nearest the docks during working hours. The holding area restrooms were reserved for use between shifts and for those occasions when the dock facilities were otherwise occupied or unusable.

Still, she felt terribly embarrassed, as if stepping into a men's room was some sort of obscene act.

Don't be silly, Rosie, she scolded beneath her breath. *It's just a men's room and you're a grown, married woman.*

She gave the door a shove, causing it to swing inward.

And then unexpectedly stop.

Rosie gasped and reared backward. There, in the doorway, stood Lieutenant Jack Riordan. The stubbly beard he'd sported the night before had been cleanly shaved and his tall frame was clad in a navy blue flannel suit, which he wore without an overcoat.

"Oh!" She drew her hand to her mouth.

Riordan propped the wooden door open with one hand and tipped his hat with the other. "Mrs. Keefe."

"Lieutenant Riordan. I was . . . I was just—"

"Looking for the ladies' room? It's the next door over."

"Oh, look at that." She feigned surprise. "Why, it is, isn't it? I'm so sorry. I didn't mean to—"

Riordan let go of the men's-room door and held both hands aloft. "No, it's okay."

"I, um . . . well, I guess I'm a bit scatterbrained what with everything going on."

"What, you mean you've never been a suspect in a murder investigation before?"

She was caught off guard at the flippancy of the remark. "No, I, uh, I'm afraid I haven't. . . ."

Riordan immediately apologized. "I'm sorry. That was . . . that was out of line. I was trying to be clever, but I'm an idiot."

Rosie's eyes narrowed. She had known only a handful of policemen in her lifetime, and although she had never witnessed any of them working a case, she was fairly confident that none of them would try to joke with and then apologize to the lead suspect in a murder investigation. Was Riordan trying to tell her that she was no longer the lead suspect? That he had found someone with a stronger motive? Or was he making light of the situation in order to trap her?

Riordan, prompted by her silence, cleared his throat awkwardly. "So, I hear you have your job back."

"You were listening?"

"Not on purpose. At least not at first. I was on my way out of the men's room when I heard people talking. When I figured out who it was and what was being said, I thought it best not to interrupt. I'm glad I didn't. That was quite the speech you made. I especially liked the whole 'innocent until proven guilty' part."

"I had to do something to convince Tony Del Vecchio to hire me back."

"It was still a nice touch."

"Well, it's true. That's how the system works, isn't it? Otherwise I would have been locked up last night."

"The police have to build a case against you and until they do you are presumed innocent, yes. However, as I'm sure you realize, there's also the court of public opinion."

Rosie frowned as she slid her eyes toward the metal doors that led to the yard. "I suspect that jury has already handed in their verdict."

"Yeah, I can only imagine the welcome you must have gotten. Which makes me wonder. Why did you fight so hard to get your job back? If everything you told me last night is true, I'd have figured that this was the last place you'd want to be."

Rosie's gaze met Riordan's. If the lieutenant suspected the true motive behind Rosie's return to Pushey, there was no trace of it in his dark blue eyes.

"Where else am I supposed to work? Do you know of any other places that are willing to hire a murder suspect? I only ask because I've never been one before and thought, perhaps, you might be able to offer some pointers." Although she had added the last comment as a serious gibe, she could feel, for a few moments, the hint of a smile spread across her lips.

"I guess I had that coming to me." Riordan hung his head. "And what about Mr. Keefe? What does your husband think of you coming back to work?"

"My husband enlisted right before Christmas. He has no idea I was ever working here in the first place."

"Enlisted, huh? Brave fellow."

"Mmm," Rosie grunted in reply. How she wished that he would change the subject.

"So he doesn't know about Finch and the, uh, murder either?"

She shook her head solemnly.

"Well, at least you have your sister to lean on."

"She . . . she has her own problems to contend with." Rosie looked away lest she burst into tears. "Can I ask a bold question, Lieutenant?"

"Sure."

"Do you believe I'm innocent?"

"Of course. It's my job to believe you're innocent until I can prove otherwise."

She looked him squarely in the face. "That's not what I meant. I want to know if you've found anything that might have swayed your opinion in one direction or the other."

"I can't tell you that, Mrs. Keefe. Even if I wanted to, I couldn't."

Rosie nodded somberly. "I understand."

"However"—Riordan paused dramatically—"that doesn't mean that you shouldn't feel free to tell me what you find during your little investigation."

She nearly jumped out her skin. "My what?"

"Investigation. Unofficial investigation, of course, since you can't dust for fingerprints or gather evidence. But you'll probably be talking to people here at the yard about Finch. You might overhear some things, too, but I'm sure you realized that before you asked to be rehired."

"No," Rosie answered flatly. "No, it, um, it never occurred to me."

"Really? I had you figured as being pretty sharp. Ah, well, good thing I prepared you, then," Riordan replied with a broad grin. "That way you can keep your eyes and ears open."

"Yes. Yes, I'll be certain to do that," Rosie agreed absently. Had Riordan been aware of her plans all along?

"If you hear anything interesting—anything at all—give me a call at the precinct. You still have the card I gave you?"

Rosie nodded and pulled the rectangular piece of cardstock from the pocket of her sweater.

"Good. Be sure to keep it handy."

"I will. . . . Um, well, I'd best be going. My sister will be wondering where I am." She excused herself and inched tentatively toward the front door. "Good day, Lieutenant."

"Good day," he replied with a tip of his hat. "Oh, Mrs. Keefe? Aren't you forgetting something?"

She spun around, her face a question.

Riordan pointed a finger at the set of wooden doors behind him. "The ladies' room is over there."

Rosie's face registered surprise, but she quickly plastered on a gracious smile. "Thank you, Lieutenant. See what I mean? Absentminded."

Riordan folded his arms across his chest and grinned as Rosie Keefe swung through the wooden ladies'-room door. "Uh-huh."

Chapter Six

After a few minutes had elapsed, Riordan watched as Rose Doyle Keefe exited the ladies' room and, with an icy "Good-bye," made her leave of Pushey Shipyard and stepped onto the cobblestone path beyond. The heavy metal doors creaked slowly shut behind her, blocking out the brilliant spring sunshine and leaving the stark, artificial light of the holding area to create a surreal and foreboding chiaroscuro landscape.

Riordan extracted a pack of Lucky Strikes and a book of matches from his inside jacket pocket. Placing one of the cigarettes between his lips, he fumbled with, and subsequently extinguished, two different matches before managing to get the tip of the slender white cylinder to glow red.

Flicking the third extinguished match onto the concrete floor of the holding area, Riordan took a long drag and wondered if he shouldn't give up smoking altogether. There was a time, just a few short months ago, when he had found the habit most enjoyable. There was, of course, still pleasure to be derived from the tobacco itself: the aroma, the flavor, the slight burn of that initial swirl of smoke as it reached the back of his throat. However, the ritual that led to that memorable puff—opening a stainless steel case to reveal an array of artfully arranged cigarettes, selecting one, and then igniting it with a shiny naphtha lighter—had been abandoned. One of the first casualties of the war.

Urged by the United States government to conserve and salvage strategic materials for use by the military, Riordan had surrendered both his cigarette case (a gift from his former fiancée) and lighter (a gift for fifteen years of police service) at a scrap metal drive in early March. Like other dutiful Americans, Riordan did not begrudge the sacrifice; indeed, he was sorry that, at age forty-three, he was considered too old to fight. Still, doing what he could for the cause didn't mean that part of him didn't mourn the loss of what was such a simple, daily pleasure.

And so, just a few days after the scrap drive, he set about devising a new ritual. Inspired by a George Raft film, the newly lighter-free Riordan tried his hand at striking a match against the heel of his shoe and then using it to ignite his cigarette. After several failed attempts, he discovered that the trick didn't work with the pocket-friendly safety matches found in diners and restaurants, but instead required old-fashioned wooden friction matches. Known as "Lucifers" by the local kids, friction matches earned their name from the fact that they exploded violently and often unexpectedly, which made them particularly dangerous when carried in one's coat pocket, and even more hazardous when carried in the pocket of someone also toting a firearm.

However, even if Riordan was willing to risk both hands and digits, the match-and-shoe trick was impractical for city living. Whereas George Raft had as much camera time as needed to stop, reach down, and light his cigarette, Riordan often found himself being hurried along a busy city street. Stopping to balance himself on one foot, if even for a second, would impede the flow of foot traffic and would result in him being knocked over by the passing crowd.

And so, having relinquished the idea of establishing a new smoking ritual, the lieutenant reluctantly accepted that the world around him was rapidly transforming from one with little money and lots of time, to one where every minute and every dime was spent on making war. It was a world where practicality came before tradition and style, a world of matches, not lighters. A world where a gentleman presented a lady, not with an open cigarette case, but an open pack of Lucky Strikes. And even that wasn't the classically styled, handsomely familiar pack of Lucky Strikes to which he had grown accustomed, but the drab white "gone to war" variety, since the ink used in the signature green and gold packaging was laden with chromium and copper, which could be put to better use in shell casings.

Riordan snuffed the partially smoked cigarette in a nearby ash stand and walked to the rear doors of the building. Upon poking his head out, he was greeted with the whirs and bangs of rivet guns and hammers. "Remind Mr. Del Vecchio that I'm still waiting to speak with him," he shouted to the officer standing guard outside Finch's office.

The uniformed officer nodded and Riordan, eager to return to the relative quiet of the holding room, swiftly shut the sound-muffling solid steel door. Alone with his thoughts, he reflected upon his conversation with Rosie Keefe. The chance encounter had answered few questions, but it had done much to solidify his belief in the woman's innocence.

First, there was her bid to be rehired. If Mrs. Keefe

was guilty of Finch's murder, it was unlikely that she'd return to the scene of the crime. One might suggest that she sought to interfere with the police investigation. But, in Riordan's experience, such schemes were strictly the stuff of books and films. In real life, all but the coldest killers had an aversion to revisiting the crime scene. Even if they managed to overcome their feelings of disgust, they would find that tampering with evidence was extremely difficult, if not impossible. Upon arriving at a crime scene, law enforcement officers immediately cordoned off the area and set about collecting physical evidence; anything "discovered" after the initial search was treated with a good deal of skepticism.

Second, Rosie Keefe didn't, in Riordan's mind, quite fit the profile of the killer. Physically, she was petite—five foot four at best—with slender wrists and a narrow waist. Her ability to land a stapler on Finch's temple was the combined result of Keefe's need to escape and Finch being caught off guard.

The scene later that day would have been much different. After lying in wait for hours, Keefe might have still been angry and seeking vengeance, but she would have been operating under far less adrenaline than she had been during her initial confrontation with Finch. As for Finch, he might not have anticipated retaliation from Keefe herself, but he still would have practiced caution during the walk home, just in case an angry brother, husband, or boyfriend was waiting for him at the end of his shift.

Taking into account the location of Finch's body and the number of shipyard employees on the streets at 5:00 p.m., one could only conclude that Finch had been lured beneath the dock and then murdered. Riordan refused to believe that Finch, given the morning's events, would have followed Keefe anywhere, never mind beneath a dark pier on a cool, overcast April evening. But if, for the sake of argument, he had, he certainly would have been wary. If there was the slightest indication that things were not as they seemed, Finch would have lashed out and it would have been Keefe's, not Finch's, body that was discovered beneath the pier.

Even from a psychological standpoint, Rosie Keefe didn't fit the role of killer. Although not an expert, Riordan had read enough case studies to recognize the rudimentary signs of an unhinged personality. In an attempt to get her to let down her defenses, he had thrown a variety of comments in Keefe's direction, all of which she'd fielded without undue or inappropriate emotion.

Riordan's thoughts were interrupted as the rear doors of the brick building swung open abruptly, allowing a tall, uniformed policeman and the short, stocky figure of Tony Del Vecchio admittance. "You wanted to see to me?"

"I did. I've wanted to all day." Riordan motioned to one of two benches that bordered the side of the room.

Del Vecchio plopped onto a backless bench and stretched his legs out in front of him. Meanwhile, the uniformed officer stood behind Riordan, notebook and pencil at the ready.

"Yeah, I know. Sorry about that. I've been trying to calm everyone down and get 'em back to work."

"That's all right." Riordan extracted the newly white package of Lucky Strikes from his pocket and tossed it to Del Vecchio. "How do you like the new job?"

Del Vecchio took a cigarette and tossed the pack back to Riordan. "Ask me in another week or so. It's not easy steppin' into Finch's shoes at such short notice."

"Very short notice." Riordan replaced the pack in his pocket and lit his cigarette, this time using just one match. "I checked the records in Finch's office. You passed the foreman's test just two weeks ago."

"So?"

Riordan watched as the heavyset man pulled a stainless steel lighter from the top pocket of his blue canvas work jacket. Not everyone, it seemed, was willing to make sacrifices. "So, it's almost as though you knew there would be a job opening up."

Del Vecchio took a drag on his cigarette. "What are you gettin' at?"

"Nothing. Just saying that the timing's pretty strange."

"Nothin' strange about it. I went to Finch a few weeks back and asked for a raise. I have a wife and three kids to feed and the two boys—say, you got kids?"

Riordan shook his head.

"Then you got no idea how expensive they can be. My two oldest—the boys—are ten and thirteen. Eatin' me out of house and home. Every day I go home, the icebox is empty. So, I go to Finch and explain that I need more money so the wife can buy more groceries. He tells me that I'm already makin' as much as a riveter can make. The next step is foreman, but I need to take a test. So, I take the test." He proudly hiked his jacket collar up with his thumbs. "Passed on the first try, too."

"Congratulations, but Finch was already foreman. How would taking a test help?"

"Finch was the *shift* foreman," Del Vecchio pointed out. "But there's a shipbuildin' foreman, a weldin' foreman, a framin' foreman . . . each one is in charge of different things."

"Hmm, but Finch didn't promote you even after you passed the test."

"There wasn't a job to promote me to."

"No openings, huh?" Riordan picked a flyer from the wall above Del Vecchio's head and displayed it. "This here says there's an opening for a day-shift welding foreman."

"I'm a riveter, not a welder. See, the test I took was for shift or shipbuildin' foreman. Framin' and weldin' have their own tests."

"Shipbuilding foreman?"

"Yeah, he inspects all the other departments. Makes sure their work looks good. Kinda the top dog. You need to do a stint as another foreman before you make it to that."

"And the shift foreman?"

"The shift foreman is in charge of schedulin', supplies, hirin', and any employee stuff that can't be handled by the other foremen."

"In other words, the only job you could have taken was Finch's."

"No. There's a second-shift foreman and there's been talk of addin' a third shift, but so far we haven't needed one."

"So your only hope of promotion was if Finch or the second-shift foreman moved up to shipbuilding foreman."

Del Vecchio seemed to realize the importance of his words. "Ummm . . . well, yeah, I . . . I guess you could look at it that way."

"But you didn't? It never dawned on you that there were just two slots—maybe three—that would earn you the cash you wanted?" Riordan grinned.

"Well, yeah, I mean no, I . . ."

"What were the odds of either Finch or the second-shift foreman moving up?"

"Finch might have. But not the second-shift guy. He's too new."

"Leaving just one slot: Finch's."

"Hey, I know what you're tryin' to do, here. Look, I didn't bump off Finch to get his job. I just did what any other guy would do. I got some work on the side and hoped that the third shift got added."

"A second job? Where?"

"A pal of mine owns a warehouse nearby. I go after my shift and help sweep up."

"A janitor?"

Del Vecchio moved his head from side to side as if mentally weighing the significance of this new job title. "Yeah . . . I guess you could call it that."

"And it didn't bother you that you had to get a second job cleaning up after people?"

"Would I rather leave my shift here and go home to my family? Sure. But pushin' a broom a few extra hours a day ain't bad. There are worse ways to make a buck."

"So, this job? Is that where you were after your shift last night?"

"No, as a matter of fact, I took last night off."

"Oh? You just got the job. You could afford to take a night off?"

"Like I said, my boss is a buddy."

"What time did you leave here?"

"Oh, didn't I say? Delaney, Hansen, and me all left early. The guy we got to fill in for Keefe could only work till three and Finch couldn't get anyone else till this mornin'. You can't have a three-man rivet gang, so we all went home."

"And you were there all night? At home, I mean."

"Yep, with the family." Del Vecchio smugly grinned. "That's why I asked for the night off. Didn't make sense to come all the way back here."

"No, I suppose it didn't. Your, uh, family can vouch for you?"

"Sure they can." Del Vecchio's smile evaporated. "But I don't know that I like the idea of you draggin' them into this."

"I'm not 'dragging' them into anything. But if we need to corroborate your alibi—"

"Why would you need to do that?" He rose to his feet. "Finch's murderer just walked outta here. Heck, she probably strolled right past you."

"Oh, you mean Mrs. Keefe? Yes, she did just leave. But it's funny, I didn't think you had her pegged as the murderer."

"What? Why wouldn't I? You heard what she did to Finch yesterday morning, didn't ya?"

"Naturally. What confuses me is when you hired her back, you made it sound like it was the other guys who thought she was guilty. You, on the other hand, seemed more sympathetic."

"You . . . you heard that? Don't you need a warrant or writ or something before you can listen in on other people's conversations?"

"Not when those conversations take place in a wide open area in front of a men's room door."

"Okay. All right. You got me. I gave Keefe her job back. What of it?"

"Aren't you worried about the safety of your other employees?"

"Well, I . . ." Del Vecchio stammered. "Well, sure I am. But I figure she did what she did 'cause she was steamed at Finch. It's not like she's crazy or anything."

"No? I'd say bashing a guy's head in is pretty crazy."

"Yeah, but she's not gonna do it again."

"You seem pretty certain."

"No, it . . . it was a question. She's not gonna do it again, is she?"

Riordan shrugged. "You tell me. You're the one who put a possible murderer back on the payroll."

"Hey, now! Look, I felt sorry for her, okay. That's all. Her husband's a creep. A real hustler. Told her he's enlisted. Meanwhile, I've seen him at least five times in the past month. Each time with a different broad. I figure she wouldn't have been here in the first place if she didn't need the dough."

Riordan frowned. *No wonder Keefe didn't respond when I complimented her husband's bravery.* "You, um, you always feel sorry for people you think are killers?"

"Can't say I've known any others," he replied glibly. "Hey, we done here? I have to get back to the yard."

The lieutenant was still thinking about Rosie Keefe. "Huh? Oh. Yeah, we're done."

Tony Del Vecchio stood up and headed to the back door.

Riordan, however, couldn't shake the feeling that there was something the new foreman wasn't telling him. "For now."

Chapter Seven

Rosie hopped the IRT back to Manhattan, her mind traveling as fast as the engine that carried her home. Had she given any thought at all to Lieutenant Riordan, she would have realized that he'd most likely be at the shipyard that afternoon. It was, after all, the last place Finch was seen alive. But so focused was Rosie on being reinstated that she couldn't have been more surprised by Riordan's presence if he had been magically transformed into Cary Grant.

Although she had found it more than a bit jarring to open the men's-room door and see Riordan gazing back at her, Rosie couldn't help but wonder if it wasn't so much the surprise of their encounter as much as the content of that meeting that she found disconcerting.

That was not to say that the exchange they shared was unpleasant. Indeed, if anything, it was *too* pleasant. And therein lay the problem. If Riordan had been gruff, cold, and examining toward his main suspect, Rosie would have understood. Instead, the lieutenant came across as polite, sociable, and utterly charming. So charming, in fact, that Rosie, despite her potential impending trip to the gallows, raised a smile.

But why? Why should he be nice to her? Why should he bother to make small talk? Perhaps this was his way of getting her to confide in him. Maybe he was even trying to wheedle her into signing a confession. If persuasion was the name of his game, Rosie had to admit he was quite effective. Although she had committed no crimes for which she could confess, back in the holding area she had nearly told him about Billy and his disappearance. It was only upon reminding herself that Riordan's priority was solving the case that she finally bit her tongue.

It was open to speculation whether or not Riordan had a desire to convict Rosie. When asked whether he believed her to be innocent, Riordan had been purposely vague, not about his duties as a police officer but about his feelings regarding those duties: *"Even if I wanted to tell you, I couldn't."* Was he trying to say that he had found something and wanted to tell her about it?

Then there was his comment about her investigation. How had he guessed that was the reason for her return to the shipyard? And why did he encourage her to share her findings with him? Was he asking her to help him exonerate her or to help him prove her guilt?

The train came to a halt at the Eighth Avenue/ Twenty-third Street Station. Rosie grabbed her handbag, stepped out onto the platform, and, after scaling the steps back to the surface, began the short walk home. A strong wind had kicked up since she had left the shipyard, but the brilliant sunshine helped to ward off the chill. Neighborhood children, having swapped their school uniforms for playclothes, filled the sidewalks and alleyways to make the most of the hours before supper.

Rosie entered the front door of the brownstone and

made her way upstairs where Katie, having donned a bright yellow apron over her red and white day dress, stood over the stove, and Charlie, in his playpen, cooed and screeched.

"Something smells good," Rosie complimented as she hung her coat in the front closet.

"Beef stew. I wanted to use up some vegetables before they went bad."

Rosie nodded. "Where's Ma?

"She went home," Katie explained.

"Oh. She's not still sore at me for going down to the shipyard, is she?"

"No, I asked her to leave."

"You did? Why?"

"Because I wanted to talk to you—alone."

"Uh-oh, that can't be good." Rosie leaned over the wooden rail of Charlie's playpen and delighted the infant by shaking one of his rattles.

"I want to know why you went to the shipyard today."

Rosie placed the rattle in her nephew's chubby hand before flopping onto the sofa. "I already told you. I went there to ask for my job back."

Katie wiped her hands on her apron and moved into the living room area. "But why?"

"Because we could use the money." She leaned forward and wiggled a finger at the baby through the bars of his playpen. "Yes, we could, couldn't we, Charlie?" she sang in a high-pitched voice. "That's right, we could."

"That's not the whole story and you know it."

Rosie's voice dropped to its normal timbre. "I know nothing of the sort. I asked for my job back because there aren't many other jobs around for someone who can't type, can't take dictation, and doesn't know how to operate a switchboard. At least, none that pay well."

"Yeah, and we both agreed that by moving in with Ma, you could take a lesser-paying job that didn't have you climbing scaffolds like a monkey. So what gives?"

"I just thought it would be nice to be able to afford a few little luxuries. Wouldn't you like that?"

"Sure I would. Let me know when the War Department says it's okay to have them again," Katie scoffed.

"All right, so we can't get stockings, but the extra money can buy us a heck of a lot of eyebrow pencil for drawing seams on our legs."

Katie rolled her eyes.

"I'd like to do more than just make do, Katie-girl. That's all."

"*Is* that all?" Katie folded her arms across her chest.

"Of course it is. What else could there be?"

Katie disappeared into the bedroom and came back with the evening paper, which she proceeded to toss onto Rosie's lap. "How about this?"

The publication had been folded to display the top of the fourth page where a bold-font headline announced:

SHIPYARD WORKER KILLED
IN BROOKLYN BLUDGEONING.

Rosie picked it up with trembling fingers.

"You told me he had been stabbed," Katie reminded.

"Yes, I did," Rosie answered quietly.

"Why did you lie to me?"

"Because I didn't want you to worry."

Katie gave an exasperated sigh and threw her hands in the air. "I'm your sister, Rosie! I'm supposed to worry about you. That's the way it works."

"I know, but you were already upset about Finch assaulting me. I didn't want to worry you even more."

Katie shook her head and plopped onto the sofa beside her sister. "The police, they know that you hit Finch in the head with a—"

"Stapler? Yes."

"Do they think you did this? Is that why that man came here last night?"

Rosie frowned. Katie's husband had been one of seven hundred men who drowned when the USS *Houston* went down in Indonesia at the end of February. The loss had caused the normally cheerful young blonde to take to bed with the shades drawn for the better part of a week. It was only upon moving in with Rosie and leaving the apartment she'd shared with Jimmy that Katie's depression had finally started to lift. Over the past few weeks, Katie had gradually returned to her old self, but how would she react if she knew that Rosie, the new anchor in her life, might soon be lost, too?

"Rosie," Katie urged. "Rosie, tell me the truth. I know you're looking out for me, but I'm not a little girl anymore."

Rosie recalled Riordan's words earlier that afternoon: *"At least you have your sister to lean on."*

"I want to look out for you the way you've always looked out for me, Rosie. The way you've looked out for Charlie and me since we moved here. And you need to talk to someone. You can't carry it all on your shoulders."

Perhaps Riordan was right. Here she had been pining for Billy to come back and "rescue" her, but, in truth, even when she was at her lowest, Katie offered more comfort than Bill Keefe ever could. "All right." Rosie sighed. "I'll tell you everything, but I don't want Ma to know."

"I won't breathe a word. Why do you think I sent her home in the first place?"

Rosie told her sister about the previous night's interrogation and the afternoon at the shipyard.

"So the police actually think you did it? And the guys at the yard, too? How could anyone believe such a thing?"

"The police are watching me as a suspect, yes. As for the guys at the yard, I can't say I blame them, or anyone else, for thinking I might have done it. Everyone within a hundred yards of Finch's office heard him shouting. A lot of them even saw the blood."

"Which is exactly why you wouldn't have clubbed Finch to death. You'd use a gun or a knife or poison, but you wouldn't have hit him in the head. Not again. That would be like leaving a signed note at the scene of the crime. How stupid do they think you are?"

"Who says they think I'm stupid? They could think I'm just plain crazy."

Katie shrugged. "But the women think you're innocent."

"No, not necessarily. They're on my side because I stood up against Hansen and because 'Finch had it coming to him.' Whatever that means."

"They'd take the side of a potential murderer over that of a dead victim? Gee. Makes you wonder what Finch did to them, doesn't it?"

"I know what he did to me. I'm sure he didn't treat them with any more respect."

"What a creep," Katie remarked. "How did a guy like that sleep at night?"

Rosie's mind wandered to Billy and the possibility that he was not overseas but, in the words of Del Vecchio, "shacked up with some dame." "How do lots of people live with the things they do?"

Katie clicked her tongue and shook her head somberly. "So, you checking out the shipyard—is that because you think someone there might have done it? You think they might have seen what happened with you and Finch and—"

"And bashed him on the head in order to pin it on me? The thought has certainly popped into my mind. But I'm also checking it out because it seems like the most logical place to start. Finch spent most of his time there."

"And what if the killer is someone who works at the shipyard? What if they get wise to what you're doing? Aren't you scared?"

"I'm terrified," Rosie stated honestly. "But I'm probably more terrified at the prospect of doing nothing and waiting for the police to come and arrest me."

"This cop you talked about—Lieutenant Riordan—have you told him that you're innocent?"

"Of course I did. But I'm sure everyone tells him that. The prisons are full of people who didn't commit the crimes they've been convicted for."

"But why would he have given you the okay to snoop if he thought you were guilty?"

"He didn't give me the okay. But then again, I guess he didn't tell me not to snoop, either."

"What?"

"What he said was that I'd probably overhear some things while on the job and if I did, I should let him know."

"Does that mean he knows you're going investigate and wants to be part of it? Or . . . ?"

"I have no idea what he means or what he's thinking."

"Did you ask him?"

"Yes, and all I got in return was that his job requires

him to presume that I'm innocent until he finds evidence that states otherwise."

"That's good, though. Isn't it?"

"So long as he remains impartial, sure. But if he, in his heart of hearts, believes I'm guilty . . ."

"He didn't tell you what he believes."

"He can't. He won't. He's not permitted."

Katie sighed and leaned against the back of the sofa. "What do you believe?"

Rosie's brow furrowed. "What do you mean?"

"I mean, do you think you can trust Riordan? Are you going to do what he said and share your findings with him?"

"I don't know. On one hand, Riordan has the whole police department behind him, so having him follow up on leads could be helpful. On the other hand, if he's only looking to arrest me and not find the real killer . . ." Rosie sighed and scratched the back of her head pensively. "Unfortunately, only time will tell if I can trust him. Until then, I'm going to have to be careful about sharing all the information I uncover."

"You mean 'we' uncover," Katie corrected.

"Huh?"

"We. I'm going to help you get to the bottom of this thing," she explained as she sat up straight.

Rosie burst out laughing. "That's very sweet of you, honey, but I can't see you climbing scaffolds and catching rivets in a bucket."

"I won't be climbing scaffolds. I'll leave that to you, thank you very much."

"I didn't think so" Rosie continued to laugh.

"I am serious about helping you, though."

"Again, that's very sweet, but I don't know what you could do. Besides, you have Charlie to take care of."

"I know," Katie replied matter-of-factly as she

snatched the newspaper from its spot on the sofa cushion and passed it to her sister. "Who says I can't do both?"

Rosie looked over the Finch article in confusion. "What should I do with this? And what does it have to do with—"

"Just look at the article," Katie insisted. "Especially the part about where Finch lived."

"'Robert Finch, a lifelong resident of the Red Hook neighborhood in Brooklyn,'" Rosie read aloud. "That's the neighborhood right near the docks. So?"

"So, I was thinking I could go down there and talk to a few people who knew Finch. See what they have to say."

"And how were you thinking of talking to them? You can't go door-to-door like the Fuller Brush man."

"Of course not. Don't be silly! I'll just run my errands there instead of here."

"Oh, Katie, you can't do that."

"Why not? There must be a grocer and a butcher in the neighborhood. Where better to catch up on neighborhood gossip than at the market?"

"The people in that neighborhood don't know you. Why would they tell you anything about Finch?"

"Why would they not?"

"Because they'll think you're a busybody. Or worse, a reporter."

"No, they won't. I'll have Charlie with me. Now tell me, who's going to suspect a pretty blonde pushing a baby carriage of such deception?" Katie challenged with a grin.

Rosie took turns eyeing her sister and nephew. Fair-haired, blue-eyed, and smiling, they made an irresistible pair. "Only a blind person."

"And if I meet one, I'll tell them that I'm a war widow. That should win them over."

"Don't do that," Rosie said in earnest. "Don't use your hardships. Not for sympathy."

"I won't be using anything. I'm proud of Jimmy. I want the whole world to know how brave he was."

"And you should tell his story, but not for my sake."

"If not for your sake, then for whose? If Jimmy had his say, he'd want me to do everything in my power to help you."

"I know, Katie, but traveling to Red Hook every day? That's quite a ways to go for simple errands."

"It's not that far," Katie argued. "Nothing is too far when it comes to saving my sister."

Chapter Eight

While a cloud-obscured sun ascended over the rain-washed city, Rosie boarded the crowded early train back to Brooklyn. Arriving at the shipyard at 6:45 a.m., she entered the holding area to wait out the fifteen minutes until the start of her nine-hour shift. The scene that lay before her was the same as it had been since she began her job ten days before. However, this time, instead of fading into the crowd, Rosie's journey over the threshold and across the hard cement floor caused the collection of coverall-clad Pushey employees to fall silent and then part like the Red Sea.

Rosie stood alone in the center of the room, the male employees gathered in front of her, the females clustered behind. She tried to project a sense of calm confidence, but it wasn't easy. Not only did her new status as shipyard pariah make her feel painfully unwelcome, but it would make the interview part of her investigation next to impossible.

Thankfully, a voice came from the rear of the room. "You're back." Nelson, dressed in a pair of gray canvas slacks, a blue work shirt, and a red headscarf, entered the space occupied by Rosie. "How did you manage it?"

"A bit of blarney. And a whole lot of luck."

"Well, no matter how you did it, I'm glad you're here. We all are."

Rosie surveyed the expressionless group of women. "Hmmm . . . they appear to be handling their excitement quite well."

Nelson waved a dismissive hand. "Don't worry about that. They just don't want to get into trouble with the new foreman. I'm sure you've seen most of them in the two weeks since you started, but if you haven't, I'll introduce you."

Rosie remembered her investigation. "Yes, I'd like to meet everyone at some point. Hear their Finch stories."

Nelson nodded in agreement and then pointed over Rosie's left shoulder.

Rosie spun around to find Michael Delaney standing just a few inches away. "What do you think you're doing here?" he demanded.

"The same thing you are. Waiting for my shift to start."

"Yeah, Del Vecchio told me you came to him looking for your job. But I thought for sure you would have come to your senses by now. Between throwing rivets at Hansen and what you did to Finch—"

"I didn't kill him, Delaney."

"That doesn't matter. It's enough that you ran away and left him bleeding. Don't you understand? These fellas don't want you here. They never did."

"And don't you understand that I need a job? This is about the only one I can get that pays a decent wage."

"Yeah, but Ma told me about you and Katie moving back to Greenpoint. Without having to make rent, the money Billy sends you will go a lot farther. That means you don't have be . . ."

As Rosie's eyes lowered, Michael Delaney realized

the impact of his words. "Ah, jeez. He's not sending you money, is he? I'm sorry, I didn't . . . I just assumed he was taking care of you. Or at least trying. I know if you were my wife, that's what I would do."

Ordinarily, Rosie would have leaped at the chance to rib Delaney about his bachelor status. However, there was such a wistful sincerity to his words that she didn't have the heart to tease. Luckily, Del Vecchio started announcing the day's work assignments, thus eliminating the need for further comment.

"Miller . . . Jones . . . Murphy . . . machine shop. Drummond . . . Gaikowski . . . Phillips . . . Snyder . . . graving plate. Nelson . . . Scarlatti . . . hull welding. Kopecky, heater . . . Keefe, passer . . ."

The voice of Rudy Hansen rang out from the crowd. "What the hell is that woman doing here, Del Vecchio?"

"We need bodies, Hansen. Jackson's gone, four of our guys have been called up for service, and McCarthy is down with the grippe."

"We may need bodies, but we don't need hers. Finch fired that crazy broad right before he got his head smashed in."

"Yeah, and I unfired her," Del Vecchio stated boldly. "I warned Keefe about gettin' into trouble. If she pulls any funny business again, she's outta here."

"That's all it takes to work here now, huh? A promise to behave yourself?"

"No, you have to be a hard worker, too. I was on the same crew as you and Keefe. She kept up with the rest of us."

"I don't care if she worked circles around us. She's a murderer. But if that don't matter to you, I have a cousin up in Dannemora. All we have to do is break him and a few of his buddies out and our manpower problems will be solved." Hansen slid his eyes toward Rosie. "Notice I said 'manpower,' not 'womanpower.' Gonna beat my head in for that?"

Rosie glared back. She desperately wanted to retaliate, but she knew it was in her best interest to hold her tongue.

"Settle down, now. We don't know for sure that Keefe's guilty," Del Vecchio reasoned.

"What? You mean to say you don't think she—"

"That's not for us to decide, Hansen. The cops are on the job and they'll get to the bottom of things. Till then we gotta act as though she's innocent."

"I don't 'gotta' do anything."

"Hey, call me crazy, but doesn't this country believe that a man or, in this case, woman, is 'innocent until proven guilty'? Why are we even fightin' this war if people like you are so quick to throw away those beliefs?"

Rosie couldn't believe her ears. Tony Del Vecchio, self-proclaimed political mastermind, had used her words, verbatim, in an argument against Hansen. What's more, those words were effective. As some employees whistled in approval and others mumbled and nodded in agreement, Hansen stared down at the concrete floor and scratched the back of his neck in awkward silence.

"Still don't like it," the tall blond Swede finally replied.

"You don't have to like it," Del Vecchio acknowledged. "But we don't need to hear about how much you don't like it neither. Now, where was I? Oh yeah. Kopecky, heater . . . Keefe, passer . . . Dewitt, bucker . . . Kilbride, riveter. Gang one, Pier Number One."

At age fifty-four, Wilson Dewitt was one of the most senior employees at Pushey Shipyard. Having started at the yard as a cleanup boy in the days prior to pneumatic rivet guns and worldwide warfare, Dewitt discovered his vocation when he was called on to fill in for a bucker whose foot had been crushed by a riveter's hammer.

In the thirty years since, Dewitt had come to be known for his dependability, strong work ethic, and easygoing nature, characteristics that would have earned any other shipyard worker promotions, raises, and the respect of supervisors and colleagues. Of course, in order to earn such things, those "other" shipyard workers would have had to be both male and white, and while Wilson Dewitt fit the former criterion, his dark brown skin stood in stark contrast to the latter.

Like Jackson and the other Negroes who worked in the shipyards, Dewitt's primary role was, and always had been, to assist the white employees, first as a maintenance worker then as a bucker. Despite his intelligence and aptitude for the shipbuilding trade, his employers would never train him to rivet or weld, and even if he had somehow managed to acquire those skills elsewhere, they wouldn't have done him much good since, as a Negro man, he was not permitted to take the exam required for promotion.

Moreover, despite his years of devotion and hard work, Dewitt could never earn as much as the other buckers in the yard, since whites and Negroes were paid according to two separate wage scales. Meaning that at the end of a hard week, a female welder with two weeks' experience often took home a larger paycheck than he did.

Rosie was acutely aware of the yard's established pecking order. At the top of the social ladder stood white male workers, but even within this group there existed a certain hierarchy. Men of Anglo-Saxon,

Scandinavian, and German descent, although comprising the minority of the workforce, formed the shipyard elite. The Irish and Italians occupied the second slot. Sharing a common faith, the two groups had formed an uneasy partnership with each other and, through sheer number, had climbed to a position of relative power within the dockside community. Beneath them, with each group occupying a different rung on the ladder, came the Slavs, Jews, Portuguese, Greeks, Hispanics, and other ethnic groups.

Strangely, or at least it was strange to Rosie, these ethnic groups chose to stand alone rather than unify for the betterment of the whole. Never was there talk of a coalition. Each group was possessive of its spot within the hierarchy and determined to protect itself from those below.

After the men came the women, who were grouped into one of two categories: white or Negro. White women, lumped together regardless of their ethnic or religious background, held a position lower than white males, yet slightly higher than Negro males. Negro women, however, possessed the lowliest status in the yard, below even that of Negro males.

As Del Vecchio finished the remainder of the morning's announcements, Rosie contemplated her new assignment. Dewitt, although seemingly courteous, was just one of four Negro men working at Pushey, and the only one to have made the transition from maintenance to riveting gang. Kolecky was a Czechoslovakian Jew who socialized with neither group and spoke to no one. Although some had attributed his silence to an inability to speak and understand English, Kolecky's ability to take instruction from superiors belied that theory. Kilbride was a hard-drinking Irish Nationalist from

County Wicklow who came to America shortly after the split of his homeland, in 1921, into northern and southern components. One of the fastest riveters in the yard, the boisterous Kilbride's "80 Proof" lunch incited him to intersperse his afternoon riveting with rebel songs ("A Nation Once Again" was a popular favorite), limericks, and anti-establishment rhetoric. He was also notorious, at the end of the day, for leaving his tools on the platform rather than signing them back into the toolshed—a habit that had driven Finch to distraction.

As the morning announcements wrapped up and employees began to filter into the yard, Rosie reflected upon her work assignment and immediately recognized why she had been placed with such a ragtag team. Although Del Vecchio might have agreed to put her back on the payroll and even paid public lip service to her return, she was at the very bottom of the Pushey pecking order. And for the riveting gang saddled with the presence of a potential murderer, Rosie's assignment served to re-establish their low social standing.

"You sure you know what you're doing?" Delaney asked.

"No," she confessed. "But there's not much I can do about that now."

"You can turn around and leave, that's what you can do. But I know you won't. Do me a favor, though. If anyone gives you a hard time, come and get me."

Rosie nodded.

"Promise?" Delaney pressed.

"Yes," Rosie snapped.

Shaking his head and muttering to himself, Michael Delaney disappeared through the holding area doors.

"Brother or boyfriend?" Nelson ventured.

"Neither."

"Hmph. Well, I'll catch you during break. Till then, good luck."

"Thanks." *I need all the luck I can get*, she thought as she exited the red brick building and made her way to Pier Number One. Approximately forty feet from her destination, she spotted Kolecky, short, somber, and bespectacled, setting up his forge. Rosie flashed a weak smile in the man's direction. As expected, Kolecky returned the smile with a blank stare.

Rosie chided herself. These people thought she was a murderer. If she went around smiling at them, they'd truly believe her to be deranged. With a grave expression on her face, she scaled the scaffold where Dewitt and Kilbride stood waiting.

"Mornin'," Dewitt quietly greeted.

Kilbride, however, flashed a wild grin. "Clinton Kilbride at your service. This here is Wilson and that down there is Kolecky. I don't abide by last names, only Christian ones—the world is dehumanizing enough—but I haven't caught Kolecky's yet. Mostly because he hasn't pitched it. Now what should we be calling you?"

"Rose. Rose Keefe."

"Rose. Just Rose?"

"Well, most people call me Rosie."

"Rosie? That's not very poetic for a fellow country-woman." Kilbride's reddish blond brow furrowed. "You sure it isn't Rosemary or Rosamund or—"

"Rosaleen," she replied, although she was unsure as to why. "Rose is short for Rosaleen."

"Ah, that's better. That's what I'll be calling ya, then. Rosaleen."

Rosie felt her mouth pucker. The only person who called her Rosaleen was her mother.

"Ah, don't like being called that, do ya now? Sorry, luv, but I won't change me mind. Rosaleen you are and Rosaleen you'll stay. So welcome, Rosaleen, to the riveting gang of Drunkard, Darkie, and Mute. If you need me to point out who's who, then ya aren't as bright as you look. And now that we're done with the introductions, let's get to work and see if you can keep up."

"Keep up?"

"Haven't you heard? I'm the fastest riveter in the yard. I suppose since you're here as punishment, they didn't warn you." Laughing maniacally, he swung over the other side of the scaffold.

"He'll have you running crazy in the morning," Dewitt clarified. "He'll slow down some after lunch, though. Always does."

Over the course of the next few hours, Rosie discovered that Dewitt's description was quite accurate. With the cone in her left hand and a pair of tongs in her right, the morning found her dashing from the ship to the edge of the wooden boards, catching a handful of red-hot rivets, and then scrambling back to insert them into the predrilled holes. All the while, Kilbride's voice could be heard urging her to hurry up.

When the noon whistle finally blew, Rosie threw both cone and tongs onto the boards in relief.

"Look, Wilson," Kilbride teased as he swung over the side of the scaffold and caught a glimpse of Rosie bent over and rubbing her knees. "I think we broke her."

She met both Kilbride and the statement with an icy stare.

"Uh-oh. Now I've done it. I'd best be careful leaving work tonight."

Determined to keep her cool and, in all honesty, too tired to fight, Rosie stood up and descended the scaffold to meet Nelson for their thirty-minute lunch break.

Kilbride watched her in confusion. "Hmph. That's not the reaction I expected. Not the reaction I expected from that one at all."

Chapter Nine

While her sister shuttled back and forth across the narrow boards of scaffolding that lined Pushey Shipyard's Pier Number One, a few blocks away Katherine Brigid Doyle Williams pushed her son's baby carriage down the uneven cement sidewalk that led to Simonetti's Butcher Shop.

Wearing a robin's-egg blue dress that played perfectly against her blue eyes and fair complexion, Katie wondered whether or not her plan would succeed. Would she enter the butcher shop to find a flock of women speaking, in hushed voices, about the "accident"? (Accidents. That's what people tended to call murders or suicides while in polite company, wasn't it?) Would they allow her to listen in on their conversation? Or would they snub her as an outsider?

And what if there was no talk going on? What if the locals chose to treat Finch's death with quiet respect? What would she say or do to start conversation? And moreover, what should she say or do in order to move that conversation toward the subject of Finch?

As Katie neared the shop she felt her heart begin to race. Although pleasant and cheerful, she had never been particularly outgoing. Growing up, Rosie typically spoke on behalf of her younger sister, informing their mother that Katie wanted lemonade instead of milk, or complaining to Katie's first-grade teacher about the boy who constantly pulled her sister's hair.

Then, after Rosie, came Jimmy. Tall, strong, and blue-eyed, but with the thick dark hair of the black Irish, James Dermot Williams was the life of every party. Always quick with a joke or a humorous anecdote, he could charm even the most difficult individuals and had a way of putting those around him at ease. All Katie needed to do was prompt Jimmy, and doors, as well as mouths, opened.

As Katie tilted the carriage up and back in order to scale the store's front step, she whispered a small prayer to her late husband. "Jimmy, if you're watching, I could really use your gift of gab right now."

Just then, a woman emerged from the butcher shop. She was in her late forties to early fifties and—from the small felt hat with veil that rested atop her perfectly coiffed dark blond hair to the low-heeled leather pumps that covered her stocking feet—dressed from head to toe in black. Dabbing at her eyes with a lace-trimmed handkerchief, she hurriedly pushed past Katie, jostling Charlie's carriage in the process.

The bump sent the carriage rolling backward, off the step, awakening the sleeping child inside and prompting him to cry.

"Sorry," the woman in black said absently before taking off down the street.

"Well . . . I . . . umm . . . that's okay," a flustered Katie stammered.

An olive-skinned man in a white butcher's coat appeared in the doorway. "I'm sorry, miss," he apologized with a faint trace of an Italian accent.

"Oh, that's all right, it's not your fault." She tipped the carriage up and back in another attempt to scale the step.

"Still, I am very sorry." He held the door open to allow her admittance. "She should not have done that. But Mrs. Finch, she's been through a terrible shock."

"Mrs. Finch?" Such was Katie's astonishment, that she let the carriage drop again, causing Charlie to cry louder. "The . . . . the one in the paper?"

"Sì. Let me 'elp." He reached down and lifted the front of the carriage through the open doorway.

Katie lifted up the handle end of the carriage and followed him inside. Although Simonetti's shop occupied two storefronts, the L-shaped counters (one refrigerated, the other lined with scales and chopping blocks) and the assortment of hams, sausages, and smoked meats that hung from the rafters gave the space a "closed-in" feel.

"Vincent," the butcher shouted to an unseen employee. *"Un biscotto per il bambino."*

As Katie took Charlie out of the carriage and soothed him, a young man emerged from the back of the shop. He looked exactly like the butcher, only thirty years younger. In his left hand, he held a biscuit, which he gave to Charlie with a smile.

The baby immediately clutched at it and happily put it into his mouth.

"Ah, the teeth," the butcher commented. "They're coming in."

Katie thanked Vincent for the cookie and then returned to her mission. "Poor Mrs. Finch. I'm surprised she's out and about so soon after what happened. It was day before yesterday when it happened . . . wasn't it?"

"Sì, day before yesterday. She came to order sandwiches for after the funeral tomorrow. Oh! That reminds me. Vincent"—he turned to the boy—"cut a few links of that sausage Mrs. Finch likes, wrap it up, and deliver it to her with our, uh . . ."

"Condolences?" Katie suggested.

"Sì, condolences."

"Aw, Pop," Vincent complained in perfect American English. "Do I have to? I'm nineteen. I'm not a delivery boy anymore. Besides, I don't even know where she lives."

The butcher smiled and held up one finger to Katie. "*Uno momento, per favore.* Um, one moment, please." He then turned to his son and spoke to him quietly but sternly. "What do I pay you for if you don't do what I tell you to do? You know exactly where she lives: 253 Van Brunt Street, the upstairs apartment. Now, bundle up those sausages and get running before I chase you with my meat tenderizer, eh?"

With a heavy sigh, Vincent returned to the back of the shop.

"*Dio mio*, I think maybe the army is just the thing for that boy. It may kill his mama, but it might straighten him out. Kids, eh?" he said to Katie, all the while smiling at Charlie. "He's little now, but you'll see. *Sarà la morte di me!* He'll be the death of me! So, what can I get for you today?"

"Well, a small roasting chicken, for starters."

"One small roasting chicken," the butcher repeated as he made his way behind the counter. "I, uh, I don't remember you coming in here before. Are you new to the neighborhood?"

Katie felt her face flush, but she did her best to remain collected. "Yes . . . yes, I am."

"Ah, you're the one who rented the apartment from Mrs. Arthur."

Had the butcher been watching, he would have seen Katie lick her lips nervously. "Um, no. I'm—I'm staying with an aunt." Realizing he might ask the name of her aunt, she added quickly, "My husband died when the *Houston* sank and she's helping us get back on our feet."

As expected, the comment brought the conversation to a screeching halt.

"*Sono spiacente* . . . I'm sorry." The butcher looked up from the chicken he was trussing. "I did not know . . ."

"No. It's okay. You have no reason to apologize. But that's why I was so interested in Mrs. Finch. What with us both losing our husbands and all."

The butcher held up a hand. "No, your husband was a hero, but Mr. Finch . . . eh, it's not good to speak ill of the dead."

Katie's eyes grew wide. "Oh! Was he as bad as all that?"

Simonetti—at least Katie assumed he was Simonetti—looked around the shop as if to ensure that no one else was listening in. "Okay, since it's just you"—he invoked the sign of the cross—"I talk. Mr. Finch, he . . . he wasn't a nice man."

Katie pulled Charlie closer. *He wasn't nice? Was that all? Well, if—*

"He was *il bruto* . . . a brute. Mrs. Finch, many a time she had the *annerire l'occhio* . . . the black eye. And the other women? *Così molto!* When I heard that the shipyards were hiring women? *Dio mio!* That was the last thing Mrs. Finch needed."

Simonetti plopped the dressed, trussed, and wrapped chicken on the butcher's scale. "'at's four pounds. What else?"

Katie was completely nonplussed. "What else? What do you mean? Oh! You mean meat. Umm . . . ummm . . . cube steak? About a pound?"

"Good choice. That marbling? She's beautiful." Simonetti drew his fingers to his lips and kissed them.

"You were saying that Finch—"

Simonetti's facial features rapidly changed and his accent thickened. "Ah, yes. Finch. He 'ad an eye for the ladies, that one. Coming 'ome with long hairs on his jacket or stinking like the perfume. But when Mrs. Finch, she ask him about it, he yells at 'er and gives 'er the black eye."

Katie shivered as she recalled what had happened to her sister on that fateful morning. She had no trouble believing that Finch was the type of man who might bully and beat his wife, a fact that was disturbing enough in itself. What was even more upsetting was the idea that many of the hairs that traveled home with Finch each night, like Rosie's, might have been removed by force. "Umm, how do you know all this? Not that I doubt what you're saying, but people do gossip—"

"It's no gossip. I 'ear it straight from Marie Finch. We talk all the time. She's my best customer and a very nice lady. . . ."

So it was "Marie" now, was it?

"Can you believe Finch 'ad the nerve to come 'ere and *accusarmi di dormire con sua moglie.* He accused me of carrying on with his wife. *È ridicolo!* I love my wife. And I'm a man of honor."

"Well, you've been quite the gentleman while I've been here," Katie remarked. Inwardly, however, she wondered if Simonetti and Mrs. Finch didn't share more than a simple customer relationship. From what Katie had seen of the woman, Mrs. Finch was attractive, slender, and approximately the same age as the butcher. For Simonetti's part, he seemed to know a lot more about Mrs. Finch than just her favorite cuts of meat. He knew the details of her marital woes, her precise address (including the fact that her apartment was located upstairs), and her Christian name.

The butcher dropped both his mallet and the steak. "*Sono spiacente!* Oh, Signora, I'm so sorry! You wanted to talk about Mrs. Finch, but I'm sure you didn't mean to 'ear all this."

Simonetti was right. All things being equal, Katie didn't want to know about the ugly things people did and, given a choice, she would have grabbed Charlie and run back to Greenpoint as quickly as possible, rather than get involved with murder, adultery, and abusive spouses. However, with her sister's life on the line, she needed to hear all the dirty details. "No. No, that's . . . that's okay. I need to know what's going on . . . since we'll be staying here for a little while."

"Ah . . . grazie. Grazie, Signora." He wrapped the steak and handed over the white paper-wrapped parcel. "Anything else today?"

Katie shook her head. She had already spent slightly more than anticipated in an effort to keep Simonetti talking, and there were still vegetables to purchase. "No, that should keep us well-fed for a few days." She leaned down and placed Charlie back into his carriage. "Oh, except you might tell me where the funeral will take place tomorrow. I don't know Mrs. Finch, but since I'm part of the neighborhood now, I'd like to pay my respects and maybe offer her a listening ear—one widow to another."

"Ah, that is most kind of you, Signora. I'm sure she would like that very much. It's at nine o'clock at The Church of the Holy Trinity over on Montague Street. It's a"—Simonetti looked around again before adding in a whisper—"an Episcopal church, not a Catholic one."

"Oh, won't you be there, then?"

"Oh no, I will be there, but, uh, not in the front row,

eh?" He escorted Katie to the door and helped her lower the baby carriage back onto the sidewalk outside the shop.

After an exchange of good-byes, Katie set off down the street in search of a grocer who could supply her with potatoes, onions, some canned vegetables, and perhaps some more information on Finch.

Rosie stopped at the holding area's ladies' room to fill her thermos with fresh water before wandering behind the small building that served as a makeshift bomb shelter. There, obscured from the prying eyes of the men, a handful of female shipyard workers stretched, fixed their lipstick, ate their lunches, and commiserated about children, men, and their workloads.

The morning clouds had yielded to sunny skies, serving to help dry the rain-soaked asphalt. Navigating around the remaining puddles, Rosie finally plopped down onto a small patch of pavement directly opposite Nelson. As the brunette lit a cigarette, Rosie gave a smile and pointed to the wall against which Nelson leaned. There, a few feet above her head, yellow-stenciled letters warned, "NO SMOKING. KEEP CLEAR."

"That's not for us, honey," Nelson scoffed as she took a long drag off her Camel. "That was put up there by men, for men."

"Yeah," agreed a tall blonde who stood farther along the wall. Her face was made up perfectly and the lapels of her coveralls lined with a variety of rhinestone-studded animal-shaped pins. "They say we're not *real* shipbuilders. If that's the case, then we shouldn't have to follow shipbuilders' rules."

A petite young woman with light brown hair and a

cleanly scrubbed face sat down beside Rosie and immediately undid her shoes. "If that's not shipbuilding we're doing, I'd like to know exactly what it is. My feet are killing me!"

"Oh, it's shipbuilding, all right," declared a beefy woman with auburn hair as she unwrapped a sandwich and took a bite. "It's just not *their* idea of shipbuilding."

"I tell ya," the blonde opined, "between the age of the buildings and the old-fashioned attitudes around this place, it's like we work at a museum. And don't even get me started about the rules. Why, I was a typist at Doubleday, Doran & Company before I came here. No one there squawked if we lit a cigarette at our desks or took a moment to chat with a coworker."

"If you had it so good there," challenged the heavy-set woman with the sandwich, "then what are you doing here? Why don't you go back?"

"I can't go back. My boss's wife found out I was sleeping with her husband."

Nelson shook her head and rolled her eyes.

"Don't get all high and mighty with me," the blonde ordered as she sat down beside Nelson and unpacked her lunch. "I got two pretty decent raises that way. Still, it wasn't as much as I'm making now. Let's face it— that's why we're all here, isn't it? There's no other job in town that pays as much as this one does. You work long and hard for it, but it's not like you wouldn't be working hard anywhere you go these days."

"And at least here we're working for a good cause," the petite woman added as she rubbed her feet. "My husband's over there right now. By working here I feel as though I'm helping him somehow."

The beefy woman placed a comforting hand on the petite woman's back. "You are helping him, honey. You're helping him to come back safe."

Rosie frowned and extracted her sandwich from the inside pocket of her jacket. The young woman's affection for her husband was so fresh, so new, whereas Rosie's was fading by the day. "How long have you been married . . . ? I'm sorry, I don't even know your name. I don't know anyone's name actually."

"Helen Thompson. Oh! I mean Scarlatti! Helen Scarlatti." She giggled. "I've been married four weeks and three days. Frankie and I eloped before he shipped out."

"And barely got to consummate the marriage," the blonde joked.

"Yes, we did," Scarlatti blushed. "Well, once."

"That, my dear, is why you need to start tucking some money away now. So when Frankie comes back, you can surprise him with a French silk negligee (black market, of course) and a room at the Biltmore. I even have some Lucy Agnes Hancock books you can read to prepare you."

"Oh, good Lord." The woman with the auburn hair sighed in disgust. She reached a hand across Scarlatti. "Mildred Mason. And Miss Fifth Avenue over there is Jeannie Wolfe."

Rosie shook Mildred's hand, greeted Jeannie, and then looked at Nelson, who was eating soup from a metal thermos.

"Huh? Oh, the first name's Betty, but you can still call me Nelson."

"Betty—I mean, Nelson—thinks that if we refer to each other by our last names, the same way the men do, we might get more respect," Helen explained before biting into an apple.

"Personally, I think you had the right idea, Rosie," Mildred opined. "Any man gets in our way, we give 'em hell."

Jeannie lit a cigarette and inhaled. "So, um, did you do it? Did you kill Finch?"

All eyes slid toward Rosie.

"No. No, I didn't." She went on to explain what had happened in Finch's office as well as her sudden, violent departure.

"That sounds like Finch, all right," Nelson confirmed. "Since you've been brave enough to tell us your story, I'll tell you mine. It was last week, during an air raid. I was down in the hull, welding. Scarlatti was at the other end. Well, Finch comes down to 'inspect what we're doing'—"

"I remember that," Helen spoke up. "I thought it was strange that he was down there. I didn't think shift supervisors did inspections."

"They don't. I don't know why he was down there in the first place, but when the air raid sirens went off, he got a few ideas. Real fast." Nelson's lip quivered as she fought to maintain her composure. "See, even down in the hull we shut the lights down during an alarm. Finch was at my end of the ship when the power went off. He stood right behind me in the dark, put his arms around my waist, and told me that he could do whatever he wanted to me right there and then and that there was nothing anyone would do about it."

Scarlatti leaped from her spot and, in her stocking feet, rushed to Nelson's side. "Oh, Betty, honey. I had no idea. You must have been so scared."

"At first. Then I was disgusted. I can still feel his breath on my neck."

"If I had only known, I would have—"

"I know."

"Did he . . . did he?"

Nelson didn't answer. "After the disgust wore off, I became angry. I remember holding that welding

torch and thinking of how I might use it against him.
Thank goodness the lights came back on when they
did, because I might have . . . I might have . . ." Nelson
looked up at Rosie, her eyes cold and emotionless. "You
see now why I said Finch got what was coming
to him?"

Rosie returned Nelson's gaze and nodded. She did
understand. The anger, the disgust, the thought that she
might have . . . that *he* might have . . .

Before she could say a word, the shipyard whistle
blew, signifying that it was time to return to work. The
quintet of women picked up their belongings and
trudged back to their respective posts.

Rosie climbed the scaffold at Pier Number One to
the strains of Kilbride's singing:

> *O My Dark Rosaleen,*
> *Do not sigh, do not weep!*
> *The priests are on the ocean green,*
> *They march along the deep.*

Upon her arrival on the platform, Dewitt predicted
in his soft-spoken manner, "He'll be a lot slower now
than he was this morning."

Kilbride, meanwhile, prepared for his afternoon
descent into the ship and continued his serenade:

> *There's wine from the royal Pope,*
> *Upon the ocean green;*
> *And Spanish ale shall give you hope,*
> *My Dark Rosaleen!*
> *My own Rosaleen!*

"A lot slower?" Rosie asked of Dewitt.
Dewitt nodded slightly and blinked.

"Say, Rosaleen!" Kilbride, like a young boy, called. "Your mum ever sing that song to you?"

Rosie answered honestly. "No, because she couldn't carry a tune in a bucket. Oh, and I'm not dark. In case you hadn't noticed."

"No, you aren't, but your heart is." Kilbride grabbed his rope swing and carried it up the scaffold to the top of the ship. "Dark with worry."

In the light of Nelson's confession, the comment was eerily well timed. Kilbride's next remark, however, sent Rosie's mind reeling: "Don't worry. I know you didn't kill Finch, darlin'. If you had murdered that imperialist bastard, I'd ask you to marry me on the spot. Ha, ha!"

With that, Kilbride leaped over the ship's edge and Dewitt began to lower the swing. All the while, the Irishman's voice echoed through the shipyard:

> *My love shall glad your heart, shall give*
>   *you hope,*
> *Shall give you health, and help, and hope,*
> *My Dark Rosaleen!*

Chapter Ten

Friday morning saw Katie assaying to squeeze into Rosie's charcoal gray dress. Although far from heavy, the young blonde's figure had become a bit more curvaceous since Charlie's arrival. "I feel like a pork sausage," she complained.

"You're not," Rosie reassured as she struggled to pull up the back zipper. "You just had a baby six months ago. You're never going to look exactly the same as you did before."

"Gee, thanks."

"And you wouldn't want to. You're beautiful now." Rosie had managed to get the zipper to approximately an inch from the top. "That's as far as she'll go. Are you sure you don't have anything else to wear?"

"Positive. The black wool dress I wore to Jimmy's service shrunk after Ma tried to wash it. And everything else I own is in a color that's not appropriate for a funeral."

"Maybe it's a sign that you shouldn't go," Rosie suggested.

"We went over this last night," Katie stated as she

donned a white cardigan. "There. Can you tell it's not zipped all the way?"

"No. You look fine. I'm just worried about you. It's so soon after Jimmy."

"Jimmy never had a funeral. He had a memorial service, so this will be different. Besides, given Finch's reputation, I'm not sure how much mourning will be going on."

"Yeah, but I'd still feel better if I were with you."

"How? You can't call in sick; you only just got your job back. And let's not forget, you have your own sleuthing to do. You need to find out why Kilbride called Finch . . . what he did." Katie would not repeat the word. "And whether there are other women at the yard who had the same experience as Nelson. Oh, and you need to find out what happened to Jackson, too!"

"I know. But first, I'd better get to work. Good luck," Rosie bade before running out of the bedroom.

"You, too."

"Oh." Rosie peeked her head around the doorframe. "And thank you. For everything."

Katie smiled her reply and, as soon as Rosie had left, set about the task of dressing Charlie and packing up the necessities for the day before catching the eight o'clock train to Brooklyn.

Upon arriving at the Brooklyn IRT station, she pushed Charlie's carriage the three blocks to the corner of Montague Street and Clinton. There, the bells of The Church of the Holy Trinity, a brownstone Gothic Revival masterpiece, summoned Finch's mourners to mass.

As Katie approached the low front steps, she spotted a familiar man in a gray fedora standing outside, just to the right of the church's heavy double doors. He reached into his jacket pocket and extracted a pack of cigarettes and a book of matches.

Lieutenant Riordan! If either Simonetti or Marie Finch thought she was working with the police, they wouldn't give her the time of day.

Moving as quickly as she could, she bumped the carriage up the steps, causing Charlie to whimper. At the sound, Riordan turned around, but Katie disappeared into the church before he could get a good look at her face.

Whew! She thought as she paused a moment to let her eyes adjust to the dim lighting of the church's interior. Once her pupils had dilated and the green spots disappeared, Katie was treated to the imposing site of stone walls, fan-vaulted ceilings, pointed arcades, and row upon row of stained glass and clerestory windows.

If Finch was heading into the afterlife to face his final judgment, this was the perfect place to start the journey.

Preferring to sit at the back of the church where she could observe both the service and its attendants, as well as make a hasty exit should Charlie cry or fuss, Katie selected a rear pew seat on the left side of the altar and behind one of the building's many imposing columns. With one hand on the handle of the carriage and the other gripping a handkerchief to conceal her face from Riordan, she kept a watchful eye on the main entrance.

It was not long before the widow, Marie Finch, arrived on the arm of a man in a black morning coat and waistcoat, white shirt, and dark gray tie. He escorted her to the front of the church, stopping every so often so she could thank a particular guest for attending.

Halfway up the aisle, to the right of the altar, sat

Simonetti. Katie nearly didn't recognize him without his white butcher's coat and apron. Upon arriving at his pew, Marie Finch shook his hand in greeting. Simonetti stood, bowed, and transferred a small, square, white object from his right hand to hers. So quickly and smoothly did the exchange take place that, unless one were watching intently, as Katie was, it would have been missed.

Marie palmed the item and, with a polite nod to Simonetti, continued her journey to the front of the church. Once she had been seated in the first pew, the gentleman in the black waistcoat bowed and then hastened to the back of the church.

The funeral director, Katie guessed. Given Marie's sole presence in the front of the church, neither she nor her late husband had relatives attending the service. However, since the church was half full and guests continued to trickle in through the front doors, it was apparent that Marie did have friends . . . and perhaps, judging from Katie's conversation with Simonetti, as well as the recent exchange, there was one friend who was closer to her than all the others.

What had Simonetti given to Marie? A note? Couldn't he have waited for a more discreet time to . . . ?

Her thoughts were interrupted by a voice emanating from her left. "Miss Keefe?"

Katie nearly jumped out of the pew.

"I'm sorry. I didn't mean to startle you."

She looked up to see Lieutenant Riordan standing beside her. He had removed the gray fedora to reveal a thick crop of chestnut brown hair. "How did . . . ?"

"Oh," he said. "I came in through the chapel. I'm friends with the Father; this used to be my beat back in the day. I'm sorry about calling you Miss Keefe, too.

I realize that's not your name, but I didn't know how else to address you."

"That . . . that's all right. I'm, um, Katie . . . I mean, Mrs. Williams. And your name again?" She knew full well who he was, but thought it best to feign nonchalance.

"Riordan. Lieutenant Jack Riordan. Mind if I sit down, Mrs. Williams?" He squeezed past her and sat next to her.

Katie glanced around nervously. No one seemed to be watching. "Um, no. No, not at all, Lieutenant . . ."

"Riordan." He peered into the carriage and smiled. "What's his name?"

"Charlie. He's, um, he's six months old."

"I had a great uncle on my mother's side named Charlie. He lived to be almost a hundred. Good strong name."

"I always thought so." She expected him to question her presence at the Finch funeral, but instead he leaned back in the pew and waxed philosophical.

"You know, you can tell a lot about the way a man lived by the send-off he receives."

Katie thought about Jimmy. His body hadn't been recovered from the *Houston*, but if it had, she was positive that the church would have been overflowing with mourners. As it was, the memorial service had drawn the attention of all of Greenpoint.

"See how Finch's widow is sitting by herself," Riordan pointed out. "That would make you think that the two of them had no children. However, I happen to know that they have a son. He's grown now, twenty-two years of age; lives in Connecticut."

"Well, where is he?" Katie asked.

"Good question. Could he not afford to make the trip? Or did he dislike his father so much that he couldn't be bothered?"

"Oh! Well, if he felt that way about his father, he might have—" She stopped mid-sentence. This was the man trying to put her sister in jail. She shouldn't be discussing the case with him.

A faint smile crossed Riordan's lips. "I already checked. He was at work all day."

"Oh," Katie replied in disappointment.

At the sound of middle C being played upon the massive Skinner organ, the funeral mass commenced. The mourners rose while, to the strains of Verdi's *Requiem*, the pine coffin that carried the body of Robert Finch was wheeled down the center aisle of the church.

Riordan leaned closer to Katie. "Notice how most of the people here are women?" he whispered. "Probably friends of Mrs. Finch, wouldn't you say?"

Katie recalled Simonetti's description of Finch and his many affairs. "Most of them, probably, but some might be—" Once again, she caught herself on the verge of telling Riordan more than she had intended.

Luckily, her sudden silence coincided with the appearance of the priest, who immediately launched into the greeting, followed by a prayer, and then the *Kyrie Eleison*. As the congregation replied to the cleric's chants with the response of "Lord, have mercy," the main doors of the church opened, piercing the dark Gothic interior with a long shaft of bright light.

Beneath the worshippers' curious stares, the figure in the doorway hastily closed the heavy wooden doors and slid from the center aisle into Katie's pew. Approximately thirty-five years of age, with fair skin and long black hair that had been tucked into a fine mesh snood, she was more exotic than good looking and her gray suit, although well-fitted, showed signs of pilling at the elbows.

With a final, "Lord, have mercy," the priest signaled the mourners to be seated before he delivered the eulogy. Katie had never before attended a funeral where the deceased's final tribute was spoken by someone who wasn't a close friend or family member, but given Finch's reputation, finding an individual to issue a few kind words would probably have proven difficult. After all, the man was murdered for a reason.

"Today we celebrate the life of Robert Andrew Finch," the Father announced before expounding upon the details of the man's birth, childhood, and start, as a teen, in the shipbuilding industry. When he went on to describe Finch's role as a "caring, devoted husband and loving father," one could hear the clearing of throats and the awkward shuffling of feet against the gray stone floors.

More dramatic, however, was the reaction of the mysterious woman seated on the other side of Katie. At the mention of Finch's wife and son, she rose to her feet and opened her mouth as if to speak. But before she could utter a sound, Charlie, in his carriage, let out a loud gurgle, followed by a happy coo.

The dark-haired woman was instantly transfixed by the infant. She watched as Katie lifted the baby from the carriage and cradled him in her arms, the expression on her face shifting from anger to surprise, and then, finally, grief. As quickly as she had risen from her seat, the woman took off down the church aisle and out the arched church doors.

A dumbfounded Katie flashed a quizzical glance at Riordan. *Surely someone should follow the woman.* Yet there the lieutenant sat, his only reaction a vague shrug.

Leaving Riordan to watch the carriage—the only task for which he seemed prepared—Katie slid out of the pew and, balancing Charlie in her left arm, pushed through the Gothic church doors with her right. Outside, she spotted the mysterious woman with her back leaned against the church and her face in her hands.

At the sound of Katie's footsteps on the pavement, she looked up and walked hastily down Montague Street, her scuffed black pumps clicking against the cement sidewalk that ran alongside the church.

With Charlie in tow, Katie took off in pursuit and called after her. In keeping with her gentle, somewhat retiring nature, Katie's voice was soft and quiet. "Hey," she said in a near-shout, to no effect. She had to talk to her. She had to find out who she was and why she was at the funeral. Rosie's life depended upon it.

With a renewed sense of urgency, Katie drew a deep breath and released the air over her vocal cords with all the force she could muster. "Hey!"

The sound surprised Charlie, prompting him to cry, but it had also stopped the mysterious woman in her tracks. She turned on one heel and faced Katie.

"I just wanted to give you a handkerchief and see if you were all right." Katie extracted a lace-trimmed hankie from the pocket of her cardigan sweater and dangled it from her extended arm.

The woman drew closer and accepted the square piece of fabric. "Thank you. I . . . I'm sorry you had to shout like you did. I'm sorry you had to make him cry."

Katie smoothed her son's fine, silky hair over his forehead and rocked him back and forth. Within a matter of seconds, the child quieted down. "He was just frightened. See? He's already better. You, on the other hand . . ."

"I'm okay."

"Really? You didn't strike me as okay."

"I just . . ." Her voice trailed off as her eyes slid toward Charlie. "I don't know why I'm talking to you. I don't know you."

"Who better to talk to than a stranger?" Katie reasoned. "At least you know I won't be biased. Besides, I know how emotional funerals can be. You see, my husband passed away recently."

The bid to earn the woman's sympathy worked. "Oh, dear, I'm sorry. And now here you are at another funeral."

"Oh, I only came to be neighborly. We're staying with my aunt and, since she can't get around anymore, I thought I should pay my respects on her behalf. I don't know the Finches and, from what I've heard about him, it's probably just as well."

"Hmph," the woman snorted. "Got that right."

"You knew him?"

"I, um . . . yeah, but . . ."

"You can tell me. I swear I won't say a word to anyone. Heck, I don't think I'll even be in the neighborhood long enough to tell anyone. My sister and I are looking to share a place in Greenpoint."

This part of Katie's story, at least, was true.

The woman looked longingly at the baby. "Greenpoint is a lovely neighborhood. That will be good for him. Say, what's his name?"

"Charlie."

"Charlie." She smiled. "The fresh air in Greenpoint should be good for Charlie. He'll have more room to run around, too. Boys need lots of space to play."

"I'm sure. He's already pretty active. I can't imagine what he'll be like when he starts crawling and then walking. Tell me, um . . ."

"Lois."

"I'm Katie. Tell me, Lois, do you have children?"

"No." The woman frowned. "I've never even been married. And now I . . . well . . . I can no longer have children."

Katie felt awful for asking. "Oh! I'm sorry. I didn't

mean to—I mean, I wouldn't have pried, only you didn't seem that old."

"I'm not. Age had nothing to do with it. It was all stupidity."

Katie's face looked a question.

"Well, since I've gone this far, I guess I might as well tell you. Bob Finch and I were friends. *Close* friends."

Katie's eyes grew wide. "You mean—?

"Yeah. I'm not proud of it. But you gotta understand that Bob could be a real charmer when he wanted to be."

Be it her naïveté, her unflinching devotion to her late husband, or the fact that her brother-in-law had run around on her sister, Katie could not fathom how some people could even think of cheating on a spouse. However, this was not the time for moral judgments. "When did you meet him?"

"About a year ago. I was moving into the building two doors down from Bob's when he spotted me. He said hello and helped me carry my things upstairs. Once I was settled in, he invited me to have dinner with him and his wife."

"He did? You didn't go, did you?"

"Of course I did. It was the first day in the neighborhood. There was nothing going on then. I had only just met him and he seemed like a . . . gentleman. And Marie was sweet, too. Over the next couple of months, I'd go over there and ask for Bob's help with some things around the apartment. My landlord is okay, but he's slow to make repairs. Bob was always at the ready with his toolbox. It was nice. And nice is tough to come by these days."

"Oh! So you and Bob—er, Mr. Finch—really *were* just close friends."

"Oh, honey, you're sweet, but you really need to get out more!"Lois laughed. "No, no, no. What happened is this: the first few times that I stopped by to ask if Bob could fix my sink, or help me set a mousetrap, Marie was happy to see me. But after a little while, she was . . . well . . . displeased. Looking back, it was probably because she knew what her husband was up to. But Bob told me she was sick. That she'd fly into fits of rage and then get so melancholy she'd spend days inside, all the lights off, just crying."

Lois drew a heavy sigh and then continued the story. "I just felt so bad for them. Bob especially. He seemed so lonely, like he had no one in the world to talk to. So I started to ask him over to fix things, only nothing needed fixing. Instead, we'd talk over coffee, or I'd make him lunch. During one of our meetings, we kissed. Well, one thing led to another and . . . well, you know. After about a month or so of us getting together, Marie started to balk about Bob coming over. I'm not sure whether she was jealous or whether she had gotten wise to what was going on, but we decided to meet in secret."

"How could it be secret if Mrs. Finch already knew you were . . . lovers?" The word made Katie blush.

"Bob promised Marie that he wouldn't see or talk to me. But meanwhile, he gradually began leaving earlier for work each morning. Bob always ate breakfast at a coffee shop near the yard, so Marie slept in. She was none the wiser."

"And he went to see you?"

"Yes, we'd have about an hour or so together before he left for work."

"He saw you every day?"

"Well, every day the yard was open. Five days a week at first, but since the war started, six days. Not that we . . . um, all the time. Sometimes I'd just make breakfast or coffee. Other times we would . . . well, you know."

Katie's eyes narrowed.

"Like I said, I'm not proud of what I did, but I was lonely and thought he was lonely, too. . . ."

"But he wasn't?"

"I don't think Robert Finch was capable of feeling anything as deep as loneliness. He had one thing on his mind and one thing only."

"Why do you say that? What did he do?"

"He gave me the clap," Lois whispered.

"The . . . the what?"

"The clap. Gonorrhea. It's a social disease. I . . . I didn't even know I had it until I got pains in my stomach," she stated as tears ran slowly down her face. "When I went to the doctor, he sent me to the hospital right away, but it was too late. I needed an emergency hysterectomy."

Katie rested a consoling hand on Lois's shoulder.

"I know what you're thinking. 'She got what she deserved, the hussy. Sneaking around with someone else's husband.'"

"No! Not at all. I can't imagine being told that you'll never—"

"It's more than that. Bob was the only man I ever felt that way about. . . . I trusted him. I loved him. I thought he felt the same way. But all the time, there were other women. He was just using me and I was too blind to see it."

"Love can be blind," Katie said gently.

"Yeah. I'll say," Lois said in disgust. "Do you know? The whole time I was in the hospital, Bob never once bothered to check on me. When I got out, he didn't even stop by to see if I needed anything."

"So he had no idea what had happened?"

"Oh, I finally told him. I waited outside his building one morning just so I could see him."

"And?"

"He thanked me for telling him and said he'd make

a doctor's appointment as soon as possible. No 'I'm sorry.' No 'how are you?' No sense of remorse. Nothing. I thought he might at least be sympathetic, but he was just worried about getting to the doctor. Worried about himself. My God, what an idiot I was!"

Katie was reminded of her conversation with Rosie, just three days earlier. "You're not an idiot because you loved someone, Lois. You just chose the wrong someone to love."

"Yeah, but now my life is ruined," Lois sobbed. "By *him.* I hope he rots in hell!"

"If that's the case, what were you doing here today? Why would you even consider paying him your respects?"

"Respects? Who said I was paying my respects? I came here to let everyone know what a weasel he was! And I was about to when . . . when—"

"When Charlie caught your attention," Katie recounted.

"Yes. And everything came flooding back again . . . how I can never have that. How Bob took that possibility away from me."

The church bells rang out. Slowly. Somberly. As if in mourning, not for Robert Finch, but for the lives that had been indelibly altered by his existence.

Realizing that Finch's widow would soon be on her way to the cemetery, Katie, eyes cast downward, spun around, only to witness her petite five-foot-one-inch shadow being slowly engulfed by that of Lieutenant Riordan.

She looked upward. His right hand, which had clutched his gray fedora inside the church, now had a firm grip on the handle of the baby carriage. "Charlie's chariot," he announced. "I thought you might be needing it."

Nonplussed, Katie placed her son into the carriage and, with a murmured thank-you to the lieutenant and Lois, barreled toward the front of the church. She arrived just in time to see Marie Finch exit through the heavy wooden doors.

"Mrs. Finch," she cried, as she abruptly blocked the woman's path with the carriage.

The sudden appearance of the obstacle caused Marie to stop short and teeter a few moments, hands high in the air, before regaining her balance. Those few moments of lost footing, however, were enough to cause the woman to drop her handbag.

"Oh, Mrs. Finch, I'm so sorry," Katie apologized as she scrambled to collect the purse and its contents from the church pavement.

Lipstick . . . compact . . . change purse . . .

"I'm new to the neighborhood and wanted to give my condolences. . . ."

Emery board . . . apartment key . . .

"I lost my husband not very long ago. . . ."

Katie spotted Marie Finch's comb, as well as the white object passed to her by Simonetti just two feet to her right.

"Oh?" Marie responded. "I'm so sorry to hear that. Umm . . . oh . . . I . . . I can get those things. You don't have to do it."

Katie lunged for the items and managed to secure the comb, but a brown shoe, belonging to a man in a dark brown suit, kicked the white object another six inches north.

"Oh no," Katie replied, "I insist." She leaped forward and collected the item in question and pretended to place it, along with the comb, inside the handbag.

Standing upright, she fastened the clasp of the handbag and presented it to Mrs. Finch. "As I was saying, I know what it's like to suffer the loss of a husband, so if you need anything, anything at all . . ."

"Well, thank you, umm . . ."

"Katherine," she inserted.

"Katherine. That's most kind, but . . ."

The firm hand of the funeral director escorted Mrs. Finch toward the open door of a black car. "Ma'am, we need to be on our way."

A perplexed Marie Finch stepped into the backseat of the car, all the while her gaze fixed on Katie, who, clutching the mysterious object in a white-gloved hand, rocked Charlie's carriage and attempted to mold her facial expression into an expression of sympathy until the funeral procession began.

Once the limousine had pulled a safe distance away from the curb, Katie opened her gloved hand to reveal the folded object, approximately two inches by two inches square, that she had, by recalling the magic tricks of her father, successfully palmed.

But before she could revel in her victory, a set of masculine fingers snatched it from her palm.

"Hey! That was mine," Katie complained.

"No, I believe it actually belongs to Marie Finch," Riordan corrected.

"But I—"

"Lifted it from her handbag? I know. I watched you. Nice work. If Charlie here grows up to have one half of his mother's sleuthing skills, I look forward to having him on the force."

"My father had many talents: magician, amateur boxer—"

"Detective?"

"No. Now, will you please give that back? I'm the one who got it."

"You did, but sorry, no. Can't. Police evidence. But you know what, I'll open it up and we can read it together. How's that sound?"

"I guess so."

Riordan carefully unfolded the sheet of paper and Katie peered eagerly around his arm:

Maria, mi amore,

How I wish I could be with you right now, but at least I sleep easier knowing that you are rid of that horrible man.

Someday, we will be together—always! Until then, stop by my shop Monday morning after you return from your sister's house.

Vincent will be making ristorante deliveries and we can be alone.

Yours,
S xoxo

"'S'? Who's 'S'?" Riordan asked.

Katie shrugged innocently.

"Come on, now. Don't be that way."

"Why should I tell you anything?"

"Because if you don't, I can have you arrested for obstructing justice."

"You wouldn't!"

It was Riordan's turn to shrug.

"Okay . . . It's Simonetti, the butcher."

"He signs a love letter using his last initial?"

"Maybe that's his first initial, too. His first name could be Steven . . . Sean . . . Sergio . . . Simon . . ."

"Simon Simonetti?"

"Well, I don't know. I'm guessing. I'm lucky I got as far as I did."

"But you're positive this is from the butcher?"

Katie closed her eyes and crossed her heart. "One hundred percent. I saw him pass her the note when he paid his respects. Vincent is his son. I met him yesterday."

Riordan raised an eyebrow.

"Umm . . . I came down to check on Rosie and thought I'd do my shopping at the same time."

"Uh-huh. And what about your friend?"

"My friend?"

"The one you followed out of the church. The one you were talking to just a few minutes ago."

"If you're so curious, why didn't you follow her?"

"Because, given how she stared at your son, I thought you'd probably get farther than I would. Not to mention that she was already spooked by something. Having a cop on her tail would only have made her run faster."

Katie stared at Charlie, who was sleeping in his carriage. She had to admit the lieutenant made sense, yet she was somewhat irked by the fact that he let her do the legwork while he sat by idly.

"So," he continued. "Who is she and what's her story?"

Katie shook her head and folded her arms across her chest. "First you steal the note that I found—"

"Stole," Riordan corrected.

"—and now this. Why should I tell you anything? You'll just use it to put my sister in jail."

"Is that what you think? This is an investigation, Mrs. Williams, not a frame-up."

"Then you're not trying to pin Finch's murder on Rosie?"

"I'm trying to find the truth. If evidence bears out that your sister killed Finch and should go to jail, then . . ."

"But that's not how it happened. She didn't do it!"

"Then the quicker I uncover the truth and find the real killer, the better. And you, Mrs. Williams, can help me do that."

"By telling you about Lois," Katie presumed.

"If that's the name of the woman you were speaking to, then yes."

"Oh, all right." She recounted Lois's tale, using words that were as close to the woman's own as possible.

When she had finished, Riordan asked: "And this 'Lois,' did she have a last name?"

"I don't know. I didn't ask."

"That's not a problem. If she lives two doors down from the Finches it should be easy to find her. Now, is that all the information you have?"

"Yes."

"Are you sure?"

Katie nodded her head in earnest. "I already told you about Simonetti and Mrs. Finch. That's it."

"Okay. What about your sister?"

"What about her?"

"Last I saw her, she was trying to get her job back at Pushey Shipyard."

"Yes, what of it?"

"Well, given everything that happened, it struck me as odd that she'd even entertain the idea of going back there."

"My sister insists that I stay home with Charlie, yet we need money, so I suppose she figured going back was the most logical thing to do." Katie shrugged. "A paycheck is a paycheck, she always says."

"Sometimes it is, but not always. Sometimes a paycheck is supplemented with other . . . benefits."

"I'm not sure I know what you mean."

"When I ran into your sister at the yard, I got the distinct impression that she had requested to be rehired in order to investigate Finch's murder. That feeling was confirmed when I walked into the church and saw you."

Katie looked away.

"She wouldn't have sent you out sleuthing without

doing some detective work herself. So," Riordan continued, "what has she dug up?"

"I don't think she'd want me to tell you."

"Of course not. She doesn't know if she should trust me, does she?"

"No."

"But you do. You trust me now, don't you?"

She looked up at Riordan, her blue eyes almost pleading. "I . . . I think we need to trust someone."

"My dear Mrs. Williams, I couldn't agree with you more." He reached beneath the back of his suit jacket and removed his wallet from his rear pants pocket. From there, he extracted two crisp dollar bills and handed them to Katie. "Here, go get yourself and Charlie some lunch."

"That . . . that's very nice of you, but I couldn't—"

"Yes, you can and you will. There's a luncheonette around the corner that makes great chocolate malteds. Have a sandwich, a malted, head home, and don't come back."

"Don't come back? But I need to investigate. Rosie needs my help!"

"And you have helped. Tremendously. You've uncovered two separate leads and three new suspects. Now that your work here is done, I think it's time for you to put sleuthing aside and focus on taking care of that boy of yours. You're the only parent he has left."

"I know, but—"

"No buts. I don't want you mingling with potential murderers any longer. I'm sure your sister feels the same way I do."

"She didn't even want me to go this far," Katie acknowledged. "But what about Marie and Simonetti? And

Lois? Who's going to find out whether one of them killed Finch?"

"I will. Not only is it my job, but I'll make it my personal promise to you. So long as you promise to stay home and keep safe. Deal?"

Katie nodded with a faint smile. "Deal."

"Okay then, get going and enjoy your lunch. And if John's behind the counter, tell him Riordan said not to skimp on the ice cream."

"Will do." She giggled as she swiveled the carriage so that it faced down Montague Street. "Oh, wait! You wanted to know what Rosie discovered."

"I do, but I think I'd rather hear it straight from the horse's mouth, so don't expect her home for supper tonight."

"You mean . . . ?" Katie drew a hand to her mouth.

"No, I'm not taking her down to the station." He laughed. "I'm going to talk to her, that's all. And it's not that I don't trust you, either, but your sister might have, um . . ."

"Sugarcoated things to protect me?"

"Exactly."

"Yeah, she does that a lot. Come to think of it, most people do. I'm not sure why."

It was Riordan's turn to smile. As Katie pushed Charlie's carriage past the church and turned toward the bumpy sidewalks of Clinton Street, he tipped his hat and uttered his usual, "Uh-huh."

Chapter Eleven

Rosie stood on the scaffold of Pier Number One and, like the day before, dashed from planking edge to hull, catching rivets in her cone and then placing them in predrilled holes. Today, however, the process, although still exerting, seemed to require slightly less effort, most likely because she knew what to expect.

With Kilbride on the other side of the steel, humming a cheerful air as he lost himself in his riveting duties, Rosie decided to ask Dewitt for his perspective on Finch. Up until this moment, the two had only chatted about the job or the weather. Rosie hoped that posing some pointed questions didn't cause the man to retreat into silence.

"You know, I haven't seen Jackson since I've been back," she prefaced as she loaded the first of three rivets into place. "What happened to her? Was she fired?"

Dewitt put the bucking bar over the rivet and held on tightly while Kilbride flattened the other side with a pop of his pneumatic gun. "Don't think so. Would've heard 'bout it."

Dewitt removed the bar, allowing Rosie to load the

next rivet. "Maybe she's sick. There are a few bugs going around, what with the weather being so changeable."

He shook his head and bucked the second rivet. "She don't have a phone, most folks workin' here don't, but she woulda sent her son to tell me 'bout it."

"You? Oh, you live nearby?"

"Close 'nough. But she woulda told me cause that's how it's done round here. Mr. Finch didn't want no Negroes sendin' their friends and family to him sayin' someone wasn't showin' up for work, so he made 'em report to me."

She placed the third rivet in the predrilled hole and then went to fetch more. "You're a foreman, then?" she asked upon her return, bending to place the first of the new set of rivets into a predrilled hole.

Dewitt laughed and applied the bucking bar. "A Negro foreman? No, ma'am. Ain't such a thing. I just do their talkin' for 'em."

"Like a spokesperson? Hmm," she mused and placed the second rivet. "So if Jackson had decided to quit her job, she'd tell you that, too."

"Sure would. Don't see how she could quit, though. Can't afford it. Not with a boy to raise and no daddy around."

"I didn't know she was alone. No wonder she was in such a panic when Finch reassigned her from the hull of the ship." Rosie placed the third rivet and then retrieved more.

"Yup, her boy's sick a lot, too." Dewitt waited until she had returned from the scaffold's edge to continue the conversation. "That kinda pay cut woulda hit her hard. Real hard."

"Did she calm down any as the day went on?" She picked a rivet up with her tongs and placed it in the first of the next line of holes.

"Don't know. Didn't talk to her 'cept to say good night." While Kilbride, on the other side of the hull, shouted for more pressure, Dewitt pushed hard against the bucking bar.

"And you haven't seen her since?"

"Not since the day you . . ." He caught himself. "Not since the day Finch changed her assignment. I stopped by her house twice now, but no one answers the door."

Rosie inserted the next rivet. "Is that normal for her?"

Dewitt shook his head and braced the bar with the full weight of his body. "Nope. Shelby—em, Miss Jackson— is always havin' visitors in. She likes it when friends come round. Not like her at all to turn folks away."

"Maybe she's afraid to come back to the docks after what happened to Finch, but she's too ashamed to admit it." She reached her tongs into the cone for another rivet.

"No way she coulda known 'bout Finch that fast, ma'am. I didn't know 'til I got here the next mornin'."

She placed the rivet into the drilled hole. "Very strange. Are you sure she's okay? I mean, have you seen her son to ask about her?"

"Haven't seen either of them." He bucked the bar against the red-hot metal. "Jackson since that evenin', like I said, and her son the day before."

Rosie scuttled across the planks and caught the next batch of rivets; this time she returned to the hull with four glowing fasteners instead of the customary three. "Aren't you worried? You said this isn't like her. Maybe you should call the police."

"Police ain't gonna care about some missing Negro woman."

Rosie pushed the rivet into the predrilled hole, this time more forcefully. "And you?"

"I'm worried. I'm plenty worried," he confessed and pushed the bucking bar with all his might.

"Take me by there tonight," she suggested.

"Huh? No. Oh no, ma'am. I couldn't do that."

"Why not? Because I'm white?"

"Well, that for a start. But . . . really, Mrs. Keefe. You don't want to be getting yourself involved in this. You'd best look out for yourself."

"I am. That's why I want to go to Shelby's place after work tonight."

"I dunno . . ."

"Please?" she said, her eyes wide and beseeching.

"All right, I'll take you. But if she doesn't open the door—"

"I'll walk away without a word," Rosie promised.

With that, Kilbride rose above the top of the hull. "No words, my dear? Why, that's the best bargain I've heard all day. The past half hour, all it's been is yap, yap, yap."

Rosie and Dewitt both stood upright.

"We've still kept pace, haven't we?" Rosie challenged.

"You have. But your attention should be on the metal and not some darkie who's abandoned her job."

"What does it matter, so long as we get our work done?"

"It matters a great deal, Rosaleen. When you stop thinking about what you're doing, my dear, and start nosing about in things that don't concern you, people are apt to get hurt."

Rosie narrowed her eyes. Something in the Irishman's tone made the statement sound more like a warning. Before she could reply, the noon whistle sounded and Kilbride, without further eye contact, dismounted from his hanging bench, shoved past Rosie, and climbed down the scaffold to the yard below.

With a hangdog expression, a silent Dewitt followed Kilbride to ground level and made his way to the outdoor toilet reserved for Negroes. Rosie, meanwhile, grabbed her lunch pail from the end of the plank and made her way to the back of the bomb shelter.

There, she found her female coworkers occupying similar locations as the day before.

"Hey, Rosie," Nelson greeted as she leaned against the brick wall of the shelter, puffing on a cigarette. "How are you making out in the gang of ghouls?"

"Oh, fine, I guess." She plunked her lunch pail onto the asphalt. "How are you ladies doing?"

"It's only just gotten warm and my feet are already burning," Scarlatti stated as she stripped off her boots and socks. "It's going to be a loooong summer."

"Your feet aren't the worst part of it. I can't imagine how hot those scaffolds are gonna be. The sun reflecting off that metal and no shade?" Mildred Mason whistled as she unwrapped her sandwich. "I'm telling you, brother!"

"My! I didn't even think of that." Scarlatti rubbed her feet feverishly. "And down in that hull? With no air to be had . . . oh, that will be awful."

Wolfe, meanwhile, stood against the bomb shelter wall and stared into the distance.

"Say," Mildred ventured. "What's with you?"

"Huh?" The blonde was startled from her reverie.

"I said, what's eating you?"

"I . . . well, I was thinking. Since Nelson came clean yesterday, I want to come clean, too."

"Come clean?" Nelson questioned.

"Yeah, about Finch. About what . . . what he did to you."

The brunette let her cigarette fall from between her lips. "You mean he did the same thing to you?"

"Yeah. Yeah, he did. Only . . . only I gave in."

"Of course you did," Mason quipped.

"It's not funny, Mildred."

"She's right," Nelson agreed. "It's not funny. Go on, Jeannie."

"Well . . . he—I mean, Finch—called me into his office one day and made me an offer." Wolfe suddenly fell silent.

"What kind of offer?" Rosie prompted.

"If I . . ." She drew a deep breath. "If I performed certain favors, I'd get a promotion."

Mason clicked her tongue.

"I don't need your comments or your condemnation, Mildred! I've been working on a riveting gang four months now. I'm capable of doing a lot more than catching molten metal in a bucket, or welding in cramped, dark quarters where no grown man can fit, or sweeping up the garbage that *they* leave behind. We all are."

The four other women in the group looked off in the distance and nodded silently.

"And no, I'm not proud of it, but I have slept with bosses before. Sometimes to get ahead. Other times so that I wouldn't be lonely for a night." She gave a self-deprecating chuckle. "The thing is, the bosses I've slept with in the past were . . . different. They were courteous, gentle."

"Oh, don't get me wrong," Wolfe continued. "It was still a business transaction. And they made sure you knew it. But at least, between the steak dinner, the private car, and the room at the Ritz, you could imagine it was something more. And at the end of the night, when the car would drop you off at your apartment alone, you knew that the very next morning you'd receive what had been promised to you."

"But not with Finch," Rosie ventured.

"No." Jeannie bit her upper lip. "Not with Finch. The moment I said yes, that was it. The next thing I knew, I was pinned on his desk and he was . . ."

Mildred, who hadn't taken a bite of her sandwich since Wolfe's story had started, was instantly on her feet. "Oh, Jeannie," she exclaimed as she placed a comforting arm around her friend. "I'm so sorry, sweetie, for saying what I did."

Wolfe embraced her and began to sob. "No . . . no . . . I don't blame you. I didn't argue with Finch, either. I know full well what I am. He did, too."

"Yeah, so, you're easy. That's still no reason for Finch to—" Nelson shivered slightly. "To do what he did."

The group fell silent, during which time Mason quieted Wolfe and Rosie consoled Nelson with a thermos of water and a steady hand on her shoulder

Two minutes elapsed before Scarlatti broke the silence. "I'm confused."

It was just the mood breaker needed. The quartet immediately broke into raucous laughter.

"God love ya, bug," Mason exclaimed between giggles.

"Bug?"

"Yeah, cute, small, and very annoying."

Scarlatti pulled a pout.

"Oh, come on now, that was a compliment," Mason cajoled. "Go on and tell us why you're so confused."

Helen Scarlatti sighed. "I'm confused because Jeannie said Finch offered her a promotion, but all the riveters are men and none of them have been fired recently. So, whose job were you going to get?"

Wolfe, her eyes red from crying, looked blankly at Scarlatti and replied: "Yours, dear. Yours."

Having spent the remainder of the lunch break in awkward silence, Keefe broke away from the company of Nelson, Scarlatti, Mason, and Wolfe and climbed the scaffold to complete the remainder of the day's work.

When she reached the platform, Kilbride was waiting for her. "Have a nice lunch?"

"Yes, I did. Thank you. I hope you did as well." She hastened to the end of the platform to deposit her lunch pail, but before she get far, Kilbride grabbed her by the wrist. "And just where do think you're going, missy?"

"Setting my pail down and getting back to work. Isn't that what you want, Kilbride? Production is the name of the game."

"That's not all I want, Rosaleen," he leered.

"You're drunk," she declared. "And where's Dewitt?"

"I told him to take another ten minutes while I spoke with you . . . in private."

"Go ahead and talk," she stated coolly. Internally, however, all she could think about was the repulsive feeling of Finch's hands upon her.

"Well, now, aren't you the bold one?"

"My husband has taught me a great many things," she replied, all the while fighting the urge to scream. "None of them more important than the fact that reason and politeness don't work with drunkards. So, what is it you want?"

"First, I'll thank you very much to put down that lunch bucket."

Without realizing it, she had lifted her left arm and appeared ready to wield the galvanized steel bucket at a moment's notice. Reluctantly, she squatted and placed the bucket onto the boards with a thump.

"Much obliged," Kilbride said in a mocking tone. "And now that I can be sure you're not going to cream me, I ought to tell you that you'd best be watching yourself around here. Some folk don't take kindly to having you nose around in their secrets. Trust me, I know of what I speak."

The reply caught her off guard. "A warning? You've grabbed me by the wrist and scared the bejesus out of me just to issue me a warning? Call me ungrateful, but you have a funny way of showing your concern."

"My relationships with the fairer sex have taught me a great many things. None of them more important than the fact that reason and politeness don't work with stubborn redheaded women." Kilbride kissed the hand that was within his grip and relinquished it with a smile before launching into song:

> *All day long, in unrest,*
> *To and fro, do I move.*
> *The very soul within my breast*
> *Is wasted for you, love!*

Her mind awash with both confusion and more than a bit of fear, she watched as Kilbride lowered himself over the ship's hull:

> *The heart in my bosom faints*
> *To think of you, my Queen,*
> *My life of life, my saint of saints,*
> *My Dark Rosaleen!*
> *My own Rosaleen!*

Chapter Twelve

Rosie spent the rest of the afternoon eagerly antici-
pating the four o'clock whistle that signified the end of
her shift and the start of the next. She wondered what
would come from her visit to Shelby Jackson. Would
the young Negro woman open her door to a white
woman who was a veritable stranger? Or, having heard
of Rosie's fight with Finch, would Jackson feel safe
disclosing the reason behind her isolation?

And what if that reason was murder? What if Jackson had lured Finch to the docks and then killed him?
Rosie would need to contact the police, but Dewitt had
made it clear that Jackson had no phone service in her
apartment.

Rosie frowned and wondered if she should call
Lieutenant Riordan before leaving the shipyard and
ask him to meet her and Dewitt at Jackson's home.
But she quickly rejected the idea. The object of the
meeting was to get Jackson to open up about Finch
and her sudden disappearance. Bringing a tall, intim-
idating police lieutenant would be counterproductive
to that aim.

Besides, she still hadn't decided whether she should

trust Riordan. For all she knew, he'd take over the interview with Jackson and use those answers to point the finger of guilt back at Rosie.

No, she resolved as the four o'clock whistle blew, Riordan should definitely not be informed of this visit. If it turned out that Jackson was, indeed, Finch's killer, she'd just have to figure out, then and there, how to proceed.

Wishing to avoid another possible confrontation with Kilbride, Rosie gave a nod to Dewitt and descended the scaffold before the Irishman's platform could be raised to the top of the hull. After a quick stop in the holding area ladies' room to splash water on her face and strengthen her resolve, she moved to the front gate to meet Dewitt.

Alas, it wasn't Dewitt she encountered, but Kilbride. His work shirt having been removed in order to keep cool under the combined heat of sun and steel, he stood in his white sleeveless undershirt, his slightly sunburned shoulders and biceps resting against the shipyard fence.

The sight was not altogether displeasing, yet Rosie felt compelled to look away.

"Oh, I do apologize. I've offended your delicate ladylike sensibilities," he stated and, with a smirk, donned his blue denim work shirt. "So where is my Rosaleen off to on this soft spring evenin'?"

"I'm not your Rosaleen. I'm not *your* anything. And you should be more concerned about putting your tools away at the end of the day instead of where I'm going."

"Don't ya be worryin' that pretty head of yers. I left my rivet gun in the toolshed, just as I should." He glanced upward as if in an effort to recall his actions. "At least I think I did, anyways. So, where are you off to?"

"I'm going for a walk and then home for supper."

"Might ya be interested in some company on your walk? I promise not to sing, unless, of course, ya'd fancy me to."

Rosie's felt her face grow warm. *The insolence!* "I most certainly would not!"

"Is it the walkin' or the singin' that offends ya?"

"Both! I'm a married woman, Kilbride."

"I'm well apprised as to your marital status, my darlin' Mrs. Keefe. And though I find ya more than worthy of my romantic attentions, my invitation was for your benefit."

"*My* benefit? A bit full of yourself, don't you think?"

"Hmph. Suit yourself, darlin'. After our conversation this afternoon and your diggin' about, I thought ya might feel safer with an ornery Mick at your side. But if you're going to be cheeky about it . . ."

Rosie's jaw dropped.

"What's the matter, Mrs. Keefe? Disappointed that I'm not the scoundrel everyone makes me out to be?" he said with a gleam in his eye.

"No, not disappointed. As for you not being a scoundrel . . . well, I . . . I wouldn't go quite as far as that," she stated quietly.

Kilbride responded with a raucous laugh. "Right ya are and smart as well for recognizin' it. And since we're speakin' plainly, before ya go asking questions about me and Finch, I'll tell ya the truth, right here, face to face: I despised the man. Loathed him."

"That's a fairly strong sentiment."

"Finch was the sorta fella that brought out strong sentiments."

"Why?"

"He was a cruel bastard, that's why. They'd hang

people in the old country for the things he did. I'm thinkin' ya knew enough about the man to agree."

Rosie recalled the day in Finch's office. *Was Kilbride aware of the fact that Finch had tried to . . .*

"The look on your face tells me I'm right," he said.

"How do you . . . ?"

"Because Finch did the same thing to someone I knew. Someone dear to me. Only she hadn't your strength, Rosaleen. She hadn't the strength to fight him off."

"Was she your . . . wife?"

"Nay, but she might have been—in time." The strong, bold features of Kilbride's face softened into a hint of a smile, not the taunting smile he often displayed on the scaffold but a smile of genuine tenderness and affection. "She was beautiful. Long, blond hair; sweet disposition . . . She came here to bring me lunch. A surprise, it was."

"Lunch?"

"It shocks ya to know I ate in those days, eh?"

Rosie shrugged. "I hadn't noticed you didn't eat now."

"Liar," he stated blandly.

She grinned. "What was her name?"

"Molly. Margaret was her Christian name, but I called her Molly."

"You loved her."

"I did."

"What happened?"

"She came here. Cold autumn day. She made lamb stew, best in the city. So in love was she that she poured some into a tin and walked here to bring it to me. That's the kind of woman she was. Of course, when Finch saw her, he decided to have a pull."

Rosie's face was a question.

"He flirted with her."

"Oh."

Kilbride's eyes flashed with an intensity Rosie had never before witnessed in a man. "But that weren't enough for a sod like Finch. No. He walked her out of the yard and asked to escort her home. She turned him down as well as she could—she weren't the forceful type. Still, he followed. The more she said no, the more persistent and angry he got. A few blocks from here he shoved her into an alley, placed a hand over her mouth, and . . ."

"I'm sorry, Clinton." The use of his first name caused the man to look up in surprise. Rosie reared back. "Oh! I didn't mean to . . ."

"Ya didn't. It was . . . I . . . I just haven't heard anyone call me by anything other than my last name in a very long time, 'tis all."

After a few moments of awkward silence, Rosie picked up the conversation. "Did Molly call the police and tell them what he had done?"

"No. She were too ashamed."

"What—what happened to Molly? I notice you talk about her in the past tense."

"She went out of her head. Completely out of her head. Couldn't sleep. Couldn't think. Couldn't do anything. She so wanted peace, she took a sleeping draught, and then another, and yet another . . . After a few minutes, she fell asleep and never woke up again."

Rosie felt the flesh on her arms rise into bumps and tears well in her eyes. She felt terrible for Kilbride and Molly. And yet, as selfish as it might seem, she couldn't shake the fact that what happened to Molly might have happened to her. She struggled to find the right words. "That's . . . I . . ."

Kilbride looked her squarely in the eyes. "Ya needn't say it, darlin'. I know."

"I'm so sorry. So very, very sorry."

"Ya have no reason. Molly wouldn't have been at the yard if it weren't for me."

"Don't even think that! What happened wasn't your fault."

"It is. I knew she was weak, I could have . . . I should have . . . I'm mighty glad ya had the strength to fight him off, Rosaleen. I just hope you're dat lucky when you run into Finch's murderer."

Rosie's eyes grew wide. "You mean . . . you mean you don't think I did it?"

"I know ya didn't do it. Just as I know I didn't do it. If either of us had, we'd 'ave done far worse than crack his bloody head open."

Dewitt emerged from the gate and stood behind Rosie, his arms folded across his chest.

"Hmm," Kilbride said. "Looks to me like ya already got a bodyguard, eh, Rosaleen? No harm done, Wilson me lad. The lady and I were only havin' a chat."

Katie turned around to see the tall Negro man. "Huh? Oh no, he's not—"

"Nope. Can't say I blame ya. True, I'd fight to the death to protect ya from the nefarious characters of Brooklyn, but the real question is who'd be around to protect ya from the likes of me?"

With that, he kissed Rosie's hand, bade Dewitt good evening, and made his way down Beard Street singing loudly:

*Ma'am dear, did ye never hear of pretty Molly
	Brannigan?
In troth, then, she's left me and I'll never be a
	man again.*

Not a spot on my hide will a summer's sun e'er
   tan again
Since Molly's gone and left me here alone
   for to die.

Rosie sighed heavily, prompting Dewitt to ask, "You okay, ma'am?"

"Yeah, just tired."

"Kilbride can do that to ya."

"He certainly can." She chuckled.

"If you're too tired, we can go tomorrow. Saturday's a half day."

"No," Rosie declined. She was eager to speak with Jackson and possibly clear her name. "Let's go now. I'm not that tired and I have things to do tomorrow afternoon."

She trod off through the Pushey Shipyard gates only to look back and see Dewitt still standing against the fence. "Aren't you coming?"

"You go first. I'll follow and give you directions as we go."

Rosie backed up. "Why are you following me? Why not just walk alongside me?"

"Oh, I couldn't do that. I couldn't let you be seen walkin' nexta me. Nexta a Negro man? People would talk."

"Wilson Dewitt, I have spent the last week being pelted with rivets, assaulted by my boss, interrogated by the police, and being serenaded by a drunken Irishman. Being called a 'darkie lover' or 'Negro sympathizer' or some other mean-spirited name used by narrow-minded people is the least of my concerns."

Dewitt shook his head.

"When we're up on the scaffold we work side-by-side,

don't we?" she argued. "Neither of us is better than the other."

"That's different."

Rosie waved her hands impatiently. "All right. Fine. I'm tired of arguing with you. We won't walk together, but instead of you following, wouldn't it be easier if you led the way?"

"Maybe, but I'd feel better you goin' first just the same. I can keep an eye on you that way."

"You think I'm going to run away?"

Dewitt laughed. "You might when you see that you're the only white person in the neighborhood."

From the shipyard, Dewitt directed Rosie to the nearest B61 bus stop. After a short ride on a north-bound vehicle (where Dewitt rode in the row behind Rosie) they connected with the B52 line, which they rode to the corner of Gates and Throop Avenues.

Since the completion of the subway line between Harlem and Bedford in 1936, the neighborhood of Bedford-Stuyvesant (named for Bedford's expansion into Stuyvesant Heights) had seen an influx of Negroes who had left Harlem in search of greater, and less expensive, housing options.

Rosie and Dewitt walked a few blocks to the Putnam Avenue brownstone apartment occupied by Shelby Jackson and her ten-year-old son. As they approached, however, they were both surprised to see a tall man in a gray fedora standing outside.

Rosie stopped dead in her tracks.

First Kilbride. Now this.

Lieutenant Riordan stepped out from the shadows cast by the long row of circa 1890s apartment buildings and tipped his hat. "Hello."

"Hello," Rosie replied, although it sounded more like a question.

Dewitt leaned forward. "Who's that?" he whispered.

"Lieutenant Riordan. He's on the Finch case."

"The police? I didn't know the cops were gonna be here."

"Neither did I."

"I ain't bringing the cops to Shelby's door. I don't want her to think that I—" Dewitt didn't stick around to finish the sentence. As Riordan approached, he turned on one heel and ran back down the street.

"Dewitt!" she called after him.

"Who's your friend and what's his hurry?" Riordan asked.

"He's on my riveting gang at the shipyard. You seem to have scared him off."

"Was it the hat or the tie?"

Rosie glanced at Riordan's tie: satin brocade in a burgundy and white flower-box pattern. "It might have been the tie. But I think it was most likely the badge."

"Oh, forgot about that. So, what brings you to Bedford-Stuy? A little ways from home for you, isn't it?"

Between putting in a full day at work, hopping two different buses, and hearing both Wolfe's and Kilbride's tales of misfortune at the hands of Finch, Rosie was in no mood to play Riordan's games. "Never mind," she groaned and began to head in the same direction as Dewitt.

"Where are you going?"

"Home. For dinner and then bed."

"*I Love a Mystery* is on tonight. Eight o'clock, I believe."

"That's swell. I'll leave you to what you were doing so you can get home in time to warm up your radio," she quipped.

Riordan suppressed a smile. "Well, if you must

go . . . but I do think it's a shame you came all this way only to leave before you could introduce me to Jackson."

The comment had the desired effect. Rosie stopped and turned around. "Me? Introduce you?"

"You're right. Maybe that wouldn't have been the right way to go about it. I suppose I was trying to think of a way to put Miss Jackson at ease so that she'd tell us what happened to make her lock herself in her house the past few days."

"How do you know she's been locked up? Maybe she left town."

"Nope. She's in there. I asked the neighbors. No one has seen Miss Jackson, but they have seen her son take out the trash and then go right back inside. And the upstairs neighbors hear noises coming from her apartment."

"Do you think she . . . ?"

"Murdered Finch and is now holed up and waiting for us to arrest her? Strange reaction, but then again, people in that situation do crazy things. Oh well." He shrugged and descended the steps that led to the basement-level apartment. "I guess I'll find out on my own."

"Stop. I know what you're doing."

"What am I doing?"

"You're trying to get me to go with you to interview Jackson. Most likely because you know she'll talk to me before she'll talk to you. In other words, you want me to do your dirty work."

"Me? I would never!"

"Oh, wouldn't you?" She trudged down the basement stairs with a sigh. "Okay, you win this time. I'll go with you. Not because I want to talk to her, mind you, but because you seem to need me."

"Uh-huh," Riordan replied with a grin and proceeded to knock on the basement door.

There was no reply, but Rosie noticed the sound of movement from behind the paneled wood door.

Riordan knocked again and then called out. "Miss Jackson. Lieutenant Riordan, New York City Police Department. I need to speak with you, please."

No answer.

"I have a warrant, Miss Jackson. If you don't let me in, I will break down the door. I'd rather your son didn't see that happen."

Still nothing.

Riordan waved Rosie back and readied his right leg to kick the door in. "Okay, I'm coming in . . . one . . ."

Silence.

"Two . . ."

As the lieutenant was about to say the word "three," the door slowly opened inward to reveal a boy of approximately ten years of age. Dressed in short trousers and a neatly pressed white cotton shirt, his wide, frightened eyes somehow made his thin frame seem even more frail.

Riordan lowered his foot and removed his hat. "Hello."

"Hello," the boy murmured in reply.

"I'm Lieutenant Riordan. And this is Mrs. Keefe." He waved a hand at Rosie. "And you are?"

"Malcolm."

"Hi, Malcolm. There's nothing for you to be scared of; we're just going to come inside and talk to your mom. Okay?"

Malcolm nodded and opened the door wider. Before he could open it wide enough for Riordan and Rosie to enter, Shelby Jackson rushed from the back of the apartment. "Malcolm! I thought I told you to stay in your room."

"He was gonna kick the door in, Mama," the boy explained quietly.

"I know, but you get to your room now, and get to studyin'. You ain't been in school these past days, but I ain't gonna let you fall behind, neither."

Malcolm shuffled away from the door, pouting all the way.

Shelby looked up at Riordan and then spotted Rosie standing behind him. "Oh! Her! She . . . she . . ."

"Hit your boss with a stapler when he tried to assault her?" Riordan challenged. "I already know that. And you already know that Robert Finch wasn't the nicest of men."

"She . . . ?" Shelby took turns glancing between Riordan and Rosie. "Is that . . . that what happened?"

Rosie nodded earnestly.

"And did you . . . ?

Rosie shook her head emphatically. "No, I didn't kill Finch. Did you?"

"No! Oh no! It weren't anything like that," Shelby said.

"Well, unless you're willing to share this story with the whole neighborhood, I suggest we go indoors, huh?" Riordan asked.

Jackson was still skeptical. "I . . . I . . . I didn't hurt nobody. I've just been so afraid. That's all."

"I know. And I'm sure you've had every reason to feel afraid. But there's safety in numbers. Besides, you and Mrs. Keefe here could probably find some comfort in commiserating with each other."

Shelby's body language relaxed. With a nod of her head, she led them into the lower-level apartment. Featuring hardwood floors and carved wood trim, the space was small but gracious, and the windows, although smaller than those in the upper-level apartments, still allowed for adequate light. The gently used furnishings—lace curtains, delicately carved tables and seating, and upholstery in an array of feminine fabrics—reflected both the gender and petite stature of the primary adult of the house and, although mismatched, created a sense of cozy warmth.

Jackson waved them to an antique Victorian settee upholstered in a dark red fabric while she, herself, took the only other seat in the room, a chintz slipcovered armchair.

Rosie looked at the fragile-looking piece of furniture, her face a question. "Are you sure it's okay?"

"No, no, you go ahead and set. That there belonged to my grandmama. You ain't the first to set down and you won't be the last."

Riordan and Rosie eyed each other surreptitiously before following their hostess's orders. The settee was narrow and its back rigid, forcing its occupants to maintain perfect poise and posture. But the most unnerving feature of all was its lack of length. At just forty-four inches long, with two-inch arms on either side, the slight seating space forced Rosie and Riordan to sit hip to hip.

"So." Riordan cleared his throat. "Miss—"

But before the lieutenant could pose a question, Shelby rose from her chair. "Where are my manners? Can I get you anything? Maybe some ice water?"

"I'm fine, thanks," Rosie instantly rejected the offer. In truth, she was as dry as the Sahara, but she wanted this ordeal over and done with.

Riordan, meanwhile, cleared his throat again. "Some ice water would be great. Thank you, Miss Jackson."

Dewitt was certainly right about Shelby's hospitality. She tottered off to the kitchen as if this were a social call instead of a police investigation.

Rosie and Riordan, meanwhile, sat in awkward silence, neither one looking at the other.

"I'm sorry," Riordan finally said. "I know you want to get home, but—"

"That's okay. You're thirsty," she said. "It is rather warm outside, isn't it?"

"Mmm. Especially for April. Seems like we went from winter right into summer."

"That's what usually happens. Though I notice it a lot more now that I'm working on a scaffold."

"Yeah, you do look like you got a bit of color today. Better make sure you wear a hat so you don't burn. Perhaps something with a wide brim—like what your sister wore this morning." He grinned broadly.

"My sis—" She hadn't time to ask, since Shelby had returned with a tray bearing a pitcher of ice water and three mismatched glasses.

"Thank you, Miss Jackson," Riordan said graciously.

"Yes, thank you," Rosie echoed, her mind all the while on Katie.

Riordan stood up to pour himself a glass, but Shelby shooed him down. "You set and let me fix that."

"Thanks again. I can't tell you how much I appreciate it. When I was a beat cop, most folks told me to drink out of their garden hoses."

"Some people have no decency," she proclaimed and poured a green hobnail glass to a half-inch from the brim.

"I'd like to think that most do, Miss Jackson, but you're right. There are those rare few who seem to delight in the misfortunes of others. I feel sorry for them, though, in a way."

"Well, that's the Christian way—not to hate but to take pity," she agreed as she passed the green glass to Riordan.

"Thank you," he said as he took the glass into his hands. "Oh, it's more than that. It's that people who act that way miss out on the good things that life offers. Like your boy, for instance."

Rosie slid her eyes toward Riordan. *This was supposed to be a hard-nosed police investigation. What on earth is he talking about?*

Although her female guest had stated she didn't want water, Shelby poured some into a short, pink glass and absently passed it to Rosie. "Why, thank you, Lieutenant Riordan. I try. Lord knows I try, but it's tough without his daddy around."

"I know it is, but you're doing a great job."

"Oh, but he gets sick. He gets sick a lot."

"So did I once," Riordan said.

"You?" Jackson laughed. "You couldn't tell now! You're as big and healthy as an ox."

"Exactly. Feed him well, let him play out in the sun, and he'll grow out of it."

"Why, that is music to my ears. You have no idea how much I owe in doctors' bills." She rested in her chair without pouring a glass of water for herself.

"I can only imagine. My mother had the same problem," he sympathized. "She took any old job in order to help us to get by. Some were good and others . . ."

Jackson stared into the distance. "Yeah, I hear you."

Rosie was at a complete loss. Here she had wanted to run the interview and shut Riordan out, but he seemed to be getting farther than she was.

"So tell me about Finch," he urged. "I know he cut your wages."

"He did," she confirmed. "He pulled me outta the hull and for no good reason. No good reason at all."

"And insulted you on top of it," Rosie added.

"I know." Shelby's voice rose. "To tell me I gained weight and then say what he did about—about my people! I . . . I gotta say I wasn't feeling very Christian then."

"Can't say I blame you," Riordan sympathized. "It would take a saint to overlook something like that. Was that the first time Finch had ever acted in an untoward manner?"

"No . . ." Shelby frowned.

Riordan glanced at Rosie; she took her cue. "What is it, Shelby?"

"I . . . I . . ."

He stood up. "I beg your pardon, Miss Jackson, but is there a washroom I could use?"

"Of course. Go out of this room, through the kitchen, and it's just there on your right."

"Thank you." Riordan rose from the settee and strode out of the room.

While he was gone, Rosie continued the conversation. "That wasn't the first time Finch behaved as less than a gentleman toward you, was it?"

Shelby shook her head solemnly.

"What did he—" Rosie nearly choked on her words. "What did he do to you?"

"I'd rather . . . I can't say."

"Yes, you can. And you should," Rosie urged. "Would it help if I told you what he did to me?"

"No, I couldn't ask you to do that. . . ."

"But I want to. I want you to know you're not the only one."

"I'm not?"

"Not by a long shot." Rosie proceeded to tell Shelby what had occurred in Finch's office.

"And that's . . . that's why he was bleedin'. You hit him in order to keep him from . . ."

Rosie nodded. "I knew I had to get out of there. I had to do whatever I could to escape."

"I had no idea. . . . Here I thought I'd done somethin' wrong. Somethin' to make him do what he did."

"What did he do?"

"We was down in the hull one day. It was cold and rainy, so I stayed down there to eat my lunch 'stead of climbin' out. You know we only get thirty minutes; unless you have to go to . . . you know. It doesn't pay to climb out. Well, Mr. Finch came down to check the work we was doin' and asked if I was there alone. I said 'yes,' but Lord, how I wish I hadn't. He . . ." Her eyes welled with tears.

"Go on, Shelby. It's okay," Rosie encouraged. "Let it out. You'll feel better."

"Mr. Finch leaned down all low like and whispered in my ear. He said he could break me in half and then he . . ."

She was sobbing by now. Rosie got up from the settee and knelt in front of the woman. "It's okay." She offered a white handkerchief from the pocket of her dark blue coveralls.

Shelby wiped her nose. "He licked my neck to see if I tasted different than a white girl."

Rosie felt her stomach turn.

"I thought he was gonna . . . gonna . . ." Shelby stammered.

"I know. I know what you thought. But did he?"

"No. He said I tasted the same. Not like chocolate

the way he thought I would. Then he laughed and went back up top."

With a clearing of his throat, Riordan announced his approach to the living room.

"This will be our secret, Shelby," Rosie promised. "The police don't need to know all the sordid details."

"Thanks, Mrs. Keefe. I do appreciate it. I don't know if I could tell it to another living soul."

"You don't have to, but if you ever need to talk again, you let me know."

"I will, Mrs. Keefe."

Rosie nodded and sat back on the settee, just in time for Riordan to join her. "Sorry for keeping you waiting," he apologized.

"That's okay," Rosie said as Riordan wedged himself onto the cushion beside her, causing the color, once again, to flow into her cheeks. *Why couldn't he question Jackson while standing up?*

"So, Miss Jackson, why don't you tell us what happened the day Finch was murdered?"

"After the mornin' announcements, I went to work sweepin', just like Mr. Finch told me to. Finished out my day. But I still couldn't believe I wouldn't be in the hull. Sweepin' wouldn't make me enough money to pay for groceries, let alone pay for Malcolm's doctor bills."

"What happened at the end of the day?" Riordan asked.

"I followed Mr. Finch," Shelby admitted. "But not to do him harm! I swear it."

"No one's suggesting you did," Rosie said soothingly.

"I know, but I just . . ."

"You worry."

"Uh-huh. I do . . . always. Sometimes so much that I don't sleep at night. Anyways, I talked to Wilson—you know, Wilson Dewitt—about what had happened and he told me to speak to Mr. Finch directly. Course, I hadn't told him 'bout . . ." Shelby's eyes slid to Rosie's.

Rosie nodded sympathetically.

"So I did like Wilson said. I followed Mr. Finch outta the yard thinkin' I'd be tough, be strong, and ask him for my old job back. You know, down in the hull."

"Did you?" Riordan ventured.

"Didn't get the chance. I watched Mr. Finch leave, waited a few minutes, and then followed. But he'd disappeared. Just disappeared. I'd seen him walk down by the docks after work a few times before—"

"You had?"

"Uh-huh."

"Did other people at the yard know this? Because no one I spoke to mentioned it to me."

"I'm sure a lot of folks knew 'bout it. At least those who'd been at the yard any length of time or walked the same way he did to get home at night."

Riordan, deep in thought, bit his lip. A few moments passed before he spoke again. "So you checked out the docks, thinking Finch might have gone there?"

"Yes, sir. It was mistin' out, so it was hard to see at first, but when some of the fog cleared, I saw . . ." She drew a trembling hand to her mouth.

"It's okay. Take your time, Miss Jackson."

"He—he was dead! There was blood everywhere and his head, it was . . ."

Riordan got up and poured some water from the large hobnail pitcher on the coffee table into a small, clear glass tumbler and handed it to Shelby Jackson. "Here. Drink up and take a deep breath."

"Thank you, sir." Shelby did as instructed and handed the glass back to Riordan.

"Feel better?"

She nodded. "A little. I'm sorry for gettin' so worked up."

"No need for apologies." Riordan placed the glass back on the tray and sat down on the settee.

This time, Rosie didn't mind his presence at all.

"Why didn't you tell someone what you saw? Why didn't you call the police?" he asked.

"I was scared. I was so scared I couldn't move at first. Then, all I could do was run. I had to get away from there and see my boy. I needed to know he was okay. I wanted him to know I was okay."

"So you came home?"

"Yes, sir."

"You didn't stop anywhere?"

"No, sir. If that bus coulda flown, I woulda paid the driver to do it."

"And what time was this?"

"Oh, I don't rightly know. I was so—so besides myself. . . ."

"A guess. It doesn't have to be completely accurate."

"I left work around ten after four, maybe four fifteen. And . . . well, it must have been the four twenty bus I caught. But I didn't take note of the time when I got home. I didn't think of it. I couldn't. All I remember is thinkin' of Malcolm. When I got here and saw him in his room safe and readin'? Well, I hugged him so tight you'd think I hadn't seen him in days. After, I got around to wonderin' if I should call the police. But by then, so much time'd gone by, you might think I did it. You might think I killed Finch. A Negro woman killin' a white man? If you'da thought that, I'd most likely get the chair. And who'd take care of Malcolm then? I have a sister in Chicago, but I don't want him goin' anywhere without me!"

Rosie thought of her own situation. If she were to go

to jail, at least Katie and Charlie would have Ma, but that didn't mean she didn't feel accountable to them. Katie had gone to her, not Ma, after Jimmy's death. Her. "No," she stated suddenly. "No, you want to look after him yourself. I . . . I understand, Shelby. I do. I can't imagine seeing what you did. You must have been terrified."

"I was. That's why I came home and locked the doors. I didn't want anyone comin' here and takin' me away from my boy. I even pulled him outta school so they couldn't keep him from me."

"And that's why you haven't been at work and why you haven't answered the door when Dewitt came by?"

"Dewitt's a nice man. Very sweet, but he ain't always the smartest. I didn't wanna tell that sweet dumb oaf what I saw, let alone what had . . . had happened in the hull." Her eyes slid to Rosie. "He'd have gone to Finch himself and then we'd both have been outta jobs."

"No," she went on, "I thought it best to lock the door and stay put. In my head I knew it was silly. I knew it was only a matter of time till you came lookin.' I knew that no locks could keep you out if you wanted in, but . . . but for a little while, it made me feel safe."

"And now?" Riordan asked. "How do you feel now?"

"Better. Better for havin' let it all out, but still scared that you're gonna take me away in your police car. Scared you're gonna take me away from my boy. Scared you're gonna think I did it. But I didn't. I didn't kill Mr. Finch. I swear to Jesus I didn't!"

"I believe you, Shelby," Rosie said quietly. "I believe you."

Riordan turned to Rosie, his face soft, yet questioning.

He looked away abruptly. "I, um, I think we're done here for tonight, Miss Jackson," he announced upon rising from the settee. "Thank you so much for answering our questions."

Shelby stood up, her mouth agape. "You mean . . . ? You mean you're not gonna take me away?"

"I don't see any reason to at this moment. We'll look into your story and see if everything checks out. If we have any more questions, we'll contact you. Just be sure to let us in on the first knock this time, all right? Malcolm shouldn't have to see the bottom of my foot any more than he has to."

Shelby smiled slightly. "I'll be sure to let you in, and Dewitt, too."

"Good. Oh, and no trips to the sister or any other out-of-town relatives. Not until this is all over with. At least, not without a call to me first." He handed her his card.

"I won't. I don't have a phone. I can use the one at the corner store, but I don't reckon to be goin' anywhere. Not with Malcolm in school and me without a paycheck."

"Will you come back to the yard?" Rosie asked. It was more of a request than a query.

"Oh, I . . . I don't know."

"We're still looking for help. Why, we had another man call up today."

"I've been gone so long now. . . ."

"Three days. But I'm willing to speak with Del Vecchio, the new foreman, on your behalf. I'm sure Dewitt would, too."

At the mention of Dewitt's name, her demeanor became slightly girlish. "It don't take much to talk Dewitt into anything."

"Tomorrow's Saturday—a half day. So, I'll see you first thing Monday?"

"I don't know . . . I'll think about it, Mrs. Keefe."

"Rosie. Please. Call me Rosie."

Shelby looked down at the floor for a few seconds before replying. "Okay, Rosie. I'll be there."

Chapter Thirteen

Riordan and Rosie bid Shelby Jackson and Malcolm adieu and then set off at a leisurely pace down the sidewalk.

"Lieutenant Riordan, why did you give me a look when I said I believed Shelby?" Rosie questioned.

"I did? What look was that?"

"A look as though you didn't understand what I was saying. Or why I might be saying it. Don't you believe her?"

Riordan stopped walking and faced her. "I do believe her, Mrs. Keefe. That's the problem."

"You're right, it is a problem. When I asked if you believed me, I didn't get a straight answer. You said you weren't allowed to state your opinion. And yet here you are, standing behind Shelby Jackson."

"You didn't ask me what I believed. You asked me if I'd found any evidence to make me think you were either innocent or guilty," he argued.

"No, I didn't. I asked if you believed me and you said it was your duty to believe me until proven otherwise."

"Precisely. I never said I didn't believe you."

"You never said you did, either."

Riordan glanced around at the neighbors who were taking advantage of the warm spring evening by sitting on their front steps or sweeping their sidewalks. "I'm not having this discussion here. We can finish it in the car."

"The car? You're taking me to headquarters?"

"No, I'm not taking you to headquarters. Why does everyone assume that? Do I look like the sort of guy who enjoys arresting young women?"

"I don't know. Are you?" Rosie challenged, but with a hint of fear in her voice.

"No, I'm not. It's around suppertime, so I figured we'd grab a bite to eat and then I'd drive you home."

"Dinner?" She looked down at her coveralls and frowned. "But I'm not really dressed for dinner."

He looked her up and down. "You look fine. More than fine. Um, for where we're going, I mean," he quickly amended. "Besides, this isn't dinner. It's a bite to eat and a chance to talk."

"Well, I . . . oh, I can't. Katie—my sister—is expecting me home."

"No, she's not. I already told her you wouldn't make it."

"You—? That's right, you said you saw her today! Where was it? When did you see her?"

With a smirk, Riordan stepped to the curb and opened the passenger door of his black 1941 Ford Deluxe. "Get in and I'll tell you."

Rosie sighed and took a seat in the cream-colored, leather interior. Riordan, happy to have won the battle, shut the door after her and then climbed into the driver's seat.

"So?" she prompted.

"So, what?"

"I did what you asked. Now tell me where and when you saw my sister."

Riordan started the six-cylinder engine and pulled away from the curb, heading southwest on Putnam. "At church during Finch's funeral this morning."

Rosie's jaw dropped. "You were there, too?"

"Indeed I was. How better to get a feel for Finch's life than to see who turned up to mourn his death? You can imagine my surprise when I recognized the pretty blonde in the last pew."

"She was there on my behalf," Rosie admitted. "Like you, she thought she might learn something valuable. Something that would keep me out of trouble and point the finger at someone else."

At the traffic light, Riordan made a right turn onto Throop and continued north. "I know. She and I had a nice conversation about it."

"You did?"

"Uh-huh. She filled me in on her findings, too."

"She did? Why, that—!"

"Don't be angry with your sister. It's not her fault. She can't help it if I make a very persuasive argument."

Rosie exhaled noisily. "What did you do? Threaten to throw her in jail?"

"No. Will you stop it with that? She thought the same thing, too. I'm a police lieutenant. There's more to my job than that."

"Like what?"

"Paperwork. Training. The majority of the time I work on solving cases. I rarely put people in jail. And never because they shouldn't be there."

"You won't be able to say that after you arrest me," she quipped.

Riordan brought the car to a halt, causing Rosie to

fly forward in her seat and then snap her head against the headrest. "Have I arrested you yet?"

"No," she said quietly.

"Didn't I just include you in my talk with Shelby Jackson?"

"Yes."

"Then why don't you trust me? You need to trust me . . . because I'm the only person out there who can help you." After a pause to regain his composure, Riordan turned left onto Flushing Avenue.

Once her surprise had subsided, Rosie asked, "Why? Why are you the only person?"

"Because I don't think you did it. I haven't since the night I brought you in for questioning. My captain, however, wanted me to arrest you on the spot."

"How did you convince him otherwise?"

"I didn't. I merely bought time. I promised to have the case solved in five days."

"Five days from now!" Rosie panicked. "That's not a lot of time."

"It's even less," Riordan replied, the car's acceleration matching the importance of his tone. "The five days started the day after I brought you in."

"So we're down to . . . ?"

"Two days."

Rosie sunk into her seat. "Two more days and I could be going to . . ."

"Now you know why I want you to trust me."

"Did you tell my sister this? Is that why she confided in you?"

"No, I didn't tell her. If I had, she would have kept on sleuthing until she either cleared your name or got herself into a heap of trouble. I simply explained to her that I was on your side, and asked her to share what she knew."

"And she did?"

"Yes, she said she figured the two of you had to trust someone and it might as well be me."

"So she told you everything about Mrs. Finch and the butcher?"

"She did. As well as Finch's girlfriend in the neighborhood."

"Girlfriend? I didn't know about that!"

"That happened this morning. I'll tell you about it later. Better yet, I'll let your sister tell you."

Rosie frowned. "I suppose she told you about everything I uncovered, too?"

"Nope. I sent her home to look after her son. Which I figured is probably what you'd want me to do."

"Yes, thank you," she said graciously. "I just can't believe she listened to you."

"She didn't at first," Riordan smiled. "I had to bribe her with lunch and ice cream."

Rosie laughed. "That's Katie, all right. Ever since she was a kid she's thought with her stomach."

"Nothing wrong with that. Especially when it works so well."

"Too well. Had you held out longer, she probably would have told you what I'd been up to."

"Oh, I know what you've been up to. But I wanted to hear the results from your own mouth, not the edited version you might have told Katie."

Rosie fell silent as Riordan pulled the car onto a side street just a few blocks away from the Brooklyn Navy Yard. There, at the end of the street, lay a beautiful promenade with a view of the East River and, off to the left, the Manhattan and Brooklyn Bridges, and beyond them, the sunset. Families, lovers, and shipyard employees lined the pavement, "oohing" and "aahing" as the fiery April sun sank below the horizon.

Realizing the value of such property, someone with an entrepreneurial spirit and a small chunk of operating capital had erected a hot dog stand a few short steps away from the water.

"See? I told you those coveralls were fine for where we were going," Riordan smirked and stepped from behind the driver's wheel. A few seconds later, he opened Rosie's door and the two approached the stand.

Rosie stared at the river, the golden rays of the sun casting a warm glow upon her long, windswept hair. "It's beautiful."

Upon seeing Rosie's reaction to the view, Riordan excused himself awkwardly. "I, um, I didn't take you here for that, Mrs. Keefe. It was more the dress code, the nearness to the bridge, and the fries. Homemade. With lots of salt. The view—that's just a bonus."

He ordered four frankfurters with mustard and sauerkraut, a large side of French fries, and two bottles of Coca-Cola. The clerk passed the order across the counter in exchange for a couple of crisp bills. "Keep the change," Riordan instructed before popping the Coke tops off the counter and passing the bottles to Rosie. Meanwhile, he grabbed the food, piping hot and loaded into red and white cardboard trays, and steered his female companion to a nearby park bench.

With Riordan seated at one end and Rosie at the other, they placed their meal on the bench between them.

She took a swig of her soda and leaned back. "Thank you."

Riordan devoured a large bite of hot dog and then wiped the mustard from his lips with a paper napkin. "Hey, we both have to eat, don't we?" he stated after swallowing. "It's not the most substantial of meals, but it does the job."

"Oh, it's fine. Really. I'm not even that hungry."

"You're not? After working all day outdoors, climbing scaffolds, I'd be starving by now."

"I was, but I . . . I seem to have lost my appetite."

"No, you don't. You're not going to waste away on me. Not now. Now's when you need your strength."

"I'm not going to waste away. I'm just not hungry."

"Nope. You're going to eat up and we're going to compare notes."

Like a sulking child, Rosie picked up a small French fry and reluctantly placed it into her mouth. Riordan was right: the potato was soft on the inside, crunchy on the outside, and perfectly salted. She picked up another one and attempted to conceal her pleasure.

"I was right. They're good, aren't they?" he said with a grin.

"They're okay," she said before moving on to one of her hot dogs.

"So, how are things at the yard? Tell me what you've found out."

"You first," she challenged.

"Uh-uh. That's not the way it works." He followed the statement with a swig of cola.

Rosie frowned. She felt like a traitor, sharing the personal stories of these people she had just started to know and like. Moreover, once those secrets were shared, Riordan and his men would probably pry into every facet of their owners' pasts.

"Come on, now," he coaxed.

"A lot of the things that were told to me were said in the strictest confidence. I'd feel bad betraying a trust like that."

"I understand. You've made friends and don't want to put them under suspicion. Not only is that admirable, but I'm sure you'll have the most pen pals of anyone at the New York Women's House of Detention."

"That's not a nice thing to say," she chastised.

"No, it's not nice, but it's true. Do you want to make friends or save yourself? Because that's where we are right now. With just two days left, you can't have both."

"I want to save myself," she replied morosely. "I need to. I can't go to jail."

"Good. We're on the same page." He took a bite of hot dog and gave it a few quick chews before swallowing. "That said, tell me everything you know about everyone—no matter how trivial you think it might be."

Rosie ate another French fry and then started in chronological order, beginning with the day she returned to work at Pushey. "First there's Nelson."

"Nelson?" he asked as he extracted a small notebook and pencil from the front breast pocket of his dress shirt.

"Yes, Betty Nelson. Twenty-five years old, dark hair, pretty."

"I'm writing down names and stories and then tracking these people down. I'm not drawing sketches."

"You said to tell you everything. I'm telling you everything. Including each person's full physical description."

"Hmm," Riordan shrugged. "I guess it can't hurt. How tall is Betty Nelson and what does she weigh?"

"A little taller than I am, so five foot five. And maybe one hundred twenty pounds. Surely not more than that."

"Okay. What happened?"

"Last week, Finch cornered her at the bottom of the hull during an air raid drill, put his arms around her waist, and . . . and threatened to . . ."

"You needn't go any farther. I get it. Did he succeed?"

"I don't know. Nelson didn't say. All she said was that she was scared at first, then nauseated, but then anger kicked in and she thought about attacking Finch with her welding torch. But then the lights came on and Finch left."

"Do you think Nelson's the type who might attack Finch?"

Rosie knitted her eyebrows together and bit her lip.

"I'm not asking you if you want to believe Nelson could attack Finch," Riordan clarified. "I'm asking you if you think she has the temperament to do so."

"Yes. Yes, I do. She's tough and kind of feisty."

"All right." He scribbled notes into the book and took a bite of hot dog.

Rosie ate a few more fries and washed them down with a mouthful of Coca-Cola. "Jeannie Wolfe. Blonde. Thirty-five years old. Tall . . . umm, five foot eight inches if she's a day. Gorgeous. And with a figure like a pinup girl."

Riordan raised an eyebrow and whistled. "What's her number?"

She chuckled. "You can probably find it on the men's-room wall. But you shouldn't. She's pretty, smart, funny, and boy, does she have style."

"Hmm . . . sells herself short, does she?"

"That and she seems to think she has to use her looks to get ahead in the world."

"You know, the right man might be able to put her straight. I'm willing to give it a shot," he smiled.

"You and half the men in the five boroughs."

"If that's the case, I can only guess she was an easy target for Finch."

"She was. He offered her a higher-paying job in exchange for . . ."

Riordan nodded. "Again, no need to say it. I've got it. What happened?"

"Finch gave her job to someone else. Someone younger."

"This guy just keeps getting better and better. How did Miss Wolfe react?"

"Despair. Disappointment. Disenchantment. She didn't say those things, of course, nor did she say anything to Finch, but it was apparent from the way she told the story. Her affair with Finch wasn't the first time she's slept with a boss for a promotion. The difference is that the previous bosses kept their end of the bargain, whereas Finch . . ." She polished off the rest of one hot dog.

He, meanwhile, started in on his second. "Do you think she could have murdered him?"

Rosie shook her head. "I really don't see her doing it, but I can't say for sure."

"Just wondering because, out of all the women Finch has wronged—Nelson, you, Jackson, the wife, the girlfriend—Wolfe has both the height and leverage needed to have delivered a death blow. That's not to say that a smaller woman couldn't have done it, but it would have required a lot more effort. Not to mention, Wolfe is the only woman in the bunch who, in Finch's mind, wouldn't have been a threat."

"What do you mean?"

"Well, he had beaten his wife in the past, dumped his girlfriend, and attempted to assault both Nelson and Jackson. If he had encountered any of them beneath the pier, his guard would have been up. Wolfe's, on the other hand, a completely different story. She gave in to him without a struggle, and he betrayed her, without her raising much of a fuss."

"That's a good point, and one that never occurred to me. Still, I can't say either way. After all, I barely know her. I know that she likes men and wants to be acknowledged by them."

"Acknowledged or loved?"

"Both. Desperately. I suppose 'how desperately?' is the question. Desperate enough for Finch's betrayal to send her over the edge? I can't say."

"Hmph. Makes you wonder, though. I'm sure if she sat back—"

"And let love come to her, she'd find someone," Rosie completed the sentence. "Well, first of all, she's over thirty. That's an old maid by today's standards. And second, it's not easy being a woman, even harder when you're an attractive one. When men approach you all the time, it's usually when they're on their very best behavior. It's only after you get to know them and love them when you finally realize that you've fallen for— not a gentleman but—a rogue."

Riordan fell into an uncomfortable silence.

"Oh, I'm sorry, Lieutenant," Rosie blushed. "I was only thinking aloud. I didn't mean to offend you. Not all men are like that, I'm sure."

"No, they're not. And no offense taken." He smiled. "Say, is the friend who ran away on your list?"

"Dewitt? No, why?"

"Well, it's apparent that he's—how shall we say— sweet on Shelby Jackson. If he got wind of what Finch did to her in the hull that day—"

"And then witnessed her humiliation that morning," Rosie added.

"And knew how hard the pay cut would be on Jackson and her son, he might have lashed out at Finch. Some men can be rogues, but others can be quite protective."

Rosie's cheeks colored slightly. "Yes, I suppose they

can. I never thought of Dewitt being a suspect, but what you said does make perfect sense."

"And what about the fella you bumped into on your way out of Finch's office? What was his name? Delancy?"

"Delaney?"

"Yeah, that's the one."

"You mean, could he have killed Finch because of . . . ? I . . . I guess he might have. I don't think he did, but . . ."

"You don't think he's protective?"

"No. No, he is. I just never looked at him like that. But what you said is right."

"Thanks. I thought so, too."

"Now that you've mentioned it, that whole protective rogue thing describes the next person on my list."

"Oh, really? Is he protective or a rogue?"

"Both. His name is Kilbride. Clinton Kilbride."

"Italian, obviously," Riordan joked.

"Yeah, by way of County Wicklow," she quipped. "Hmm . . . how old are you?"

"What? Why?"

"Because I'd say Kilbride's about your age, that's why."

"Ah, 'twenty seven,'" he said aloud and etched a pair of numbers into the notebook with the soft lead of the pencil."

Rosie couldn't help but laugh.

"What? You don't believe me? I can show you my driver's license."

"No, I believe you." She giggled.

"Either you're lying or you need glasses. So, back to Kilbride."

"Oh, he's . . ." She placed a level hand about seven or eight inches above her head. "Um, six foot."

"Were you wearing those shoes when you last stood

next to him?" Riordan used the pencil to point at Rosie's feet.

She looked down at her cork-heeled loafers. "Yes, why?"

"One-inch soles. Five foot eleven," he corrected. "Weight?"

"I'm a terrible judge of that when it comes to men. He's thin, but"—she felt the color rise to her cheeks as she recalled the way the shirtless Kilbride had leaned against the chain link fence of the yard—"umm, not without muscles."

Riordan noticed Rosie's sudden awkwardness and cleared his throat. "Ehem. Athletic build," he said aloud and jotted it in his notepad. "Hmph. So what's his story?"

"F-Finch . . ." She hesitated.

"This is no time for modesty, Mrs. Keefe. I'm a police officer. I've heard it all."

"He raped Kilbride's girlfriend."

Riordan sighed heavily. "Jeez."

"Yeah. She, um . . ." Rosie scratched her head and mustered the strength to utter the final words of the statement. "She killed herself shortly afterward because she couldn't bear to live with the memories."

They sat in silence for several seconds as the streetlights cycled on and the sun cast its final beams over the East River.

"Listen, I know what Finch tried to do to you," Riordan stated. "I'm sorry you have to go through this. This investigation, the suspicion, listening to these other women. And now Kilbride's fiancée? I can't imagine how those stories must make you feel."

"Lucky. It makes me feel lucky that I got out of there when I did. Unfortunately, it also makes me less than enthusiastic about finding Finch's killer. If it weren't my head on the chopping block, I'd be happy to let whoever murdered Finch go scot-free. They provided a great service to the women of this world. I know that must sound terrible. . . ."

"No. It doesn't sound terrible at all. I've had those same thoughts myself on occasion," he commiserated.

"How do you go on being a cop? How do you keep doing what you do?"

"I remember the times—and there are quite a few—when justice was served and things worked out the way they should."

"That's what gets you through? Memories? I don't know if that would be enough for me."

"Sometimes it isn't. That's when I try to imagine what would've happened if I didn't do what I do. The innocent people who might have gone to jail." He slid his eyes in her direction. "The criminals who may have gone free. The victims and families who'd go unvindicated. The system might not always work, but the majority of times it does, and I'm glad to be part of it."

Rosie had guessed that Riordan was a hardworking police officer, but she had no idea how committed he was to the concept of justice. As the crowds left the riverfront and darkness descended upon the city, she wondered how she could have misjudged him. "May I ask you something? Not about the case—well, it is, indirectly—but about your job."

"Sure."

"Well, you seem pretty dedicated to your work, so why did your captain only give you five days for this case? Why not let you solve it as you see fit?"

"That's a long, complicated story, but I'll try to summarize it in two words: Frank Costello."

"The mob boss?"

"Yeah. I've been trying to get him since putting Lucky Luciano in jail."

"That was you?" Rosie exclaimed. "I remember reading about it in the papers. Didn't you get an award or commendation or something like that?"

"Commendation, yeah. A little too soon, though."

"What do you mean? You put Luciano behind bars, didn't you?"

"I did, but he's still in control of the mob. Never mind, you don't want to hear this. . . . I'm sorry."

"No," Rosie insisted. "No, I do want to hear about it. How can someone in jail still be in control of anything?"

Riordan leaned back in his seat and drew a deep breath. "The thing you need to understand about the Mafia is that bosses can pull strings from anywhere. From prison, from another country, while in hiding. They use underbosses to do their bidding for them."

"And Costello is one of these underbosses," she surmised.

"Yeah, although with Luciano in prison he's more like the acting boss."

"So, what's the point of putting a boss in jail if someone else just takes over?"

"The point is that by putting the boss in jail, you typically shut down whatever operations they ran. Will the mob try to start something up elsewhere? Sure. But at least you've curtailed the spread of those operations."

"Okay, so by putting Luciano in jail you helped limit crime and got a crime boss off the streets. I still don't understand why the captain would give you a tough time about me. You'd think you'd be the star of the force."

"When you put someone like Luciano away, someone the public sees as a vicious killer, you are a star.

Everyone congratulates you. But when you go after someone like Costello—someone more subtle, more charismatic—you have to take a more roundabout approach."

"What does it matter? A criminal's a criminal."

"No, that's where you're wrong. Some are more influential than others. And Costello?" He took the last sip from his bottle of Coca-Cola. "He's the prime minister of the underworld, a consummate diplomat. If a politician needs to be reached or a judge fixed, Costello has just the right contacts to organize it. The trouble is when I went after Costello and named him as the city's next public enemy, I upset a lot of his friends. Friends in some pretty high places. Kinney, my captain, got the heat for it."

Rosie's jaw dropped. "I'd always heard of crooked politicians, but I had no idea it was that widespread or that it existed at such high levels."

"It wasn't. Not until Costello got into the mix."

"And so, because you went after Costello . . ."

"Kinney, and the powers that be, want me to make an example of you."

"An example of what? Convicting an innocent woman?"

"Doesn't matter if you're innocent or not. They want an arrest to prove that the system still works and that we're not just focusing on Costello, but solving 'real' cases."

"Why me? What did I do to deserve to be made an example of?"

"Luck of the draw. Truth is, they'd have chosen any case that would result in an easy arrest and an easier conviction. But don't worry, I haven't given up yet." He eyed the gathering darkness around them and smiled. "Say, I'd better get you home before we have another city scandal on our hands."

After discarding the remnants of their meal in a nearby trash can, Riordan escorted Rosie to the passenger seat of the Ford and then climbed into the driver's seat. With his foot applying steady pressure on the clutch, he gave the ignition key a turn, causing the car to jolt back to life.

After performing a three-point turn, Riordan steered the Ford Deluxe back onto Flushing Avenue. From there, it was a short drive to the Manhattan Bridge.

"So, now that I've told you everything I know, it's time for you to share," Rosie prompted. "What have you found out about Finch? Or aren't you allowed to tell me?"

"I'm not supposed to tell you, but under the circumstances . . ."

"Yes?"

"Not much. We checked into Finch's past and found a bunch of women he had been linked to at various times, but given what you've unearthed, that's not shocking."

"Do any of them seem like they might be suspects?"

"Not really. Like I said, Finch was 'linked' to them, but we couldn't learn many details. They simply weren't willing to open up to the cops the way they would to another woman. Not to mention that some of those relationships go back so far that it seems unlikely they'd take revenge now."

Rosie sighed and leaned back against the passenger seat headrest. "And you found nothing in Finch's office? Or his home?"

"The shipyard office contained nothing more than employee records and standard paperwork. Not surprising since Finch shared it with the second-shift supervisor. And his apartment was clean. So clean, in fact, that we needed to contact the bank in order to secure his financial records."

Rosie sat up. "There was no paperwork at the apartment at all?"

"Not a scrap. Which means either Finch kept his records elsewhere, under lock and key, or someone got rid of them."

"Mrs. Finch?" she suggested.

Riordan pulled a face. "I spoke with Mrs. Finch. I have no trouble believing she'd be carrying on with the butcher or anyone else who paid her a bit of attention and treated her kindly, but I don't think she has any idea what she'd be looking for when it comes to financial matters."

"Are you sure? Still waters run deep."

Riordan made a right-hand turn onto the bridge. "Not a hundred percent, but pretty certain. She's led a sheltered life. Unless she was being coached by someone else—"

"Simonetti?"

"I guess it's possible. But why would she destroy those records? Because she was tucking money aside? Maybe, but I find it hard to believe that someone like Finch wouldn't have noticed it."

"Maybe he did and that's why she and Simonetti bumped him off."

"Anything's possible," he shrugged. "But we can't make a case out of possibilities. Until we get that paperwork from the bank and give it a thorough read, we don't have proof of anything."

"When will you get those records?"

"Tomorrow afternoon, most likely."

"I have a half day tomorrow. I can stop by after headquarters after work and—"

"No," Riordan said sternly. "I shouldn't have shared what I did. You're not getting the bank information, too."

"But I don't see—"

"No arguments. I'll take care of things from here."

The trip over the bridge had taken less time than anticipated. In a few short moments, they were at the brownstone apartment building Rosie called home.

Riordan exited the driver's side of the vehicle and walked to Rosie's side in an attempt at gentlemanlike courtesy. She, however, had already let herself out.

"Thank you," she said graciously, but it was apparent she was miffed. "Thank you for everything. Dinner. The talk. I appreciate it."

"I'm not going to let you take the rap for this, Mrs. Keefe," he said earnestly. "I won't stand by and let that happen."

Rosie, however, couldn't see how Riordan had any other choice. "No, I'm sure you'll do your best," she agreed as she mounted the front steps of the building. "Good night."

He tipped his hat and watched as she stepped inside and shut the windowed wooden door behind her. "Good night, Rosie," he whispered once she was safely inside.

Rosie, meanwhile, trudged to her second-floor apartment, where Katie, clad in a blue cotton, short-sleeved nightgown, sprawled upon the overstuffed couch, listening to *Hobby Lobby*. "So?" the blonde greeted upon Rosie's arrival.

"So what?"

Katie sprung to her feet and switched the radio to off. "So, did you talk to Lieutenant Riordan?"

"I did."

"Did he convince you to tell him what you found out?"

"Yes, we had a good, long discussion."

"I'm glad. We need someone we can trust on our side. And, well, I kinda like him. I think he's nice."

"Of course, you would," Rosie teased. "He bought you lunch."

"Very funny!" Katie stuck out her tongue.

Despite her heavy heart, Rosie plastered on a smile. "I'm joking. I told Lieutenant Riordan everything I know, and he told me everything he's uncovered. Especially that you were the heroine of the day. But he saved the details for you to tell."

"Oh, that? It was nothing, really." She blushed before launching headlong into the tale of Marie Finch, the love letter, and Robert Finch's old flame.

"I can't thank you enough, lamb." Rosie embraced her sister tightly and then, slipping out of her loafers, plopped onto the sofa.

"Did it help? Will my findings keep you out of jail?" Katie asked eagerly.

"According to Riordan, they'll definitely help."

"Just help? What else do you need?"

"Nothing, honey. There are just a few financial records missing. Once we find those, I'm as good as home."

"How do we find them?" Katie sat on the cushion beside Rosie.

"'We' don't find anything."

"Oh, come on. I did a great job playing detective, didn't I?"

"You sure did. There's no denying that."

"So, what gives? Why keep me out now? Tell me what's going on."

Rosie undid the belt of her canvas coveralls and went to the kitchen for a glass of water. She knew she couldn't tell Katie about her imminent arrest, but she reluctantly told her about the lack of documents at the shipyard office and the apartment. "The police did a search of Finch's apartment and came up empty."

"Empty how?"

"Empty as in they found no bank records or other financial documents."

"Oh, is that all!"

"What do you mean, 'Is that all?' Katie-girl, sometimes you worry me."

"Huh? All I meant is that Pop always hid money and stuff from Ma."

Rosie jolted upright. "He did? I didn't know that."

"Well, if you'd have stopped arguing with Ma long enough, he might have told you." Katie smiled smugly.

"'Well, if you had' blah, blah, blah," she mocked. "You forget that most of the times I argued with Ma it was on your behalf."

"Oh, please. You two would have gone at it even if Pop and I weren't there."

"Maybe," Rosie said. "Just tell me about the money and the bills, will you?"

Katie leaned forward eagerly. "Okay, do you remember when Ma had that hat fetish?"

"Of course. Who could forget it? She saw that Hedda Hopper photo in the paper and decided she wanted to model herself after her."

"Uh-huh. Once he got a huge bill from the milliner's, Dad kept all his spare cash and other stuff under lock and key."

"Lock and key where?"

"The toolshed in the backyard. He knew Ma would never have gone back there and gotten her hands dirty. That's why he kept the racing form back there, too."

"Is *that* where he kept it? You know, I always

wondered about that. Ma would remove it from the paper in the morning and yet Pop would always have it back again by supper."

Katie nodded. "He made me promise to keep it a secret."

"Oh, and you keep *that* a secret. Meanwhile, you ratted me out for . . ." Rosie's voice trailed off. "Wait a minute. If Ma and Pop, who otherwise got along okay, kept secrets from each other, it only makes sense that Finch, a man with a lot of secrets—"

"Scads of them," Katie confirmed.

"—would have had even more reason to keep his bank records and bills under lock and key."

"Did the Finches have a toolshed at their apartment building?"

Rosie laughed. "Afraid not, but I'm sure he would have picked a hiding place he could be sure his wife wouldn't check. Now, if I could only get into that apartment. . . ."

"Oh, but you can. Simonetti's note said that Marie Finch is staying with her sister all weekend. That means their place is empty."

"You're forgetting something. I don't even know where the Finches live."

"I do," Katie happily said.

"You do? Really?"

"Yep." Katie rose from the sofa and collected her handbag, which hung from the back of the bedroom door. Reaching inside, she removed a scrap of paper and read the words scribbled hastily in pencil. "'253 Van Brunt Street, upstairs apartment.'"

"You're amazing, Katie. How did you get that?"

"I overheard it at the butcher's shop and scribbled it

down as soon as I left, just in case it might come in handy for something."

"Handy? You have no idea how handy," Rosie said appreciatively. "Hmm . . . So all I have to do is find a way to get into the apartment and hope I find what I'm looking for."

"'We,'" Katie corrected. "All 'we' have to do is find what we're looking for."

"Katieeee," Rosie sang. "No. If you won't listen to me, listen to Lieutenant Riordan."

"Lieutenant Riordan?"

"Yes, he told you you're not to do any more sleuthing, didn't he?"

"Well, maybe . . ." Katie stared at her feet awkwardly. "Since when do you listen to what he has to say?"

"I don't . . . Well, not much anyway. But he wouldn't approve of me breaking in, let alone you acting as my accomplice. It's best you stay home, sweetie."

"You've been telling me to stay home since we were kids," Katie whined, "and I'm tired of it! You said yourself that I did a great job as a detective. Besides, it seems to me that you could use a lookout when you check out Finch's place. You know, someone to give a whistle should the cops or anyone else show up."

Rosie mulled it over; the idea was not without merit. "Come on, Katie, don't push me. I can't have you with me. I'd never forgive myself if something happened to you."

"What do you think is going to happen? It's Red Hook in broad daylight and you'll be there with me."

The older sister pulled a face.

"Please?" Katie begged. "I'll meet you after work and we can go together."

"And what about Charlie?"

"I'll have Ma watch him while I go 'shopping.'"

"Katie . . . you shouldn't." Rosie felt her resolve weakening.

"I don't care if I shouldn't. I want to help you as much as I can. Please," Katie urged.

Rosie thought of the short time left until her arrest. She didn't want Katie and Charlie to see her taken away in handcuffs. "Okay," she agreed. "You can come with me, but on one condition."

"Sure. What is it?"

"You move out by tomorrow night."

"Move out? What do you mean?"

"I mean, Katie-girl, that we have only a few short weeks until the end of the month and I need that time to get my things in order. Besides, Ma's eager to have you and Charlie back in Greenpoint."

"Yeah, I know she is—she's eager to have all of us back—but what about you?"

"I'll be along at the end of the month. Until then, if I need help packing, I know who to call."

"All right," Katie reluctantly agreed. "But I still don't understand the rush to get me out of here."

"The rush, dear sister, is that it's finally spring. And it would better for you and Charlie to be breathing the smells of freshly cut grass and lilac bushes instead of the asphalt and tar used by the road crews to patch the winter potholes."

"It *was* nice today, wasn't it?"

"It sure was," Rosie concurred.

"I'll call Ma and tell her I'll be there with my things. Then I'll leave Charlie there and meet you at the ship-yard. What time?"

"Twelve thirty."

"Twelve thirty," Katie repeated. "Sounds like a plan."

As Katie went off to the bedroom to call their mother, Rosie stretched out on the overstuffed couch.

It's a plan, all right, she thought. And so far, the only one she had.

Chapter Fourteen

Saturday morning loomed as bright and unseasonably warm as the day prior to it. Having switched her heavy canvas coveralls for a pair of Sanforized cotton work pants and short-sleeved shirt, Rosie entered the employee holding area and informed a stunned Del Vecchio that Jackson would be returning to work Monday morning.

"What?!" was his only reaction. "What makes you think I want her back?"

"Because, once again, it would look very bad if you didn't take back a single mother who's been too sick with the grippe the past few days to call in."

Del Vecchio reached into the breast pocket of his work shirt and extracted a pack of cigarettes and a stainless steel lighter. "The grippe? And she couldn't call?"

"No phone. Besides, her fever was so high and she was so weak, she couldn't even make it to the door. That's why she didn't answer when Dewitt stopped by. I only got inside after having someone kick the door in." *At least that part is partially true,* she rationalized.

Still, she'd go home and say a few Hail Marys—just in case.

Del Vecchio gave a heavy sigh. "Okay, Keefe. But that's the last favor I do for you, *capisce*?"

Rosie had no idea what the word "capisce" meant, but she could infer that Jackson was getting her job back. Satisfied that at least one item on the day's agenda could be crossed off, she waited quietly beside Nelson through the day's work announcements and then set off through the yard.

Taking great care not to smile, she greeted a silent Kolacky as he heated the forge and then she scaled the scaffold of Pier Number One.

Kilbride was waiting for her. "Mornin', Rosaleen. Looks like we're in for a scorcher today."

"Good morning. Yeah, it's already seventy degrees and it's only eight o'clock. Thank goodness it's a half day."

"True. Still, e'en a 'alf day of sun can turn a person's scalp as red as those tresses of yours." He pulled a plaid handkerchief from the front pocket of his work shirt and handed it to Rosie. "'Ere, use that as a bonnet, will ya? Though it might be fun tryin' to revive ya, I don't need you gettin' faint due to the heatstroke."

"Thanks, Kilbride." Smiling, Rosie folded the square of fabric into a triangle and tied it beneath the back of her hair. As she looked up, she saw Kilbride's rivet gun lying on the platform. "I thought you said you checked that back into the toolshed last night."

"I thought I did, too. I swear it must be those filthy leprechauns. They have it in for me, don't ya know."

Rosie shook her head. "The only one who'll have it in for you is Del Vecchio. If the second-shift riveter sees your gun here and reports you, he'll dock your paycheck."

"Eh, let the little wop do his worst. I can take 'im!"

Again Rosie shook her head. Not only did Kilbride probably know more racial epithets than anyone at the yard, he used them constantly.

As if to bear out this theory, Dewitt suddenly appeared at the top of the scaffold.

"Mornin', Wilson. Gonna be a hot one. Hope you brought your suntan lotion." Kilbride laughed loudly.

"Mornin.'" The tall Negro man nodded to Kilbride and slid his eyes sheepishly toward Rosie.

"Oh, what's this? You and Rosaleen havin' a lover's spat?" Kilbride joked.

Rosie glared at the Irishman.

"Sorry, love. I suppose I ought to let you sort things out for yourselves. But in the meantime, let's get to work, eh?"

With that, Kilbride hopped onto the rope scaffold and began to sing as Rosie and Dewitt lowered him over the edge of the hull:

> *Of priests we can offer a charmin variety,*
> *Far renownd for learnin and piety;*
> *Still, Id advance ye widout impropriety,*
> *Father OFlynn as the flowr of them all.*

> *Heres a health to you, Father OFlynn,*
> *Slainte and slainte and slainte agin;*
> *Powrfulest preacher, and tenderest teacher,*
> *And kindliest creature in ould Donegal.*

As they each worked a rope, Dewitt looked at Rosie. "Sorry for runnin' off the way I did last night. I didn't want Shelby thinkin' that I . . ."

"That's all right, Wilson. I understand."

"I checked in on her after you folks left, though."

"You did? I'm sure she liked that."

"Yes, ma'am, she did. She told me you talked her into comin' back to the yard, too. Thank you for that."

"My pleasure."

"You have no idea how happy I am to have her back." He cleared his throat. "I mean—she has those bills to pay for her boy, and this is the best-paying job in town."

"I knew what you meant." She smiled. "I already spoke to Del Vecchio. He knows she'll be back on Monday. Just make sure you tell Shelby that, if anyone asks, she was at home with the grippe and too weak to get out of bed."

Dewitt nodded. "I will. She hates lyin', but I'll make sure she does this time."

"Good." As the volume of Kilbride's voice increased, Rosie rolled her eyes and laughed. "It's going to be a long four-and-a-half hours if you persist in singing through all of them, Clinton. Shouldn't you be saving your saliva, what with the hot weather?"

Even the taciturn Dewitt couldn't help but chuckle.

"Ah, aren't you full of piss and vinegar this mornin', Rosaleen," Kilbride replied and continued to sing even louder:

Dont talk of your Provost and Fellows of Trinity,
Famous forever at Greek and Latinity,
Dad and the divils and all at Divinity,
Father OFlynn d make hares of them all!

As Kilbride sang the last word, a ruckus could be heard from the yard below.

"What the hell am I supposed to do with these?" Rudy Hansen, the blond Swedish heater, picked up a handful of unheated rivets from the bucket beside him and threw them to the ground angrily. "I can't get these hot enough without losing half the shank!"

Rosie watched as Del Vecchio, his face a bright crimson, hurried across the yard to Hansen's forge. Although she could not hear the new foreman's words, it was apparent that he was desperate to silence the man.

Hansen, however, remained agitated. "What do you mean it's not the rivets?" he shouted, this time louder than before. "I'm the best heater in this yard, Del Vecchio. If I can't get those to temperature, no one can!"

Del Vecchio placed a hand on Hansen's back, leaned toward the man, and issued a quiet directive. Hansen resisted, albeit quietly, but his body language exhibited his hostility. After a few moments had elapsed, however, the tall, blond Hansen finally threw his hands up in the air and followed his short, swarthy boss into the holding area.

Riveting gangs often encountered faulty rivets on the job. The process for such occurrences was to pull the bad rivet, set it aside, note the batch it came from on a nearby clipboard, and then move along.

With his years of shipbuilding experience, Hansen should have been accustomed to stumbling upon the odd faulty rivet. So why was he so upset? And why was Del Vecchio so eager to quiet him down?

The only reason she could think of was that the entire bag might be defective. How that could possibly have occurred, she had no idea, but there was only one way to test it.

Spying the unattended bag of rivets standing by Hansen's forge, Rosie gave a quick nod to Dewitt. "I'll be right back," she announced before climbing down the scaffold.

Quick as a wink, she ran to the adjacent pier where Rudy Hansen's white-hot forge sent plumes of black smoke billowing into the air above Gowanus Bay. Reaching into the bag of rivets, she extracted the metal objects by the handful and stuffed them into the pockets of her cotton work pants before hastening back to Pier Number One.

Once there, she stopped by Kolacky's forge and offered him a handful of rivets. "Kolacky? Can you try using these first?"

Kolacky's dark eyebrows furrowed, causing his thick eyeglasses to travel up the bridge of his nose.

"It's an experiment. If you could try using them, I'd appreciate it. Please."

Without a word, Kolacky took the rivets from Rosie's hand and threw them onto the forge.

Pulling the second handful of rivets from her other pocket, she ran to the next forge, which was operated by Terrence Foster. At sixty-one years of age, Foster, gray, grizzled, his hide tanned from over four decades of outdoor labor, served as the elder statesman of the yard. Although not necessarily in favor of Pushey's new policy of hiring women, Foster had witnessed enough transformations within the industry to understand that it was useless to resist change. Instead, he rolled with the punches, did his best to remain neutral, and treated everyone with respect.

Rosie, out of breath from her spate of recent activity, rushed to him with an outstretched arm. Without a word, Foster grabbed the contents of Rosie's hand. "You making trouble again?"

Rosie smiled and nodded. "I don't make it. It just finds me."

"Yeah, well, you'd best get back up that scaffold before Kilbride finds out you're gone. Then you will have trouble."

"But what about—?" She pointed to the rivets.

"I'll let you know," he assured with a nod of his head.

"Thanks." She turned on one heel and hastened back to Pier Number One, where a gloomy Kolacky stood frowning into the forge.

"What?" she asked. "They're no good?"

Kolacky turned up his nose and shook his head.

"Hmm . . . Thank you, Kolacky," she said graciously before scampering back up to the platform.

There, Kilbride, still on his rope platform, glared over the hull of the ship. "They warned me you might be a hothead and a busybody, Rosaleen, but no one told me you were a sprinter."

"Oh, I'm sorry. I was just—"

"I know what you were doing, Rosaleen. The question is, do *you*?" With a stern look, Kilbride lowered himself down into the hull.

Rosie watched as Dewitt pulled the ropes that sped Kilbride's descent. He was right. She had no idea what she was getting herself into, but she also knew that she had no room for second thoughts.

A sudden shout drew her attention. Leaning over the edge of the scaffold, she saw Foster jumping up and down and waving. "Hey! Hey! It didn't heat. It melted."

Rosie waved a signal in return and then prepared for the day's work, all the while her mind awhirl. Kolacky, with an underhanded toss, sent the first batch of rivets sailing toward the scaffold. With a graceful bend of the arm, Rosie caught them in her cone and then proceeded to place them into the ship's predrilled holes. As she did so, she eyed each piece of white metal and wondered what made these rivets good and the other ones defective.

The occasional faulty rivet was one thing, but an entire bag of them was a different matter entirely. What had changed to make them so difficult to heat to temperature? Were they simply the wrong rivets or were they, indeed, faulty? And if they were bad, how could they have slipped through quality inspectors?

Foster, although obliging, had more years of experience than the other heaters in the yard, but unfortunately his knowledge was more anecdotal than scientific. To understand the forging process, Rosie needed to speak to someone who knew the ins and outs of steel casting and riveting.

Indeed, there was only one man in the yard who understood the technical elements behind the perfect rivet fit. And that man was Rudy Hansen.

While the average eight-hour workday was punctuated by a thirty-minute lunch break at noon, the shorter Saturday shift offered employees a fifteen-minute break at ten thirty. As the temperature soared to an uncomfortably humid eighty-two degrees, Rosie danced across the scaffold boards, catching and then placing rivets, and periodically wiping the perspiration from her brow.

After what seemed like a lifetime, the whistle sounded to signify the beginning of break. As Dewitt pulled Kilbride up from over the side of the hull, Rosie hurried down the scaffold and ran as fast as she could toward Pier Number Three.

There, she approached Rudy Hansen, who stood by his forge, guzzling water from an insulated metal jug. "Hansen," she called.

"Get away from me," he warned.

"Hansen. I need to speak with you."

"I have nothing to say to you, Keefe."

"Please, Hansen. This isn't about you, me, Finch, or what happened the other day. This is about the rivets you complained about this morning."

Hansen raised an eyebrow. "What about them?"

"They're defective. The whole batch of them. I had other heaters test them out."

"When did you do that?"

"While you were inside talking to Del Vecchio. Before the cleanup crew took the bag away."

"Why?"

"Because I knew you wouldn't say they couldn't be heated if they could."

He bit his lip, deep in thought.

"What is it?" she prompted. "What would make them do that?"

"Now's not a good time to talk," he said softly as he glanced at Del Vecchio and Delaney, standing outside the holding area door, laughing and talking.

"Okay, then when?"

"I'm not telling you anything," he scoffed.

"Come on, Hansen, please. If something's going on—"

"Something's going on, all right. You're nuts. Now get outta here." He pushed her, hard. Rosie felt herself falling backward, but before she could hit the ground, a pair of strong arms caught her and propped her up.

"Now, Rudy, that's no way to be treatin' a lady, is it?" Kilbride challenged as he helped Rosie to her feet.

"This has nothing to do with you, Kilbride."

"Ah, but it does. Rosaleen here is a part of me riveting gang. That means she took time out of our workday to test your rivets. Those tests prove that it were the rivets at fault, and not your heating skills. I think that's worthy of a reward, don't ya think?"

"You want to know what I think? I think you're crazy, too."

"True, dat. I don't know many folks who'd argue with ya. But Rosaleen isn't crazy. Indeed, the lady had a simple request and asked it nicely, so why don't ya have a listen while she repeats it?"

Rosie took her cue. "It's important that I talk to you about the rivets, Hansen. Not here. Not now, but after work."

Hansen pulled a face. "Where?"

She searched her memory for a place that would afford them a chance to speak in private, would set Hansen's nerves at ease, and yet would ensure her safety should Hansen decide to throw his weight around again. "There's a bar in Greenpoint called Logan's. It's on the corner of Greenpoint and McGuinness."

Rosie didn't frequent bars; however, Logan's, a bar near the neighborhood where she had grown up, was a favorite of Billy's. Not only did she know the proprietor, Frank Logan, from the many occasions upon which he had brought Billy home after a night of drinking, but she had gone to school with his two daughters, Moira and Colleen.

"Oh, that's a nice pub, that is," Kilbride opined. "Good folk. Nice atmosphere. You'll enjoy havin' a pint there, Hansen."

With a prolonged sigh, the tall Swede finally caved in. "What time?"

Rosie considered the time required to check Finch's apartment, send Katie off, shower, and change clothes. "How about six o'clock?"

"Okay, I'll be there."

"Good," Rosie said with a quick nod and headed back to the scaffold, Kilbride following close at her heels. "Thank you, Clinton, but I could have gotten him on my own."

"I know. I saw ya were workin' wonders when I arrived," he quipped. "Fallin' all over yerself to get 'im to talk to ya."

"Funny. Very funny."

"I think so." He chuckled. "In all seriousness, though, ya'd best watch yerself."

"Logan's is owned by friends of mine, so I should be okay."

"I didn't just mean Hansen. If someone put the fix in to make sure that batch of rivets were bad, then they're not goin' to be happy about you findin' out and makin' sure they can't do it again."

"But why would someone substitute faulty rivets? And how? It just doesn't make any sense, Kilbride."

"If I 'ad the answer to those questions, darlin', I'd be makin' more money than I do. Alas, all I know 'bout rivets is how to pound 'em into oblivion with my pneumatic gun."

"And all I know is how to catch them and then put them in place without getting burned." She frowned.

"And even that ya don't do fast enough," he teased.

"Be quiet, Kilbride," she objected. "If I were any faster, you'd fall off your rope swing."

"Now that sounds like a challenge I'm willin' to accept."

With that, the whistle blew, prompting Kilbride to grab Rosie's hand and lead her back to Pier Number One. He sang:

> *Just give me your hand,*
> *Tabhair dom do lámh.*
> *Just give me your hand*
> *And I'll walk with you,*
> *Through the streets of our land,*
> *Through the mountains so grand.*
> *If you give me your hand.*

Rosie broke free of Kilbride's grip, but she followed behind him, laughing all the way.

Two hours later, the Pushey Shipyard whistle blew to signify the end of the work week and the beginning of the day-and-a-half weekend.

A tired, sweat-drenched Rosie bid adieu to her coworkers and exited through the front gate, where Katie waited. Sporting a red-and-white-striped, whirl-skirt dirndl dress with a button front, white slingback sandals, and a red straw hat that rested at a jaunty angle upon her golden head, she looked as if she had stepped right out of the pages of the Sears spring catalog.

In her right hand she clutched her handbag. In her left, a brown paper grocery sack.

"Hey, Katie-girl," Rosie greeted "What's in the bag?"

"This is for you. I know how hot it's been today and I thought you might want to slip into something cooler." She passed the sack to her sister, who immediately peered inside.

"Oh, Katie-girl! It's no wonder you're my favorite sister."

"I'm your *only* sister," Katie corrected.

Before Rosie could tease her sister any further, a voice came from just inside the shipyard fence. "Sister? How can so much beauty be in one family, I ask. 'Tis an embarrassment of riches, to be sure."

"Clinton Kilbride," Rosie admonished. "You be on your best behavior."

"I will, Rosaleen Keefe." He turned his attention to Katie and with an outstretched hand said, "Now that ya know our names, what's yers?"

"Um, Katie." She made it sound more like a question than a statement.

"Ah, but that must be short for somethin', no?"

"Katherine," she offered happily. "Katherine Brigid."

"Ah, a name like a—"

"Poem?" Rosie hit Kilbride on the back of the head, causing him to choke on the rest of his words. "That's enough out of you. Now, I'm going to get changed. When I come back, I hope to find my sister alive, well, and bearing no visible fingerprints."

"Yes, ma'am!" He saluted cheekily.

Rosie trotted back through the gates and into the holding area ladies' room, where she slipped out of her work clothes and, after wiping herself down with a few moistened paper towels, slipped into a sleeveless blue and brown plaid sundress and a pair of strappy brown wedges.

After undoing the kerchief and brushing her auburn locks, she stuffed her work clothes back into the bag and strolled to the Pushey Shipyard gates, where Kilbride was entertaining Katie with a few—thankfully clean—limericks.

When Rosie appeared, the Irishman's eyes grew wide. "Why, Rosaleen, darlin'. Look at ya! If that ain't enough to send a man happy to his grave, I don't know what else would."

"Save your flattery for Monday morning, Clinton."

He flashed a boyish grin. "I will. I will indeed, but may I at least kiss the hand of your baby sister before I go?"

"No."

Kilbride winked at Katie. "Jealous type. I get lots of those."

"Oh, and this is yours." Rosie returned the kerchief she had used to shield her head from the sun.

He took the piece of cloth and held it close to his

nose. "Ah, the scent of your hair lives up to your name, fair Rose."

"Get out of here, Kilbride," she instructed with a playful punch in the arm.

"All right, I'm goin'. I'm goin'. Try not to miss me too much, darlin'."

As Katie giggled, Kilbride whistled his way down Beard Street.

"I like him," she stated. "He's funny."

"Yeah, he's a hoot, all right. So, how did everything go with the move?"

"Good. Ma helped me pack and then got Saul, the grocer, to bring his truck over. As of eleven thirty this morning, everything I have, Charlie included, was at Ma's place. Everything except you, that is. And go ahead and call me silly, but until you're back there with me, it's not quite home."

Rosie embraced her sister and valiantly tried to fight back her tears. "Oh, Katie, my lamb, I'll be there soon. Don't you worry."

"But I do worry," she cried.

"You shouldn't. We're going to head over to Finch's apartment, find the financial records, and put this whole thing to rest."

"Really?" a sniffling Katie asked.

Given that the police had already searched the Finches' apartment, Rosie was doubtful she'd uncover anything new, but she refused to admit that to her sister. "You bet. Now dry your eyes and let's get going."

Katie took a lace handkerchief from her handbag and dabbed at her eyes.

"So which way is it?" Rosie asked and pointed a thumb in either direction.

"I don't know. I just know the address, but I have no idea where it is."

"Oh, Katie." Rosie laughed.

"I'm sorry. I didn't look it up on a map."

"No, no. That's okay. I didn't think of that either. We'll just ask a cab driver or a train conductor or something. It will be fine."

It was, indeed, fine. After consulting with the local beat cop—a touch of irony that Rosie found amusing—they continued on to the Finches' Van Brunt Street apartment.

The red brick, semi-attached apartment building featured six windows in the front—two for each of the three floors. Granite steps, flanked by scrolled wrought-iron railings led to an off-center front door—toward the left on the left unit, and toward the right on the right unit. Long alleys running between the buildings provided space for trash cans.

"How are you going to get inside?" Katie asked.

Rosie eyed the front entrance, but soon realized that she'd most likely be greeted with a locked apartment door. "I don't know," she confessed. "You said their place is on the second floor, didn't you?"

"That's right. But how—?"

Before Katie could ask, Rosie had moved from the front of the building to the side alleyway closest to the Finches' unit, examining every possible access point of the three-story building as she did so. "Look." She pointed upward excitedly. "There's an open window in the Finches apartment, right near that fire escape."

Katie gazed up at the window indicated. The bottom sash had been left open approximately two inches, allowing just enough ventilation in to keep the red geranium on the sill from wilting in the summerlike heat, while protecting the puffy white eyelet tie-back curtains from getting doused by a passing rainstorm.

From there, she looked down at Rosie's wedge-soled

shoes in disappointment. "I guess bringing that change of clothes wasn't such a good idea after all."

"Hey, I didn't think of it either. How could we possibly have known? It's not as if we went to cat burglar school. There's not much we can do about it now, though. It's not like I'm going to strip down and change back into my coveralls." She walked over to the base of the fire escape, slipped out of her shoes, and set them and the paper sack containing her work clothes down on the asphalt. "Give me a boost, will you?"

Katie obliged by tucking her handbag in one armpit, crouching down, and weaving the fingers of both hands together.

Rosie lifted her right leg and stepped into her sister's hands. After a few failed attempts and several grunts and groans, she managed to get a foot onto the bottom rung of the fire-escape ladder. From there, she positioned her other foot on the rung and, using her arms, pulled herself upright.

"Once I'm in," she informed Katie, "I'll go out the front door. Unless you see someone going in. Then give me a whistle like when we were kids, remember?"

"The first few bars of 'Whistling in the Dark,'" Katie confirmed with a nod of the head. "Got it!"

Having grown accustomed to climbing scaffolding at the shipyard, the rest of Rosie's ascent was easy; within a minute, she was on the fire-escape landing adjacent to the open window. Opening said window and climbing in, however, required a bit more effort.

Leaning over the edge of the fire-escape railing, Rosie pushed at the bottom pane, but the spate of warm, humid weather had caused the wood of the sash to expand and its layers of white paint to stick. Trying to be as quiet as possible, she gave the window a few hard bangs with the palm of her hand and then, using all her strength, inched the bottom sash of the window upward along the tracks until there was enough space to climb inside.

Katie cringed as she watched her sister step over the edge of the fire-escape railing, balance herself, and then slide, head-first and legs dangling, into the open window. Gliding her torso over the windowsill and, inside, the cast-iron radiator, she put her hands down on the carpeted apartment floor and pulled herself to her feet.

Rosie found herself in a twelve-foot-by-twelve-foot square room. In the center rested a full-sized spool bed wrapped in a chenille coverlet bearing a floral pattern in shades of green, yellow, pink, and blue. Two nightstands designed in the Colonial fashion from orange-toned maple stood on either side of the bed and, across the room, a matching orange maple triple dresser with attached mirror was lined with a silver ladies' vanity set consisting of a tray, brush, comb, and hand mirror.

She drew a deep breath and fixed her dress. *Well, here is as good a place as any to start.*

Setting to work, she rummaged through the drawers of the dresser and nightstands, checked the bedroom closet, and examined the hatboxes beneath the bed. Finding nothing of interest, she turned her attention to the bathroom, including a thorough search of the medicine cabinet and laundry hamper. As expected, they turned up empty as well.

Having marked the bedroom and bathroom off her list, she traveled to the adjacent kitchen. To her left, a black-and-white dinette set with aluminum trim served as the eating area. To the right, a small stove and icebox acted as the heart and soul of the corner-style galley kitchen, which apart from their presence, was lined, top and bottom, with an array of white metal cabinets.

White metal cabinets that would take an intimidatingly long time for a single human being to search.

Rosie took a moment to ponder the situation. Should she start tearing into the cupboards? Or was it a waste of time? Seeing as it was considered to be the woman's, and hence Marie's, domain, the kitchen was probably the last place Finch would hide important paperwork. It would simply be too difficult for him to predict and control whether his wife would stumble upon it.

Following this assumption, she decided to head, instead, into the living room. Overlooking the street, the living room was a light, airy space that served as a warm entry to the rest of the apartment. The front picture window was accented by a set of floral pinch-pleated drapes with wide-slat venetian blinds for additional privacy. On the wall perpendicular to, and left of, the window stood the front door. To the left of that, a gilded framed mirror reflected the brilliant sunlight that streamed between the slats of the blinds, while beneath it, a solid brown sofa covered with crocheted antimacassars offered seating for three. On the wall to the right, two mismatched armchairs flanked a small, round wooden table with a large ceramic lamp. And in the center of the room rested an orange maple coffee table.

Rosie did a quick search of the room, but apart from the spaces underneath the furniture and drapes, the room appeared to lack any viable hiding spaces. Deciding to return to the kitchen, she turned around, only to spot a narrow door on her right, just between the two rooms.

A smile stretched across her face as she opened the door to reveal a coat closet, at the bottom of which rested a large red metal lockbox. It wasn't a toolshed, but perhaps if she were lucky . . .

Grabbing the box by its handle, she slid it closer and eagerly flipped open the two latches. The lid popped open, exposing a bevy of tools inside. Taking each piece out she did a mental inventory: *Hammer . . . Phillips screwdriver . . . flat screwdriver . . . adjustable wrench . . . tape measure . . . hand drill . . . level . . . a jar of nails . . . putty knife . . . hacksaw . . .*

Alas, with the removal of the hacksaw, the box was empty. Rosie picked up the box and shook it to ensure she hadn't missed anything. All was silent.

Damn! she thought. *I thought for sure—*

Her thoughts were interrupted by the sound of Katie's whistles: *Toot-too-too-too-tooooo, Toot-too-too-too-tooooooo.*

So startled was Rosie that she dropped the box with a loud clatter. Fumbling, she picked it up only to discover that the inside bottom—a false one—had tumbled onto the floor, and with it, a paper-clipped stack of approximately three bank statements.

Rosie's jaw dropped open and she was tempted to shriek and dance with joy, but Katie's second set of whistles prompted her to pack up and run: *Toot-too-too-too-tooooo, Toot-too-too-too-tooooooo.*

Hastily, she placed the tools back into the box, fastened it, and shoved it back into the closet before shutting the door. Then, amid yet another set of whistles, she ran on her tiptoes to the open bedroom window. Needing the full use of both hands, she stuffed the bank statements into her brassiere and, without a glance to the alley below, reached out to the fire-escape railing, grabbed hold, and pulled herself out the window and onto the landing.

From there, it was a simple matter of stepping over

the railing and onto the platform and then following the series of ladders to ground level.

Simple, that is, until she looked down from the top of the second ladder to see Lieutenant Riordan standing directly below her.

Rosie felt her face grow hot, her palms sweat, and her heart start to race. Part of her distress was due to having been caught breaking and entering the Finches' apartment. The other part was due to the fact that Riordan, from his position on the ground, could look right up her dress.

"Oh!" she exclaimed and struggled, with one hand, to pull the back of her skirt forward between her knees. Rosie's attempt to transform her dress into a romper had been unsuccessful, but it had been quite effective in causing her to lose her grip on the ladder's metal rungs.

"Oh!" she cried again as she forgot about her dress and tried, in vain, to keep both feet and hands on the slippery metal rungs.

With a short shriek, she plummeted to earth and braced herself for the feel of the asphalt as it smashed against her skin.

It therefore came as quite a surprise to be greeted, upon landing, by the feel of cotton and the warm scent of musk. Rosie opened her eyes, which had been tightly closed in fear, to find herself, quite literally, nose to nose with Lieutenant Riordan.

"Next time you feel like dropping in, give me a call first, will you?" He smiled.

"Oh!" Disoriented, she looked around, only to find herself cradled in Riordan's arms. "Oh!"

"I think you said that already."

Rosie bit her lip. "Could you put me down, please?"

"Absolutely." He placed her feetfirst onto the pavement.

She looked about for a trace of Katie, but the only other things in the alley were some trash cans, her shoes, and the brown grocery sack that contained the day's work clothes. "Well, I guess I should be glad she didn't take those with her."

"Sorry about that. Your sister got a glimpse of me, started whistling, and then shouted, 'I wasn't sleuthing, I promise!' before taking off."

Rosie clicked her tongue. "I should have known. She did the same thing when Mrs. McCarthy caught us soaping up her parlor windows one Halloween."

Riordan laughed. "So, um, what were you looking for up there?"

"Up there? I wasn't—" She smiled, fluttered her eyelashes, and tried to act casual, but it was no use; there was no way she could pretend she wasn't snooping. "Oh, never mind. You already know what I was doing up there. I was giving the place another search, just to make sure your guys didn't miss anything."

"You know I can have you arrested for breaking and entering, don't you?"

"That would sound more like a threat if you weren't already planning on arresting me tomorrow."

Riordan looked away sheepishly. "Yeah, I guess so."

"Of course, if you do it now, that would save you and your men the time it takes to travel to Manhattan," she teased. "Save gas, too. The government is talking about rationing fuel, you know."

"Yeah, yeah." He looked at her, eyes questioning. "So, um, did you find anything?"

"Nope. Nothing. Your men did an excellent job at cleaning up the place."

"Really?"

"Yes, there wasn't a clue left to be found."

Riordan glanced at the front of Rosie's dress with a

grin. The bank statements she had secured in her brassiere had worked their way up her dress during the fall. "Excuse me," he pardoned as he reached just below her neck and extracted the small stack of documents.

"Oh!" Rosie exclaimed. "Where did those come from?"

"Where, indeed?"

"I swear I never saw them before!"

"Uh-huh. I suppose your seamstress sewed them in there for safekeeping and they just worked their way loose."

She rolled her eyes. "Okay, you got me. I found them upstairs."

"Yeah, I figured that, but where?"

"The toolbox in the living room closet."

"My guys looked there and didn't see anything."

"That's because they didn't look hard enough. The box had a false bottom."

"And you knew enough to look for it?" he challenged.

Rosie tilted her head from side to side as she debated whether or not she should allow Riordan to believe she possessed some sort of sleuthing sixth sense. "Yes . . . no . . . well, I kinda stumbled upon it."

"Stumbled?"

"All right, I dropped the box and the false bottom fell out."

"Hmmm. Maybe I should teach that trick to my guys."

"Perhaps you should. Now"—she reached for the statements—"can I have those back, please?"

He pulled them away from her and put them in his inside jacket pocket. "No. They're police evidence now."

"Did you have a warrant to take them from me?"

"Didn't need one. They were sticking up from . . ."

He waved a finger at her bosom and blushed slightly. "You know . . . they were in plain sight."

"But I'm the one who found them! And you're getting the statements sent to you from the bank anyway. You don't need both."

"Tell you what. I won't give them to you, but we can look them over. Together."

"You did the same thing to Katie. I know you did. She told me."

"Yeah, so? What's your answer?"

Rosie shuffled her feet reluctantly. "Well . . . okay. I guess so."

Riordan pulled the statements from inside his jacket. He removed the paper clip and placed it in his mouth.

"I can't see them," Rosie complained as she attempted to peer over his shoulder.

At her request, he held the stack aloft.

The cover statement, dated from late January of that year, bore the transactions for a savings-account holding at Flushing Bank that had been opened on February 5, 1942. The familiar four-column display possessed a space for transaction date, transaction type, withdrawal amount, and deposit amount.

The withdrawal column was empty.

"Finch opened this account with $10,000!" Rosie exclaimed. "How could he possibly have saved that much from his job at Pushey Shipyard?"

"He didn't. Look at these deposits: $2,000 a week? That's not his paycheck. Not from Pushey anyways."

Rosie grabbed the papers and scanned them one by one. Each month—from January to the present—followed the same pattern. Four deposits, and a few recent withdrawals averaging anywhere from fifty to one hundred dollars.

"Finch was obviously on someone's payroll, but whose?" Riordan asked.

She shook her head. "I have no idea. No idea what those withdrawals would be for either."

"Hmph. I'll take this back to headquarters and make some phone calls." He smiled. "Care for a ride back home, Mrs. Keefe? Or should I call you Sherlock?"

"Mrs. Keefe will do. And yes, a ride would be lovely, thank you."

With an exaggerated bow, Riordan indicated for Rosie to pass him. But upon recalling the bank statements still in her possession, he cleared his throat and beckoned her return. "Ehem."

She stopped and attempted to play innocent. "What?"

"You know what," he stated as he pulled the statements from her hand and, once again, secured them in his inside jacket pocket.

Chapter Fifteen

Rosie, after a silent car ride with Riordan, returned to her Manhattan apartment to find Katie, hat and shoes removed, sprawled upon the sofa, reading the latest issue of *The Saturday Evening Post*, which bore a Norman Rockwell image of Willie Gillis reading a newspaper while on KP duty.

"What the heck are you doing here?" Rosie asked. "You were supposed to go straight to Ma's. Given the speed with which you left me, you should have been there an hour ago."

Katie threw the magazine to the floor and leaped from the sofa. "Oh, thank goodness you're home!"

"Yeah, you seemed really worked up," she teased.

"I was. I am. And most of all, I'm so sorry, Rosie!" She threw her arms around her sister's neck. "I shouldn't have left you in that apartment alone."

"Sure. You're sorry now," she teased. "Honestly, Katie-girl! I haven't seen anyone disappear like that since I caught Dante the Magician's act at the Roxy two years ago."

"I'm sorry. Really I am. It's just that I had promised

Lieutenant Riordan I'd stay at home and not snoop anymore, and when I saw him . . . well . . . well, I ran."

"And how!"

"At least I signaled to you before running off," Katie rationalized. "Not just twice, but three times."

"You did," Rosie said.

"And I remembered the secret whistle, too."

"Yes, but you were a tad off key."

"I was not!" Katie insisted.

Rosie laughed. Sometimes it was far too easy to get her sister's goat.

"And I plan to make it up to you. I called Ma when I got home and asked her to watch Charlie overnight. Why don't we go to the movies and then grab a soda? My treat."

"Katie . . ." she warned.

"Oh, come on. It's a new Andy Hardy. You know how I love those! We haven't gone out, just the two of us, since before I had Charlie. It'll be fun."

Rosie would have loved to have spent what might be her last evening of freedom enjoying a night alone with her sister. However, not only did she need to meet Hansen, but she wanted Katie clear of the apartment when Riordan came to arrest her the next morning. "No, Katie. You said you'd move out tonight if I let you come with me to the Finches' apartment. A deal's a deal, remember?"

"Yeah, but I still don't see what the big rush is."

"The rush is that I have a lot to do if I'm going to be out of here by the end of the month. And it was a hot day, I'm tired. Besides, once we're in Greenpoint, we can go out and have Ma babysit whenever we want."

"I suppose." Katie frowned, but then her face brightened. "Say, maybe we can dig up some old records and dance in the living room again. Remember when we used to do that? It's been a while."

"That's because it's hard to dance in a ten-foot-square room full of furniture." Rosie gestured to the cramped living room.

"Yeah, but Ma's house is bigger. And you'll have your old room back. It might be fun. You know, like the old days."

"I have no doubt it will. But right now, I need a shower and *you* need to get a move on."

"Okay," Katie groaned as she picked up her hat, shoes, and handbag from the scuffed hardwood floor. "Will I see you tomorrow?"

"Maybe. I'll give you a call." Rosie embraced her sister firmly.

The hug was so tight that Katie squeaked. "I guess I'm forgiven?"

"Yes." Rosie laughed. "Of course you're forgiven, lamb. You'd have to do a lot more than run away from the police to make me not love you."

"Awww. I feel the same way, Rosie."

"I'm glad. It would stink to find out my only sister was kinda fickle in her feelings."

"That's one thing you can never accuse me of."

"I know, Katie-girl. Hey, when you get to Greenpoint, say hi to Ma and give Charlie a kiss for me, will you?"

"You bet!" With a giggle, Katie left, the scent of baby powder and Chantilly perfume lingering behind her in the warm, heavy air of the apartment.

Rosie checked the clock: four p.m.

Realizing she had just two hours to get to Logan's in Greenpoint, she took a much-needed shower (her day at the shipyard and the foray into Finch's apartment had left every inch of her skin feeling damp and sticky) and then changed into a tailored short-sleeved blue dress and a pair of white peep-toe pumps before setting off for the train to Brooklyn and, from there, the bus to Greenpoint.

Logan's was a quiet drinking spot where many a laborer could find a cold beer and a hot meal at the end of a long workday. Built in the 1890s, its dark wooden booths, red leather upholstery, and rich wood paneling harkened back to the pre-cocktail-era tradition of men in fine suits gathering together at local clubs to converse over brandy and cigars. Fifty years later, the class of clientele and the dress code had changed, but the majority of Logan's customers were still male.

Rosie felt heads turn the moment she walked through the light-obstructing, painted-metal door of the bar. For a moment, she felt completely out of her element, but fortunately, Frank Logan spotted her and, with a warm welcome, escorted her inside. "Mrs. Keefe. To what do we owe the honor?"

"I'm here to meet someone. Tall, Scandinavian-looking, name is Rudy Hansen."

Frank looked surprised and awkward. "Ah, yes. He's right this way." Logan walked her to a dark corner table where a sullen Hansen sat contemplating his half-full pilsner glass. "Can I get you anything, Mrs. Keefe?"

"Yes, a lemon Coke with ice, please."

"Right away," Logan replied with a gesture of his hand.

"Thanks for meeting me, Hansen."

"Didn't have much of a choice what with your watchdog, Kilbride, barking and nipping at my heels," he grumbled.

"He's enthusiastic, to be sure, but you still could have said 'no.'"

"And have you two hounding me until I agreed to give in? Better we meet now so I can get you off my back." Hansen took a sip of his beer. "Let's get this over with. What do you want from me?"

"I want to know about those rivets today. What happened?"

"They were bad," he shrugged. "But Del Vecchio refused to listen to me."

"Bad. Bad how? I don't understand."

"Bad as in defective. As in they wouldn't heat. You've been on the job how long? Two weeks?"

"Just about."

"Then you know the process. The heater uses his forge to get the rivets to the temperature where they become soft and can be flattened with a rivet gun, right?"

"Right. Got it."

Frank Logan returned with Rosie's Coke and, after checking on her tablemate's beverage status, bid a hasty retreat behind the bar. As Hansen told his tale, Rosie sipped her soda in silence.

"So that it doesn't heat too quickly, steel is tempered with carbon, nickel, or chromium. The rivets used for ships are tempered with carbon. More precisely, high-grade steel and mild, or low, carbon. In other words, they hold up to heating without melting, and if you cool them off in water, they stay strong and don't change much."

"So they can handle being in extreme temperatures and conditions," she paraphrased.

"Right. They expand and contract instead of breaking down, which is ideal for something that's going to be in water. The problem with the rivets I got today is they melted away instead of heating."

"Meaning?"

"Meaning that they were most likely low-grade steel that's high in carbon. The carbon takes longer to reach the desired temperature, but before it can, the steel in the rivet melts away."

"Leaving you with no rivet," she presumed.

"Not only that. When you take a hot rivet that's made of steel and has a lot of carbon in it and drop it in water, it becomes hard and brittle."

"And if you use those for shipbuilding what happens?"

"For starters, you can't heat them to the same temperature you would use to heat a better rivet. They'll melt, like the ones we saw today. And if you do manage to use them by heating them more slowly, then they're likely to become brittle and snap with temperature changes and pressure."

"And if they snap?"

"You get a hole in the side of your hull," he stated bluntly.

Rosie leaned back in her chair. "Then that bag had to be a mistake. Why else would anyone take the chance of that happening?"

"Money. That's the only thing I can figure. The shipyard's probably trying to cut corners to turn a profit."

"At the risk of our boys' lives? I can't believe that—"

"You don't? You don't think this sort of thing goes on all the time? Companies are always trying to save a buck and they don't care how they do it. It's only when someone gets hurt that they decide it wasn't such a good idea. And by then, their pockets have already been lined."

"Do you think Del Vecchio knew about the rivets?"

"No idea. All I know is that I didn't receive those rivets by accident. They were left on that pier this morning for yours truly. I'm the best heater in the yard. Everyone knows it."

Rosie begrudgingly agreed.

"I can only imagine," Hansen continued, "that who-ever left that bag there wanted me to test them out in order to see if they'd fly."

"And if, like today, they didn't?"

"Then they'd know they'd have to up the quality and lower the carbon on the next batch. Not go so cheap."

"If that's the case, it's hard to believe Del Vecchio didn't know about it. He's the new shift foreman."

"Whether Del Vecchio was in on the deal or re-ceived instructions from someone else, it's tough to say." Hansen drank the rest of his beer and held up a finger to order another round. True to character, he didn't ask his tablemate if she wanted a second soda.

Rosie made a point of sucking noisily on the straw in her glass of lemon Coke, finishing the last sweet drops of liquid. If Hansen got the hint, he failed to act upon it.

"But I saw Del Vecchio rush you into the holding area," she pointed out. "If he wasn't in on it, why did he try to silence you?"

"He thought I was making trouble. At least that's what he told me."

She pondered the plausibility of this explanation. Between Rosie's attack on Finch, Finch's murder, and both scenes with Hansen, it had been an eventful week. Another outburst by Hansen, whether based on truth or not, could easily have agitated Del Vecchio's already frayed nerves.

"The bag of rivets, where did they go?"

"Sweepers took them, I guess. They were gone by the time I got back from the holding area."

"And that's the last time you saw them?"

"The last time I saw them, heard about them, or spoke about them—until now."

"Well, I guess that's it for now." Rosie pushed back her chair and rose to her feet. "Thank you, Hansen."

"Yeah. Just don't tell anyone at the yard that we met tonight, okay? I don't want them to think I've gone soft."

"I'll be sure to keep it under wraps." She smiled and made her way to the bar to pay for her soda.

"What's the damage, Frank? Do I need to tap into my Swiss bank account?" she teased.

"An even dime for tonight, Mrs. Keefe, but, um . . ."

"But what?"

"Well, I feel funny asking, but there's also the matter of your husband's bar tab."

At the mention of Billy, Rosie felt a hole develop in the pit of her stomach. "Billy's off at war, but tell me how much he owes and I'll see what I can do."

"Oh, I didn't know he got called. When did he ship out? Last week?"

Her brow furrowed. Frank Logan had celebrated his seventieth birthday that past January. Was he starting to lose track of time and people? "Last week? Heaven's no, Mr. Logan. He left three months ago."

The color rose in Logan's pockmarked face, staining it a bright crimson. "Umm . . . I beg pardon, ma'am, but he was here just two weeks ago. Patty, my cook, can vouch for it."

The ruddy face of Patty, the short-order cook and makeshift bouncer, appeared in the window of the tiny kitchen, and gave a nod.

It took several moments for Rosie's brain to process the barkeep's words, but once it did, her knees buckled slightly and she suddenly felt lightheaded.

Logan rushed from his place behind the bar and placed a steadying hand on her forearm. "You okay?"

"Yes, I . . ."

He helped her onto a barstool. "Here, sit down a minute."

"Thank you." ·

"Hey, no problem. Just stay put and I'll get you some water." He went behind the bar and filled a clear old-fashioned glass with ice and a steady stream of water from the sink's tap.

"Here," he said, as he returned to Rosie's side, glass in hand.

She took it in a trembling hand. "I'm so sorry about that. I don't . . . I don't know what came over me."

"No reason to apologize. I've never seen someone go white like that before. Must be the heat."

"That—that must be it," she replied, all the while her thoughts on Billy.

"Yeah, thought so. Got too hot too fast. Always does. Then next week it'll probably snow again." He punctuated the prediction with a disgusted wave of his hand.

"So, um, about Billy. You said he was here two weeks ago?"

"He was. Must have been a last hurrah before shipping out, huh?"

She tried to muster a smile. "Yes, that's exactly what it was."

"Thought so. I approached him about the bill, but he must have forgotten. No wonder, either. Boy, was he tight!"

"Hmm, you usually bring him home when he's like that. Unless, of course, he wasn't alone."

"Alone?" Logan's face flushed as he repeated the word evasively. "Oh . . . ummm . . . why no. No, he wasn't."

It was apparent from his flustered reaction that the companion was not male.

"I, um, I think I feel better now. How much is the tab, Mr. Logan?"

"Thirty bucks, but I don't need all of it right now, Mrs. Keefe. Just give me what you can afford. What with Billy off to war, I know money must be hard to come by."

Rosie extracted a tattered leather wallet from her handbag and checked its contents. Payday at the yard occurred every other Monday—her next check was still two days away. "I have five dollars," she announced as she counted out the last bills in her wallet. "Is that enough?"

"That's more than enough, thanks, Mrs. Keefe. I wouldn't have asked you, but business ain't what it used to be what with most of my customers being drafted."

"I understand. It's okay." She hopped down from the stool and gathered up her handbag. "I'd best be going. Thanks, Mr. Logan."

"Thank you, Mrs. Keefe. I appreciate it. And take care of yourself. If you get another spell like that, go to the doctor."

Rosie nodded absently and wended her way out of the bar. In a daze, she retraced her steps to the bus stop and boarded.

Two weeks, she thought as the bus rolled onward. *Billy was in town as recently as two weeks ago and yet he hasn't called. Hasn't stopped by to say "hello." Hasn't provided an explanation for his whereabouts.*

Lies. The whole draft story was a lie. If that was untrue, what else? Had Billy ever loved her or was she simply a trophy? Marrying one of the prettiest girls in school, who lived in one of the biggest houses in the neighborhood, would fetch Billy the glory he sought without much effort on his part.

And Billy had a serious aversion to effort. In Billy's mind, his intellect was higher than everyone else's, his looks more attractive, his charms more alluring. Why should he work? Why should he break a sweat when others should feel honored having him in their employ?

Even though he had managed to talk himself up to others and, to a certain extent, himself, beneath that cocky, devil-may-care exterior existed a desperately insecure human being. A man who put on a good show in order to hide a deep sense of failure and personal dissatisfaction. Most of the time, Billy believed the things he said. Believed that he was the prize catch he claimed to be. Believed he was the pride of Greenpoint, Brooklyn.

Then there were the dark moments, those lonely hours when the dam behind which he locked his self-doubt opened just wide enough to allow a ripple of uncertainty to wash upon his consciousness. The cause of the dam leak varied—meeting a school friend who had gone on to job success, a friend buying a new car, an argument with an employer—but the solution was always the same.

Seeking any way to quell the oncoming tide of self-loathing, Billy reached out for the best thing he could find to ease the pain and despair: alcohol. Those first few sips of beer or whiskey were like a magic elixir. The muscles in his body loosened, his mood lifted, and for a short while he forgot his demons. But that first drink only lasted so long, and its happy effects mitigated over time. And so it was soon followed by another. And another. And yet another.

In the fifteen years since he had started drinking, the euphoria produced by those first few sips now required a few bottles. And the four-beers-a-night routine had gradually grown to seven, eight, and sometimes as many as ten.

But it was a delicate balance. If he hadn't consumed enough to fall into the deep oblivion of sleep, then his jealousies and insecurities broke through the dam and swept over him like a tidal wave, plunging him into a sea of self-loathing.

It was at those moments that Rosie felt sorry for Billy. Sitting alone in the dark, he'd cry for hours, speaking to no one and feeling nothing except his own pain.

If he drank too much, his bravado reached new and obnoxious heights, spurring him to spew forth insults and obscenities at anyone who dared question his wisdom. Most of the time, Billy passed out shortly after offending those in his company. If the barkeep knew Rosie, he'd call her to collect Billy or, in the case of Frank Logan, drop the intoxicated man at her doorstep. But there were many times when, having faced the sharp end of Billy's tongue, a vengeful pub proprietor would leave him in the side alley or, worse yet, call the police.

And then there were those occasions when he didn't pass out after his eighth beer in two hours and instead, continued drinking. It was during those moments when Billy, his inhibitions lost in the haze of the alcohol and his temper and sense of indignation at full tilt, would manifest his feelings of inferiority in a physical sense.

Rosie felt the bus come to a halt outside the IRT station. Gathering her handbag, she rose from her seat, stepped from the bus, and walked up a flight of metal stairs and across a wooden platform to the waiting train. Upon showing the conductor her monthly pass, she stepped into the third car and took an empty seat in the last row before once again immersing herself in her thoughts.

Billy. She shook her head at his name. *Billy and his temper.* He had been told, from the time he was a kid, that his big mouth and temper would be his undoing. Indeed, Rosie wasn't sure how he had managed to live to the age of thirty-three without having some irate bar patron attempt to knock his teeth out of his head.

On some level, she wished some bar patron had, for it might have put the fear of God into him. Heaven only knew that Billy's outbursts had put the fear of God into her several times. Broken glasses, smashed plates, overturned furniture, holes punched into the plaster walls, and once, just once, he had even shoved Rosie into the kitchen table.

The incident had left Rosie with bruises and scratches galore and had spurred her to consider moving to her mother's house. But in true Billy fashion, once he had sobered up he apologized with a bouquet of flowers, copious amounts of hugs and "I love yous," and a vow to never hurt her again.

She, quite naturally, believed him. She wanted to believe him. That was the thing about Billy: no matter how bad things could be, he had a way of making you believe that they would eventually get better. Although she suspected that not all of his all-night outings had ended with him sleeping in an alley and that perhaps he wasn't always drinking with the boys, when he was home he made her feel as if she were the only woman who mattered.

Mattered, that is, until the next time he came home in a rage or didn't come home at all. And then the cycle of doubt started all over again.

But now, between Del Vecchio's words at the shipyard and Logan's sighting of Billy at the bar, she knew for certain that she wasn't the only woman who mattered to him.

To Billy Keefe, her thoughts and feelings—indeed, Rosie herself—weren't anything that mattered at all.

She was jolted from her reverie by the conductor's announcement that they had reached the Thirty-third Street stop. So lost in thought was she that the twenty-minute trip had seemed to take mere seconds. From the station, she slowly made her way to her apartment building and trudged up the stairs to her second-floor flat.

Finding the evening paper outside the door, she picked it up, went inside, and immediately deposited it on the coffee table before flopping facedown onto the couch. Every bit of strength and energy she possessed after talking to Hansen seemed to have evaporated the moment she received the news about Billy.

Why should she bother to fight to preserve her freedom when her entire existence was a joke?

For the first time in days, she surrendered fully to her emotions. No blinking back the tears or biting her lip to retain composure. Instead of a trickle, her tear ducts produced a steady stream of salty water and her breath came in heavy sobs.

After several minutes, she sniffed and raised her head from the pillow. Her throat was dry, the roof of her mouth soft and swollen, and her eyes burned, but the outburst was, ultimately, cathartic. Deciding she needed both a handkerchief and a drink of water, she rose from the sofa, the hem of her dress knocking the newspaper off the table as she did so.

As she bent down to retrieve it, she read, through puffy, half-closed eyes, the headline:

SENATOR TRUMAN'S CRUSADE CONTINUES.

72 POSSIBLE CASES OF WAR PROFITEERING

FOUND IN NYC; MORE SUSPECTED

Hansen's words about the faulty rivets flashed across Rosie's mind like a streak of lightning. Was Pushey Shipyard doing more than just trying to cut corners? Were they charging the United States government for ships built out of high-quality steel and then using subpar materials instead? And if they were, did Finch know about it? If so, that would help to explain the deposits in his checkbook. It might also help to explain why he was killed.

Her mind full of questions, she scanned the article and made her way to the kitchen for a much-needed glass of water. As she grabbed a glass from the cupboard, a knock came at the door.

Placing both the glass and the newspaper on the kitchen counter, Rosie moved to the door and opened it to see Lieutenant Riordan, a grave expression on his face.

"What is it?" she asked.

"Hansen," he replied as he removed his gray fedora and stepped inside the apartment.

Rosie shut the door behind him. "What about him?"

"He was assaulted on his way home from a bar in Greenpoint."

She felt the color drain from her face. "Assaulted how? Where?"

"We found him on the corner of Franklin and Meserole. He'd been beaten half to death. If not with a club or bat then by someone with hands like cured hams."

Rudy Hansen stood approximately six foot three inches tall. Rosie couldn't imagine the brutality required to bring a man that size to the brink of death. "Will he be okay?"

"Should be, but until then he's at Bellevue in critical condition."

Rosie leaned against the metal kitchen table. "Did he see who attacked him?"

"Don't know. He's still unconscious."

"Oh!" Rosie drew a hand to her mouth in surprise and horror.

"I know. Whoever attacked him really had it in for the guy," Riordan commented. "So, um, Greenpoint's your neighborhood, isn't it?"

"Originally, yes. I grew up there and my mother still lives there. Why?"

"Because Hansen's from the Bronx. I find it strange that he'd be all the way in Brooklyn at a bar that's not on his route back home."

"There's a million reasons why he might have been there: family, friends . . ."

"A woman," Riordan added with a smirk.

"Yes. Yes, I suppose Hansen could have been meeting a lady friend."

"A good-looking lady friend with red hair?"

"Sure. Why not?"

"Who also goes by the name of Rose Doyle Keefe?"

Rosie felt the color drain from her face again.

"We know you were there, Mrs. Keefe. Frank Logan confirmed it. So tell me why? Why would you meet Rudy Hansen, a guy who just a few days ago threw hot rivets in your face?"

"He invited me out for a drink."

"And you went? You, a married woman, in your old neighborhood? Weren't you afraid that might raise some eyebrows?"

"N-no." The way Riordan depicted the scene made it seem cheap and tawdry. "I mean, it wasn't like that!"

"I'm sure it wasn't. I'm sure you spoke to Hansen regarding Finch or some piece of information you'd uncovered. The question is what?"

"I have no idea what you're talking about."

"Look, Mrs. Keefe, I am about this far from arresting you." He held his thumb and forefinger aloft to approximate the distance of one inch. "Not for murder, but to protect you from the people who hurt Hansen. Now then, are you going to tell me what happened or do you want to spend tonight, tomorrow, and possibly the rest of your life in jail? Because if you don't tell me what you know, I can't help you."

Rosie wandered into the living room and came to rest on the sofa. Riordan, meanwhile, stood over her, arms folded across his chest as a sign that he meant business.

"Hansen got a batch of bad rivets this morning. Not just one or two rivets, as is typical, but an entire bag. So I met with him to try and see what he made of the situation."

"And?"

"And he suspected that Pushey was cutting corners in order to save money."

"And you? What do you think?"

Rosie frowned and then retrieved the newspaper from the kitchen counter. "Here," she said as she passed the periodical to Riordan.

She watched as his blue eyes scanned the article and then stared off at a point somewhere in the distance.

"So?" she prompted.

His eyes swiftly focused on hers. "I had a feeling something wasn't right about Pushey Shipyard."

"You did not," she challenged. "You're only saying that because—"

"I had a *feeling*," he clarified. "You, however, have presented me with a viable theory. Something I've been sorely lacking."

"Okay, so we have a theory," she stated impatiently. "What next?"

"Well, if someone at Pushey is switching materials, they're doing it during the off hours so that they don't get caught."

"Makes sense." Rosie nodded.

"When does the second shift end?"

"Midnight, usually. The sweepers might leave a little later, though."

Riordan glanced out the window at the gathering dusk. "Meaning that whoever is guilty of the switch, and quite possibly Finch's murder, will probably be hard at work in just a few short hours."

"Maybe sooner than that. There is no second shift on Saturdays. The first shift does a half day from eight until noon and then the yard is empty until Monday morning."

"So the murderer could be there right now, even as we speak."

"What? You mean tonight?"

"Yes, tonight. Criminals don't take holidays."

"I know, but . . ."

Riordan chuckled. "What, you thought he'd be taking a bath or out with his best girl watching the latest Cagney flick?"

"Well, no, but—"

"Saturday night is just as good as any," he announced as he replaced his fedora on his head and strode toward the door.

"Where are you going?"

"To Pushey Shipyard to see if I can't catch this guy in the act."

"Can I come—?"

Riordan cut her off before she could finish the question. "No, you can't. You're locking this door behind me and you're not opening it for anyone. Got it?"

Rosie obediently nodded.

"Good. Now fix yourself a bite to eat, listen to the radio, and go to bed. I'll see you in the morning and let you know how things went." With that, Riordan disappeared down the steps.

Rosie, following his instructions, locked the door tightly behind him. The day's events had left her both terrified and exhausted, but part of her sincerely wished she could have tagged along, if only to be able to look Finch's killer in the eye and tell him about the hell she had been through.

Knowing, however, that accompanying Riordan was not an option, she decided instead to don her favorite short-sleeved cotton pajamas and listen to Bob Nolan's *Radio Rodeo*. But before she could reach her bedroom door, the telephone rang.

She picked up the receiver. "Hello?"

"Oh hey, Rosie. It's Delaney."

"Oh hi, Delaney. What can I do for you?"

"Nothing. I just found out Rudy Hansen was attacked tonight and I figured I'd check in to see if you were okay. You know, what with Katie being at your Mom's and all."

"That's very nice of you, but I'm fine."

"You sure?"

"Positive."

"Okay. Well, if you need anything give me a shout."

"I will, Delaney. Thanks." She replaced the receiver in its cradle and set off toward the bedroom, but something about the conversation gave her pause.

First, as of just a few hours ago, Katie was staying with Rosie for a night on the town and moving back to Greenpoint the next morning—a plan conveyed to Evelyn Doyle. So how could Delaney have known that Rosie was alone? Second, Rosie had only just learned of Hansen's attack from Lieutenant Riordan. How did Delaney hear about it so quickly?

How would Delaney hear about anything? From *his mother, of course,* she concluded. Feeling foolish for her suspicions, yet needing to quell her fears, she decided to call her mother. Picking up the receiver, she dialed the operator. "Greenpoint-5792, please."

The operator directed the call and after a few rings, Evelyn Doyle, with perfect telephone pitch, answered. "Hello, Doyle residence."

Rosie cringed at her mother's formality. "Hi, Ma, it's Rosie, er, Rosaleen."

Mrs. Doyle's manner became quite frosty. "Oh, hello, Rosaleen. And what are you up to tonight that you couldn't join your sister for a movie and a soda? It's dish night, you know. The two of you could have gotten me that gravy boat I've had my eye on."

She rolled her eyes. "I'm tired, Ma. I've been working all week, you know."

"Yes, I *do* know. Back at that terrible place with all those lecherous, filthy men! Well, if something happens to you, don't come crying to me."

"Believe me, I won't," she swore. It was, indeed, the truth: Rosie's mother was not the sort of woman you went to for sympathy. "Say, Ma, have you spoken with Mrs. Delaney recently?"

"No, why? Is she sick? It's her gall bladder again, isn't it? You know I told her she shouldn't be eating that liverwurst from Krauss's Delicatessen. It's far too rich for her!"

"No, Ma, she's not sick. Well, she might be, I don't know." She shook her head. "I just wanted to know if you had talked to her since Katie told you she was moving in."

"No. Haven't heard a peep. I did tell Mrs. Pearce at the post office that your sister and Charlie were moving in. She might have told Mrs. Delaney. Oh! But wait . . . no, when I saw Mrs. Pearce today, I told her the whole thing was off."

"So no one knew Katie was moving in today."

"No. How could they? It's not like I received a lot of notice. Really, Rosaleen, you can be so impetuous at times! I don't know where you get it from, but you really should try to think of others before you make such plans—"

"Bye, Ma." Rosie cut her off, not just so she didn't have to hear her mother's tirade, but because Delaney's story wasn't adding up.

The only way Delaney could have known that Hansen had been attacked was if he were in on the scheme to assault him. And the only way he could have known that Rosie was alone was if he had been watching her apartment.

Where was he when he had called? Was he at home? Or was he nearby? There was only one way to find out. She'd call him at home and see if he answered. But if he were to answer, what would she say was her reason for calling? As a married woman, what possible reason would she have for calling a bachelor at his home?

I've got it! she thought as she recalled the hip flask Delaney had given her the day of Finch's assault. Rushing to the bedroom, she retrieved the object, which, thanks to Katie, had been wrapped in Delaney's newly laundered handkerchief and placed on Rosie's dresser to await delivery.

I'll call Delaney to remind him that I still have his flask and handkerchief, she plotted. *And tell him that if he'd like to collect it, he can stop by tomorrow since I'll be packing my things to move out.*

With her plan in place, she lifted the receiver and placed it to her right ear, but before she could dial the operator, something caught her eye. It was the glow of the stainless steel hip flask, sparkling in the soft light cast by the distant streetlamp.

Replacing the receiver, Rosie reached to the end table and turned on one of two matching living room lamps. Beneath the light of the incandescent bulb, she examined the flask thoroughly. Able to hold approximately eight ounces of liquid, it measured about eight inches by four inches, featured a screw-on cap, and on the front, the initials "MDD" were engraved in bold, block lettering.

But what was most notable about this particular flask was its pristine condition. Every inch of its smooth surface seemed to gleam in the light and, aside from a few greasy fingerprints, possessed no scratches, scuff marks, or other flaws.

Rosie turned the object over in her hands meditatively. Surely a man like Delaney, one who worked in the shipyards, would have inflicted a few nicks on the surface by now. Even if he hadn't dropped it, the rubbing of the flask against the pocket of his canvas work pants as he plied the bucking bar would have caused some wear and tear.

No, she decided, this flask was new. Brand new.

But how, and more important where, would Delaney have procured such a thing? All nonessential metal items had been pulled from store shelves immediately after the United States declared war on Japan, over four months ago. True, Delaney might have been one of the last lucky civilians to acquire such a luxury prior to the metal ban, but she was doubtful that the flask would have retained its flawlessly shiny finish for that length of time.

Likewise, the pressure was on civilians nationwide to turn in any and all metal items during the recent city-wide scrap drives. So great was the sense of urgency that a church in Greenpoint had turned in its bell and a local park had even surrendered a set of Civil War–era cannons to the cause. Indeed, Rosie had noticed that Lieutenant Riordan—a man who might have found a way around the law—lit his cigarettes, rather clumsily, with matches: a hint that until now, he had most likely used a lighter. Quite possibly one made of stainless steel.

There was only one place where Delaney might have acquired any product made of steel: the black market. But if he was buying black-market items, might he be selling them as well? Could he and Finch have been accomplices?

Rosie closed her eyes and tried to imagine how the profiteering scheme might have come together. Although she had a good idea of Finch's role in the plot, she could not guess the why and wherefore behind his murder. There were still too many missing details to get a clear picture. However, one thing was for certain: involved in the plan or not, Michael Delaney had something to hide.

With a sense of urgency, Rosie picked up the telephone receiver and dialed the operator. "Greenpoint-1105, please."

Within a few seconds, the phone rang at the Delaney residence. After several rings, an elderly woman answered. "Hello?"

"Oh, hello, Mrs. Delaney. It's Rosie Keefe, er, Doyle," she corrected, realizing that the elderly woman might not recall her married name. "I was looking for Michael. Is he around?"

"Oh, Rosie! How nice to hear from ya," she said in a soft brogue. "Michael had some errands to run after work and hasn't come home yet. Shall I give him a message?"

She felt lightheaded again. If Delaney wasn't home, where was he? "Umm, no . . . no, thank you. I'll call him back some other time."

"All right, then. Good-bye, dear."

"Good night, Mrs. Delaney."

She put down the receiver and moved to the window. Was Delaney down there, somewhere on the street? Had he been watching her apartment all afternoon? Had he seen her meet with Hansen? More important, had he seen Riordan stop by and then leave for the shipyard?

Without missing a beat, Rosie dashed to the phone and called Riordan's precinct.

"Seventy-sixth Precinct, Sergeant Cooper speaking," a gruff male voice answered.

"Yes, Sergeant. This is Mrs. Rose Keefe. I need to get a message to Lieutenant Riordan."

"Lieutenant Riordan is away from his desk right now. May I take a message?"

"Yes . . . I know he's away from his desk. He's at the Pushey Shipyard and I do need to get a message to him. Is there any way you can send it to him by radio?"

The sergeant fell silent.

"Hello?" Rosie prompted after several seconds had elapsed.

"Yeah, I'm here. Hold on a second, please."

She could hear him conversing with another man, most likely about her request. "Yeah, okay. What's the message?"

"Tell him that Delaney's in on the shipyard scheme. And that he might be following him."

"Okay. Hold on a second?"

"Sure," she agreed breathlessly, but as the seconds ticked away, she felt her sense of urgency grow.

After what felt like an eternity, Sergeant Cooper returned to the phone. "We tried radioing the lieutenant, but there was no reply."

Rosie's pulse quickened. "What? No! There has to be another way to reach him. Can you send a car? It's important."

"Hold on, please."

Again she heard the sergeant speaking with someone in the background. This time, however, the reply came quickly. "I'm sorry, ma'am, but I can't do that."

"You can't? Why not?"

"If he needs backup, he'll request it."

"You don't understand. He may be in danger," she insisted.

"If you'd like to speak with Captain Kinney—"

"No," she replied. The reason for the sergeant's lack of cooperation became suddenly clear. "No, that's all right."

"Good night, ma'am."

Rosie slammed the receiver into the cradle without a word. She had one option left: to go after Riordan herself.

Taking the hip flask as evidence, her apartment key, and a bit of change (the only money she had left after paying part of Billy's bar tab) from her handbag and placing it in the pocket of her dress, she set off to the train station.

The day's warmth and humidity had visually manifested itself in the shape of storm clouds forming a few miles east of the Hudson River. Amid the rumbling of distant thunder, Rosie rushed down the steps of her apartment building and onto the sidewalk. A block away from the Eighth Avenue/Twenty-third Street station, Rosie felt a strong arm reach around her shoulders and a hand clamp over her mouth. Before she could put up a struggle, a hard cylindrical object pressed against the small of her back.

"Where do you think you're going, Rosie?" came a whisper in her ear. Although she recognized the voice as belonging to Michael Delaney, its usual whining cadence had been replaced with a tone far more sinister. "Going to warn your friend?"

Rosie's eyes were wide with fear. Although she couldn't speak, she managed to shake her head slowly from side to side.

"Liar," Delaney spat back. "I saw him leave your apartment and I know where he's headed. You were gonna meet him there and warn him, weren't you? Warn him about me. You know what? I think that's a great idea. Let's you and I go join him. Okay?"

She didn't react, prompting Delaney to push the gun harder into her back.

"Okay?"

This time she nodded in agreement.

"Good. Now, I'm going to take my hand away from your mouth and we're going to take a walk to the train station. Quietly. Got it?"

Again, she nodded.

"And when I say quiet, I mean quiet. Don't make me hurt you, Rosie. I don't want to hurt you."

She nodded, this time vigorously, prompting Delaney to slowly remove his hand.

Rosie drew a deep breath through her mouth.

"That's it. Breathe." He draped his jacket over her shoulders so as to conceal the gun he had pointing in Rosie's back. "Now walk."

Putting one foot carefully in front of the other, she proceeded slowly yet surely down the remainder of the block. Delaney, walking at her side, with the gun planted firmly in her back, made sure to nod and smile to passersby.

"Okay, down the steps," he instructed as they reached the IRT station. "You first, and don't try to get ahead of me. There's nowhere you can run."

With Delaney close behind, she descended the steps to the train platform. There, he joined her, and they waited side by side in silence until the next train to Brooklyn pulled to a halt and deposited its passengers.

It being a warm Saturday night—the first of the year—the trains heading into Manhattan were packed with lovers, singles, and groups of men and women looking for a night on the town. Trains heading out of Manhattan, however, were empty and would not be full until the bars made last call at three a.m.

It was a lucky break for Delaney.

When the train had expelled its passengers and the doors had cleared, Delaney directed Rosie into the third car, which had been abandoned save for three people. Dead center on the bench that ran the length of the left side of the car sat an elderly woman who appeared to be going on an overnight trip. Diagonally across from her, at the rear of the right-side bench, an adolescent boy and girl were busy necking.

The elderly woman, visibly uncomfortable with the public display of affection, played awkwardly with the handle of her small valise and cleared her throat periodically.

Delaney motioned to Rosie to take hold of the leather strap and stood close behind her, one arm keeping the gun positioned in her back, the other wrapped tightly around the front of her waist.

The sight of what she deemed to be another set of amorous young people caused the elderly woman to clear her throat even more loudly and then busy herself with the task of cleaning out her handbag.

"Look at that," Delaney said in Rosie's ear. "The old bird thinks we're lovers. Should we give her a show?"

Rosie leaned her head away from Delaney's. She couldn't stand the feeling of his breath on the side of her face.

"But we're not, are we, Rosie?" he continued. "Not for lack of trying, though. No. I've been here all this time, loving you, wanting you," he added in a whisper. "But you've never wanted me, have you? You always seem to want someone else. First it was Billy Keefe and now this cop, Riordan."

"Riordan?" she exclaimed. "There's nothing going on with him. He's just trying to keep me out of jail."

"Liar! Liar. I saw you two by the Navy Yard, watching the sunset, and talking. That didn't seem very law enforcement-like to me."

Rosie thought she might vomit. How long had Delaney been watching her? How long had he been following her every move? How could she not have seen him there in the shadows? How could she not have known?

"And now, here you are rushing after him, trying to save him. But it's too late, Rosie."

"What do you mean?"

"I already called Del Vecchio. He'll have the warehouse emptied by the time your cop gets there. Well, empty except for Del Vecchio and his .38."

Rosie had been terrified, but at least she had hope that Riordan might have called for backup. At the prospect that Riordan might be dead, genuine panic started to set in.

She had to get away from Delaney. She had to. But how?

The train had emerged from its subterranean channel

and hummed along the elevated tracks that led to Red Hook. Rosie thought about her escape as she watched the landscape flicker past the windows. The train offered no exit route and the station only one, but the walk to the shipyard was filled with alleys, side streets, and apartment buildings. What's more, the war effort had tapped into the city's supply of skilled male workers, thus bringing infrastructural repairs to a grinding halt and leaving streets and sidewalks in various stages of disrepair.

If she could use the potholes, cracks, and missing pavement to break away from Delaney, she might stand a chance.

With the sound of escaping air, the train drew to a halt at the Romanesque revival City Hall station, which, with the work week ended, now stood eerily empty. Before the war, City Hall station had been a favorite stop of Rosie's. The curved section of track offset the elegant style of the polychrome tiled arches, brass fixtures, wrought-iron chandeliers, and three cured skylights made of cut amethyst glass. Since entering the war, those skylights, which corresponded to three gratings in City Hall park, had been blackened with tar to avoid attention from enemy bombers. The move to obliterate the light source, although strategically sound, had left the station with a timeless, dark feeling that Rosie found deeply foreboding.

Delaney pushed Rosie out the sliding doors and waited until the train left the station before directing her to walk. With the train gone, the only sounds in the empty station were the clacking of their heels against the platform cement.

As they scaled the steps that led to the green square of land in front of City Hall, Rosie mentally retraced the walk to the shipyard. Two blocks ahead, there was a hole in the sidewalk that might afford her an opportunity to knock Delaney off balance—providing, of course, that he wasn't aware of its presence. Considering her abductor traveled from the opposite direction each morning, Rosie was willing to stake money on the fact that he wasn't.

Marching forward through the wind and thunder, Rosie could pick out the pivotal spot in the near distance. Calculating where Delaney might walk, given his proximity to her, she altered her pace so that she could step daintily, and discreetly, over the small pothole while, with any luck, her abductor stepped in it.

Unfortunately, when she reached the spot, Delaney followed her lead and bypassed the hole with no difficulty.

Disappointed but not hopeless, Rosie zeroed in on the next obstacle, just a few feet ahead. A section of pavement that had buckled, causing an uneven walking surface.

Having walked this path for ten days, Rosie had learned, without even looking down, where to walk to avoid getting the toe of her shoe caught on the cement.

Delaney, meanwhile, tripped and stumbled forward.

It was precisely the break Rosie needed. Kicking off her shoes, she ran, hell for leather, down the street, doing her best to stay in the shadows.

Chapter Sixteen

Riordan pulled his Ford Deluxe to a stop along Beard Street and approached the young man standing outside the Pushey Shipyard gate. Between eighteen and twenty years old, he possessed a pencil-thin mustache that did little to hide or age his youthful countenance and, unlike the typical guard on duty, he was conspicuously lacking a uniform.

"Lieutenant Jack Riordan, NYPD." He flashed his badge. "What happened to the MP who's usually on duty?"

"Oh, h-he's out sick."

"Really? Here I was thinking that whatever is going on behind that fence might not be condoned by the United States government."

The young man's face blanched.

Riordan reached into his pocket and pulled out a piece of paper. "Here, my badge and this twenty-dollar bill say you leave here without a word and I pretend I never saw you."

The young man gazed at the bill, looked back over his shoulder, and hesitated for a moment, at which point Riordan raised his voice. "Go on! Get out of here!"

He took off like a shot, leaving Riordan, by the glow of a nearby streetlight, to figure out how to jimmy the complex lock.

Riordan rolled his eyes. Next time he would have to remember to pay off the guard *after* demanding that the gate be unlocked. For now, however, the sole of his size eleven-and-a-half shoe would suffice.

After several tries, he managed to finesse the gate and enter the yard, his Colt Detective Special at the ready in his right hand and a long, black flashlight in his left. As the impending storm rolled closer to the city, he moved to the right of the building known as the employee holding area and focused his attention on the smaller outlying structures.

Although Riordan's men had searched the shipyard thoroughly, Riordan himself, preferring to reserve his time and energy to focus on clues, was still somewhat vague about the yard's layout. As such, it was only after discovering the toolshed, worksite lavatory, and blue-print building, that he happened upon an expansive building made of corrugated steel.

Shining his flashlight in the window, Riordan saw a wooden rack system, approximately six feet deep and twelve feet high, built neatly along the far wall. The first two slots of the rack were filled with sheet metal. The rest were empty.

To the right, on a perpendicular wall, metal corrals held burlap bags labeled as containing fasteners of every size, shape, and variety. However, there were just two or three bags of each kind.

Giving the door latch a turn, he entered the building and examined its contents. In a warehouse capable of holding tons of materials, the presence of only a few pieces of sheet metal and several hundred fasteners—end of week or not—seemed dubious. Given that the country was ramping up for war, one would have thought that this storage area would be filled to the rafters with supplies.

Shining his flashlight onto the cement floor of the sheet-metal racks, Riordan bent down to take note of several lines of dirt on the front and back beams of the rack, running perpendicular to the sides of each section. Moreover, those lines looked fresh and damp, indicating that there had, indeed, been more sheet metal stacked in the area and that that metal had been moved quite recently.

Upon this discovery, Riordan checked the fastener corrals. There, too, existed irregularly shaped damp spots upon the concrete, as if multiple bags of supplies had once rested there and had recently been carted off. As recently, perhaps, as the past few hours.

Riordan stood up to check out the small-parts bins that were mounted on the wall above, but before he could do so, a shot rang out. Acting quickly, he dropped to the ground and rolled toward the sheet-metal racks, getting some shots off along the way. Squeezing into the first of the bins, he wedged himself between two thick pieces of sheet metal. The narrow opening acted as a makeshift shield, while allowing him to counter the gunfire emanating from the warehouse door.

The anonymous shooter scrambled behind one of the metal warehouse doors, but the sheltered angle made aiming at Riordan next to impossible. Looking for another hiding spot, the figure crossed the entranceway, but, after several volleys, he eventually fell over, landing face forward. Riordan, gun still drawn, rose from his spot in the sheet-metal bin and carefully approached the body.

After a few kicks with the toe of his shoe, he rolled him over.

It was the short, stocky figure of Tony Del Vecchio.

A barefoot Rosie sprinted down Wright Street, trying the handle of every door she passed along the way. The shipyard and dockworkers, however, had long left for the day, leaving the area vacant. Desperately, she decided to scream for help, in case somewhere nearby, some person still remained.

As she opened her mouth, she felt an incredible force come crashing down on her back, knocking her face first into the pavement. "You didn't think I'd let you get away that easily, did you?" Delaney taunted as he lay on top of her.

Meanwhile Rosie, having had the wind knocked out of her, gasped for air.

"Come on!" He stood up and dragged Rosie to her feet, scraping both her knees against the hard, rough surface of the asphalt. "Come on!"

Rosie stood up and, having finally caught her breath, swallowed the pool of saliva that had formed in her open mouth. The substance had the taste of dirt and salt. She raised a finger to the corner of her mouth and removed it, only to find it covered in blood and tiny bits of gravel.

"Come on," Delany urged again and shoved the cold steel of the gun in her back.

Slowly, she started to walk toward Beard Street. She felt exhausted and her entire body ached. "Why are you doing this to me? Why not just kill me? Kill me like you did Finch."

"I didn't kill Finch."

"No? You were his accomplices, weren't you? You and Del Vecchio?"

Delaney shook his head. "It's not as easy as that, Rosie. It's not that simple."

"Try me," she challenged as she spun around.

"Keep walking and I will." He waved the gun.

She obeyed and Delaney launched into his story. "It all started with the *Normandie* fire. Remember the whole scare about it being sabotaged by the Nazis or the Nips?"

"Yes, but the government found no evidence of that. They said the fire was caused by a spark from a welding torch."

"Yeah, but did anyone believe it?"

"Sure, lots of people did."

"But they still wondered, didn't they? Admit it, you did, too."

"You're right. I did. Still do."

"Do you know why? Because every day the people of this city look out at that ship's hull lying in the Hudson River. And every time they go down to the water, be it Jersey or Long Island, they see German U-boats right off the shore. As you can imagine, the government doesn't like having their navy's ability to protect its citizens thrown into question. Problem is, until all their ships are built, there's not much they can do. So they decided they needed a fleet of vessels that could temporarily handle the job of scaring off the U-boats. And because of the talk that Nazis and Nips were here on land, they needed a bunch of people who knew the waterfront and could identify potential spy activity."

"Where would they possibly find either?" she asked as the storm closed in.

"Easy. The mob."

Rosie stopped dead in her tracks. "You're telling me that the United States government made a pact with—with—"

"Yep, Naval Intelligence, the Manhattan D.A., and good old Lucky Luciano all in bed together." He prodded Rosie to keep walking. "Joe Lanza, the king of the Fulton Fish Market, now rules the harbor with his fleet of fishing boats, and Frank Costello—"

"Luciano's right-hand man," Rosie commented as she recalled her conversation with Riordan.

"—along with some guy named Anastasia is in charge of the waterfront."

"All of it?"

"From the docks, to the streets, to the very land Pushey Shipyard sits on. In exchange for all this 'protection,' Luciano gets a transfer from Dannemora to some place down south with a hedge fence instead of barbed wire."

"And the rivets . . . ?"

"Costello's scheme. You give a mobster full rein over a neighborhood and they're going to want to make money off the deal."

"I can't believe it. You mean the government would—"

"Oh, you better believe they would."

"And you? Why are you doing this? *How* could you do this? Don't you care about those sailors' lives?"

"Same reason anyone does anything these days: money. That's why you showed up at the yard in the first place, wasn't it?"

They turned onto Beard Street. "I'm doing an honest day's work for an honest day's pay. I'm not hurting anyone with what I do. It's hardly the same thing."

"Isn't it? Eh, maybe not."

Rosie recalled Del Vecchio's cigarette lighter. It was

just as shiny and flawless as Delaney's hip flask. "So you and Del Vecchio were Finch's accomplices, weren't you?"

"Yes. Finch was in on the deal from the start, but when it started getting bigger and more steel was being shipped in and out of the yard and in less and less time, he knew he couldn't handle it on his own, so he offered Del Vecchio and me a part of his take."

"Delaney," Rosie sighed. "I thought you were different. I thought . . ."

"Hey, if it was your mother who was up to her eyeballs in medical bills, you'd have done the same thing," he argued. "Don't tell me you wouldn't. The problem is Finch was getting too much attention. Between the booze, the women, and flashing fifty-dollar bills around like it was chump change, it was only a matter of time until he ended up in jail or spilled the beans."

She could see the shipyard up ahead. "But the government must have known what to expect when they turned the waterfront over to the mob. Surely—"

"It's not the government they were worried about. It was the people. It's one thing to suspect that the Mob is operating in your neighborhood. It's another thing to know they are." He shook his head. "No, if Finch had talked about what we were doing here—even the smallest slip—it would have been all over."

"So you killed Finch," she presumed.

"No, I told you I didn't kill him. That's the truth."

"Then who did?"

"Del Vecchio. He knew Finch got his payoff down by the pier each week. So he waited for him there and . . . let him have it."

"Del Vecchio," she repeated quietly. "And I'm sure he bashed him on the head because of what I had done earlier in the day."

"He may have," Delaney confessed.

"Good God."

"Hey, that doesn't make him a bad guy, Rosie. It doesn't because he isn't. He's not like that. He's a good guy. A family man," Delaney insisted. "He was just following orders. When Frank Costello's men tell you to do something, you don't argue."

"Is that how he got his promotion?"

"Part of it. Costello's gang wanted to start putting inside men in all the key spots. Because Del Vecchio bumped off Finch, I guess they figured he should get his job."

They had arrived at the Pushey Gate only to find the gate forced open and no guard on duty.

"Looks like we have company." Grabbing Rosie by the arm, Delaney raised his gun and entered the yard in search of Del Vecchio.

Dragging Rosie behind him, he peered through the windows of every building in the complex as he made his way to the warehouse. As expected, he found nothing along the way and finally entered the warehouse, only to see Riordan standing over Del Vecchio's body.

Riordan, gun still drawn, aimed it at Delaney. Delaney, meanwhile, grabbed for Rosie in an attempt to shield himself with her. It was enough to give Riordan pause.

Rosie, however, would have none of it. Recalling a technique her Dad once showed her, she took advantage of her position and gave him a hard kick to the side of the shin, just below the kneecap.

The move worked. Delaney lost his footing and crumpled to the ground, but not before getting a shot off at Riordan. Rosie watched in horror as the lieutenant fell to the ground.

"Riordan!" she screamed. But there was no time to turn back and check on him. She had to get away. She had to get help.

As the skies opened and lightning touched down over Gowanus Bay, Rosie ran out the warehouse door and toward the familiar haven of nearby Pier Number One. Once there, however, she knew the only place she could go was up.

Damning the risk of electrocution, she took hold of a bottom rung and started to climb. Raindrops crashed off the scaffold, soaking Rosie through to her skin and making it difficult to keep her hands and feet from slipping off the metal bars, making the ascent a slow one.

Yet upward she continued.

As she neared the third level of the skeletal structure, a shout came from the yard below. Delaney had caught up. "Rosie! Rosie, get down!"

Undeterred, she continued to climb.

"Rosie, please come down. I don't want to hurt you!"

"You don't? Is that why you marched me here with a gun in my back? Is that why you dragged me out of an alley?"

"I had to, Rosie. You gave me no choice. But I don't want to hurt you. Really."

"Oh, and I suppose that's why you followed me in the first place. Because you didn't want to hurt me?"

Delaney began to climb after her, the gun still in his right hand. "I wasn't supposed to follow you. It was going to be one of Costello's men, but I asked for the job. I asked for it to make sure you were safe. And when"—his hand slipped, but he recovered his balance—"And when Hansen was attacked, I made sure that happened after you had left the bar. I . . . I didn't want you to get hurt. I wanted to protect you because I—because I love you."

Breathless from her climb, but close to the planking, Rosie screamed, "Love? Is that why you were willing to let me go to jail?"

"I didn't want to . . . I didn't," Delaney sounded as though he was close to tears.

Rosie stepped onto the wooden planking. As she did so a shot rang out and she felt a burning sensation in her right hip that caused her to drop to her knees. "Oh!" she gasped.

She endeavored to get back onto her feet, but it was too late. Delaney was already at the other end of the platform, his gun pointed directly at her. "I do love you, Rosie. But even love isn't enough to protect me from Costello's men."

As Rosie lay upon the wooden planks of the platform, her hand reached behind her torso into the darkness and fell upon something cold, hard, and metallic.

Delaney cocked the gun and pointed it at Rosie's heart. "I can't let them kill me, Rosie. I'm sorry."

She tried on a sympathetic look, all the while grasping the object behind her. "I guess that's it, then. I have nowhere else to run, do I? I just have one last request."

"What is it?"

"Well, I was raised Catholic, like you were. Remember the days at St. Cecelia's?"

"I do. I knew I loved you even then."

"And I'm—I'm sorry I didn't notice." The words brought a rush of bile to her mouth. "Seeing as there's no priest here to administer Last Rites, could you at least join me in a prayer?"

Delaney shook his head gravely. "Don't make me do that, Rosie. This is tough enough."

"Please?" she begged. "I don't want to go without seeking some sort of absolution."

Delaney nodded and hung his head as Rosie began reciting the Hail Mary. "Hail Mary, full of grace, Our Lord is with thee. Blessed art thou among women, and blessed is the fruit of thy womb, Jesus. Holy Mary, Mother of God—"

With that final invocation, Rosie grabbed the pneumatic rivet gun Kilbride had left outdoors, clutched it tightly in both hands like a battering ram, and lunged toward Delaney. Pushing hard on the trigger, she sent the tip of the gun into Delaney's chest with several blasts of air.

Delaney, crying out in agony, fell backward off the platform, causing a relieved, but exhausted, Rosie to plop onto the planks and catch her breath.

He's gone. He's finally gone. She wiped the rain from her face and began to stand up so as to start her descent down the scaffold.

Just then, she felt a hand grab her right ankle, prompting her to scream.

Hanging from the platform with one hand and holding onto Rosie with the other, Delaney was either attempting to climb back up or to pull her down with him.

Screaming the entire time, she flopped onto her stomach and frantically clawed at the planks, the nearby hull, anything that would keep her from sliding off the platform.

As she felt herself being pulled closer to the edge of the platform, closer to falling to the yard below, a shot rang out. Rosie, expecting to feel another burning pain, closed her eyes and braced for the worst.

However, it wasn't a burning sensation that she felt but the sensation of Delaney's fingers loosing their grip on her ankle. Within seconds, they disappeared altogether. She opened her eyes in confusion.

Illuminated by a nearby streak of lightning, Lieutenant Riordan stood at the opposite end of the platform. Bruised, bloody, his left arm dangling limply at his side, he dropped the gun from his right hand and collapsed beside Rosie.

"Riordan!" she exclaimed. Thankfully he was still conscious. "I thought . . . I thought Delaney . . ."

"He did." He smiled. "I don't look like this for nothing."

"Where did he get you?"

"Shoulder. Left shoulder. You know, that's a helluva climb you make every day."

Half-crying, half-laughing, she nodded. "Yeah. Yeah, but Monday's climb will seem a lot easier than this one."

"I heard shots. Are you okay? Did he get you?"

"I thought he got me, but . . ." She reached down to her right hip, only to have her fingers meet, not blood, but metal. Reaching into her pocket, she pulled out Delaney's hip flask, which now bore a dent the size of a bullet hole.

Rosie stared at the object in disbelief and repeated the words Delaney had spoken upon giving it to her: "In case you need it."

Chapter Seventeen

Sunday morning materialized from the rain—sunny, clear, but seasonably cooler. After filing a report at police headquarters and having her cuts, scrapes, and abrasions tended to at the hospital, Rosie returned home, collapsed upon her sofa, and slept the sleep of a free woman.

She awoke six hours later, showered, donned a blue plaid dress with a white collar, and set off on the IRT to Brooklyn. Seeing the station in broad daylight fought off the chill she experienced as she stepped onto the platform, but she would not be deterred from her quest.

After a brief stop in Greenpoint, she then traveled to the third floor of Kings County Hospital, where Jack Riordan, his arm in a cast that stretched from his shoulder to his wrist, sat in bed, reading the morning paper spread upon his lap.

"Did we make the front page?" Rosie asked as she peeked her head in the door.

"Nope. King George VI did." He pulled a face.

"King George? Did he take a bullet to save a woman from jail, too?"

"No, he gave the George Cross to Malta. But we're on page three."

"Well, better luck next time, I suppose," she teased.

"I do hope you're joking."

"I am." She smiled and handed Riordan a white waxed paper bag of crullers she had purchased prior to her visit. "These are for you. A thank-you for saving me from Delaney."

"You didn't need to do that. It's my job. And from what I can remember, you were doing okay on your own. Well . . . except maybe for when Delaney was trying to pull you off the scaffold," Riordan teased as he opened the bag and sniffed its contents.

"Yeah, 'except' for that I was doing fine." She laughed.

Riordan chuckled and took a bite of cruller. "Mmm . . . these are good."

"Yeah, I got them from the bakery my mother wants me to work at."

"Oh, are you leaving the shipyard?"

Rosie shook her head. "No, after everything that's happened it might come as a shock, but I'm actually starting to like it there."

"Good. I'm sure the cause could use more women like you."

Rosie blushed and cleared her throat awkwardly. "Well, I'd . . . um . . . I'd better be going. I have a lot of packing to do."

"Packing?" Riordan asked with a start. "I thought you were staying at the shipyard."

"Oh, I am. But I'm moving to Brooklyn. Back to my mother's place. Katie and Charlie will be living with us, too."

"Brooklyn, huh? I'm glad."

"Why? So I'm no longer stirring up trouble in Manhattan?" Rosie joked.

"No. Because I live in Brooklyn, too. Being in the same borough will make it easier to check up on you," Riordan stated with a smile.

"Check up on me?" Rosie repeated as she felt the color rise in her cheeks.

"Sure. I've invested too much time clearing your name to let you run afoul of the law again."

"Run afoul of the law? And say, what do you mean you cleared my name? I wasn't exactly wringing my hands in despair waiting to be rescued from the gallows."

"No, you weren't," Riordan agreed, with more than a hint of admiration in his voice.

"If anything, I single-handedly solved the case," she half-jokingly said.

"Single-handedly?"

"That's right."

"Uh-huh . . . I could argue that I pitched in a little, but since I'm a gentleman and already in a considerable amount of pain, let's just call it a draw, shall we?"

"Agreed," Rosie said with a sparkle in her eye.

"Besides"—Riordan's face grew somber—"now that we know what's really going on, the question isn't 'Who solved the case?' or 'Who saved you from Delaney?' It's 'Who's going to save the waterfront from Costello?'"

Rosie shook her head slowly and frowned. "Who's going to save any of us, Lieutenant Riordan? The Nazis are taking over Europe and Africa, mobsters are taking over New York, profiteers are taking over the war effort, and our government nods its head and cries 'Victory' in spite of it all. What hope is left?"

Riordan reached into the white bag and handed Rosie a cruller. "You," he replied. "You and other people who aren't satisfied with just making do, Mrs. Keefe."

Rosie bit her lip in thought. "Well, I guess my being

at Pushey made a little bit of a difference, didn't it? At least to the women there."

"Uh-huh."

"And you—well, you make a difference every day."

"Not *every* day, but I try."

"Yeah, but if you and I can do it, we all can do it."

"Exactly." Riordan raised his cruller and "clinked" it against hers. "To you, Mrs. Keefe."

She giggled. "To you, Lieutenant Riordan."

"And to you moving to Brooklyn," he added with a boyish grin.